Drawing Mr. Darcy

Book Two: A Faithful Portrait

Melanie Rachel

Other books by Melanie Rachel

Courage Rises

Courage Requires

Drawing Mr. Darcy: Sketching His Character (Book One)

The *Drawing Mr. Darcy* books are dedicated to my parents, who adopted four children and raised us with love.

TABLE OF CONTENTS

Summary: *At the end of Book One, we left Elizabeth, Darcy, and Mr. Bennet in the study at Longbourn. Darcy has made an offer of courtship to Elizabeth, and she has accepted. While Darcy has been told that Elizabeth is not only a Bennet, but also a Russell, Elizabeth is about to reveal the extent of her present and future fortune to both men.*

CHAPTER ONE

Darcy waited for Miss Elizabeth to stop speaking. Her eyes lifted to his, both proud and apprehensive, but he could not summon any form of response. It took him several long moments even to think to glance at her father, who appeared no less stunned than he was himself.

"So," Miss Elizabeth said, sitting a bit taller and running the palms of her hands over her lap, "in summary, and based upon the letters from my solicitor waiting for me this morning, I currently have working capital of just over thirty thousand pounds."

Darcy heard the words, but had trouble comprehending them. He had originally believed she had neither wealth nor connections, but her fortune was superior to his own sister's. *Darcy, you fool*, he chastised himself. *When did you begin trusting Caroline Bingley as a source of information?*

Elizabeth had mentioned the Russells in her response to his stilted proposal, and he had recalled his father's friends, suspecting she possessed a reasonable dowry. He had only just made the connection between her and the Duke of Bedford, but still, the connection was through marriage, and the duke had a large and growing family of his own—he had not expected the connection to be an especially strong one. That the connection was a close one was unexpected, but it was hardly the thing that surprised him most.

In none of his woefully inaccurate musings had he expected she had such resources. Investment interests. A working farm, a kind of small estate, just beyond London's city limits. The land was not leasehold. There was not even a mortgage—she owned the property outright. She was not squeezed into a townhouse; she could stable her own horses—a tremendous asset in London, where most people were forced to rent horses to avoid stabling fees. She could discuss each holding in precise detail. Something shifted inside him. She was not beneath him in position, not at all.

He had looked forward to taking care of her, but she did not require it. That might take some getting used to . . .

Miss Elizabeth was still speaking. "That includes my ready cash, but not the twenty-two thousand in the funds or the longer-term investments which have yet to pay out. I expect a good return on my stake in Uncle Gardiner's enterprise when his ships return, but depending upon his wishes, I may reinvest those funds in the business." She cleared her throat nervously. "Then, of course, there is the Kensington property, where profits are approximately five hundred pounds a year. I do hope to increase production there."

"Pineapples," her father said, as though only just realizing something important, and she nodded. Darcy sent her a questioning look.

"Later," she said, glancing shyly up at him. "I have not leased the house this year, so there will be no income from it, but there is currently about eight thousand pounds in my accounts for the farm and house, thanks to Uncle Phillip. The house and park surrounding it was his, but he left it to me in his will. He set aside five thousand pounds for repairs and maintenance. I placed the lease profits in that account and I added to it on my own after his passing." She frowned, and Darcy realized she was trying to offer him a complete accounting. "There are other odds and ends, but that is the bulk of it."

She took a very deep breath. "There is one more thing. Aunt Olivia informed me just before we arrived at Longbourn that I am to inherit all from her. She has been revealing things to me gradually. She tells me I know most of it now, but John—His Grace—still supervises several of Aunt's accounts." She lifted a hand to tug her ear, dropping it immediately when she realized what she was doing.

She tugs her ear when she is nervous, he thought, charmed. *Smooths her gown and tugs her ear.*

"However," she finished, "Aunt will remain with us for some years yet, so we can let that go for now."

Darcy tried to say something, but the words stuck in his throat. He tried again without success. Miss Elizabeth lifted her shoulders slightly. "I tell you all of this not to boast." She smoothed her skirt. "I tell you because I enjoy investing, I enjoy earning money, and I do not intend to stop." She stood and held out her hand to him—he stood and reached immediately to take it. Her dark eyes searched his.

"My work is profitable and satisfying, but it takes a good deal of time and study. Sometimes it requires travel. What I need to know, sir," she said solemnly, "is whether you are prepared for such an unconventional wife." He began to answer, but her brows contracted, and he had to force himself not to smooth out the little line that appeared on her forehead. "I like to read the newspaper, Mr. Darcy, all of it, not just the society pages. In fact, it is important that I do. I read a great many papers and scientific reports that are not considered strictly proper for a woman."

Darcy was even more curious now. "What kinds of things are you reading about at present?"

Miss Elizabeth straightened. As a result, her chest pushed out and Darcy took a small step back even as he could feel Mr. Bennet's eyes on him. Elizabeth did not seem to notice this interaction.

"Trevithick's steam-powered locomotive is just the beginning, you know." Her expression lit with excitement. "I have already made money with Watt, and I read over the patent for Blenkinsop's rack and pinion system not long ago. Fenton, Murray, and Wood in Leeds have the contract to build the locomotive. I have invested there." She turned to face her father. "You may wish to as well, Papa. There is a fortune to be made, and the company is well positioned to take advantage. There are immediate industrial uses for the design, but I believe one day we will transport people all over the country without horses."

Darcy noted Mr. Bennet, now listening attentively, leaning slightly forward, one hand rubbing his chin.

Miss Elizabeth turned back to him, worrying her lower lip until he shook his head at her.

"Is this all?" he asked softly.

She shook her head. "Because my time is spent differently than most women, there are things I cannot do as your wife."

"Such as?" He was tickled. Did she really believe he would object? *To what?*

"I have given this some thought, Mr. Darcy, and I think . . ." She stopped. Lifted her free hand to her ear. He took it in his own hand instead.

"Just tell me," he said gently. "You will feel better once you have."

Miss Elizabeth squared her shoulders and took a deep breath. "Should this courtship result in a marriage, there are things I can and cannot do. I will not hold visiting hours in London three times a week, but I might hold them once a week for a few hours. I will not spend my time slavishly returning those visits or shopping on Bond Street to be seen but I will maintain an intimate acquaintance with those closest to us." Here, her expression pinched. "I will not have time to visit each of Pemberley's tenants on a regular basis, but I will introduce myself to them all and be certain their needs are met." She waited until he nodded before adding, "I would likely need to rely on Mrs. Reynolds and Mrs. White for many of the day-to-day operations of your properties. They will hire servants and dismiss them when necessary. They would need to continue with sorting out the details of entertaining. I would of course, be available to consult with them on any of these matters."

Elizabeth tilted her head to the side. "If you are hoping to redecorate any rooms, I would need to be presented with several options and simply allowed to select one." She paused for a moment, considering. "Georgie might rather enjoy gathering that information. Her tolerance for shopping is greater than mine." She smiled at his sister's name, but then frowned and met his eyes, her gaze serious. "Some of your friends or business associates might find the arrangement rather odd."

Darcy blinked. He had known she was clever, but this . . . and yet, she was full young, too, unsure he could accept that she would be a different kind of wife. Could he? Two months ago, he might have had a different answer, but now, he knew he had been a fool. Whatever kind of wife Elizabeth would be—that was the kind of wife he wanted. Needed.

"Let them," he said frankly. "It is no concern of mine."

Elizabeth is not wrong to worry, he admitted to himself. Most men would insist that she not continue her work once wed. Most men would assume they knew better and could improve upon her efforts, insisting she turn over all her assets to his safekeeping. He had not thought about it for some time, how his own mother's brilliance had been stunted by her marriage.

Never had he understood refusing to benefit from a keen mind. His tutor had taught him to calculate, but it was his mother who had taught him to love mathematics. They had engaged in heated discussions over the controversy between Newton's theory of calculus and that of Leibniz. He had argued for Newton's precedence, sure that as an Englishman, it was the correct position. His mother had instead pointed out that it was possible for both men to have independently arrived at their conclusions, but that Newton had not published his explanation for fluxional notation until long after Leibniz's publication. *Nova Methodus pro Maximis et Minimis,* she had reminded him as she sipped her tea, was the very first published work explaining the theory of calculus, and that Leibniz ought not be denied his accomplishments merely because he was German. *The world,* she had said, *is larger than England.*

In this sense, the breach between he and his father that lasted so long seemed to have done him a service—he had long been angry on his mother's behalf. His father had been a traditional man. He did not mind Lady Anne discussing mathematics within the immediate family— however, once she left the privacy of that small sphere, she was not to converse on any topic that might lead to raised eyebrows. Not with her parents, not with her sister or brother, not with her friends. She had loved her husband and did as he required. *And she hid such an important part of herself from everyone but us. What might she have had to offer that larger world had she not been forced to play such a role?* His mother would have adored Elizabeth.

It occurred to him then, as he watched Elizabeth's face break into a relieved smile, as he felt her squeeze his hands, that his mother had prepared him for just this moment. His mother was why he could never tolerate women who fawned, who had no thoughts of their own that they were willing to reveal.

"Thank you," Miss Elizabeth said, her voice breathy and low. "I did not think I should ever find a man who would be willing to accept me once he knew."

Accept you? He was amazed and grateful she would even consider him. She had plainly outlined what she saw as the drawbacks of the match for him. She insisted he be forewarned what pursuing her might cost him. She was willing to risk him calling off because she did not wish either of them to be unhappily wed. *No other woman I have known would do such a thing.*

Elizabeth desired neither his money nor his status. She did not covet Pemberley, though he knew she had been there many times to visit his sister. She had told him very clearly why he might wish to reconsider, allowing him a discreet way to withdraw. She just wanted *him*. For himself. *Provided you do not do something stupid and let her slip through your fingers.*

He felt almost giddy, but it would not do to laugh as her father had done. He simply ran his thumb along the knuckles of her hands and rejoiced when she trembled at his touch. *She is a wonder.* He shook his head. He glanced at Mr. Bennet, who lifted his thick eyebrows. *This courtship cannot last long. I will not survive it.* Surely her father saw the wisdom . . .

"Miss Elizabeth," Darcy said at last, "the things you describe, they really are not performed so assiduously for the sake of husbands."

It was Elizabeth's turn to appear baffled. "What do you mean?"

Darcy chuckled. "These activities—the visits, Bond Street, entertaining?"

"Yes?" Her tentative expression was tinged with hope.

Darcy felt his heart going out to her. She felt out of place, too, then, as he often did when he read over mathematical theorems and wished his mother was around to discuss them. "It is the women who insist upon them," he informed her, "not the men. Well, perhaps those who sit in Parliament might require the social connections for their work." He raised an eyebrow at her. "I am not in Parliament."

Miss Elizabeth squeezed his hand. "So, you would not mind that I spend much of my time reading, writing letters, selecting and managing my interests?" She blushed. "Our interests?"

"I did not say that," he replied carefully. "You must know how much I cherish fulfilling my social obligations, particularly in London."

Her face clouded over.

"A wife who earns more than she spends, who is not a slave to the latest fashions, who does not wish to make the acquaintance of every titled family in London regardless of character, who can speak intelligently about Blenkinsop's rack and pinion patent, who has shares in the firm designing the locomotives themselves? It all sounds quite exhausting." He appeared to consider it. "But I suppose I might be able to live with it."

She looked away, but Darcy saw the smile.

"Well then, Mr. Darcy," Elizabeth said quietly, bringing her free hand to rest tentatively on top of his. "I suppose we many consider ourselves courting." She smiled brightly at her father.

Mr. Bennet smiled back. "Before we tell your mother the good news and lose all possibility of intelligent conversation, I would very much like to hear more about this locomotive."

"Blenkinsop's rack and pinion system was created largely to avoid a patent challenge from Trevithick," Darcy offered as he helped her to sit and took his chair again. He was genuinely curious. "How can you be certain that no such claim will be made against Blenkinsop?"

Miss Elizabeth's lips pursed into the little bow he loved so much. "I cannot. George Stephenson has been working on just such a thing, and his drawings are most promising. I intend to follow his progress and will likely invest in his designs as well."

Darcy laughed and accepted the glass of wine Mr. Bennet held out to him. "It may be early for indulging," Mr. Bennet said, his eyes crinkling at the corners, "but I have a great inclination to toast my clever daughter."

Miss Elizabeth held her own glass and blushed again, nearly the color of the wine itself. "Thank you, Papa," she said, then turned to Darcy. He touched his glass to hers and lifted the drink to his lips, never breaking the connection of their gaze. Mr. Bennet cleared his throat and they both startled.

"The steam-engine, Elizabeth," her father said firmly. "Tell me about it."

✤

"Mr. Darcy," Elizabeth said, once they had concluded speaking about investments, "I realize we were focused on other things, but who was the man Mr. Bingley walked away from the carriage?"

He nodded. "He ran directly at the carriage, causing the driver to pull up rather severely or risk running him down. To be honest, I wished to put distance between us before discussing him. I was not entirely certain he was . . . well." He set his wineglass down. "He said his name was Mr. Collins?"

Mr. Bennet groaned, placing his own glass on his desk and leaning back in his chair. "Whatever was that fool doing accosting your coach?" His face paled. "No one was hurt, I hope?"

"No," Mr. Darcy assured him, and gave Elizabeth a questioning look. She shook her head a fraction of an inch, and he did not inform her father that both she and Jane had been thrown from their seats.

"Who is he?" she asked.

Mr. Bennet closed his eyes. "My cousin, and the heir to Longbourn."

"He was telling the truth, then," Mr. Darcy said. "Bingley and I sent him on to Netherfield."

Mr. Bennet looked at him askance. "Why would you do that?"

"Because he was an idiot of the first order," Mr. Darcy replied, as though it was the most logical thing in the world. Then he flinched. "Forgive me, sir." Mr. Bennet waved off his apology. Mr Darcy crossed his legs so that his left ankle was resting on his right knee. "Also, because it would give us time . . ."

"To complete your business with me?" Mr. Bennet broke in. He grunted his approval and reached for his abandoned tea. "I think Lizzy may not be the only tactician in the room."

Elizabeth tapped one slipper on the rug. "Mama told me she sent Mr. Collins to seek me at Netherfield. She has told him I would be pleased to marry him."

Her father almost choked. "What?" he gasped, pulling a handkerchief from his pocket and wiping his mouth with it.

Elizabeth was gratified by her father's obvious shock. "She said that she had encouraged him to ask for my hand because Jane was shortly to be engaged," she said, the bashful light in her eyes gone. "That it was wonderful that I would be mistress to Longbourn and thus returned to my real family."

Thomas Bennet rubbed his eyes with a hand and seemed to be stifling a stronger response. "My apologies, Lizzy. I did tell him to amuse himself this morning. He has been driving me to distraction, and I had work to do." He looked at her and then Mr. Darcy. "Mr. Collins showed up here three days early, saying his patroness had allowed him additional time."

"Without informing you?" Elizabeth was aghast.

"Now, I cannot accuse him of that—yet," Mr. Bennet said, motioning at a stack of letters on his desk. "I have not yet gone through this week's post. He certainly proceeded without a *response* from me. I suppose his esteemed patroness deemed it unnecessary."

Mr. Darcy cleared his throat and pulled at his cravat. "I am afraid that his esteemed patroness is my late mother's sister."

"No," Elizabeth said in disbelief, swiveling back to meet his embarrassed face. Mr. Darcy was almost boyishly disconcerted, a spot of red appearing in each cheek. *Gentlemen do not like to be told they are sweet, Lizzy. Do not tell him.*

"Lady Catherine?" she asked, though she thought she knew.

"Definitely Lady Catherine."

Mr. Bennet snorted. "Does Collins know? I cannot imagine the fawning he will subject you to."

"He bowed so low I think he may have had dirt on his nose," Mr. Darcy observed wryly, and Mr. Bennet propped an elbow on the surface of his desk, supporting his head in one hand as he laughed.

Elizabeth reached forward and touched her suitor's arm. "Thank you," she said simply.

"Whatever for?" Mr. Darcy responded. "I am afraid my thoughts were entirely on my own gain, Miss Elizabeth, and Bingley's on his."

"No, Mr. Darcy," she said, her voice quiet and composed. "Your first thought was to save me from a fall. Your second was to accompany Mr. Bingley and offer your assistance. Your third was likely to protect us all from a man whose character was not clear to you. Your last thought was to send him on his original errand while you tended to yours. You knew he would find nobody in residence at Netherfield."

"That is not precisely accurate, Miss Elizabeth," he reminded her. "My cousin is there."

Her eyes widened, and one slender hand moved to cover her mouth. "Oh! Mr. Fitzwilliam!" she exclaimed. "Whatever will he do with the man?"

Mr. Darcy's face was difficult to read, but his eyes danced. "I do not know, Miss Elizabeth," he said. "But I greatly anticipate learning."

It was some time before they left Mr. Bennet to his books. Miss Bennet and Bingley were entering the house, having taken a walk about the gardens. Kitty entered behind them and after a brief greeting, flitted off to the stillroom. As the four of them moved towards the drawing room at the front of the house, there was a commotion outside. Darcy heard a man's voice raised in irritation and, he thought, delight.

"Watch your mount, you cow-handed dandyprat!"

"Ah," he said, flashing Bingley a look, "Richard has arrived."

Elizabeth's first impression of her distant cousin, the Reverend Mr. Collins, was not an auspicious one. Her father had explained that he was a young man only a few years past ordination. He had matriculated from an august university, already secured a good living when most of his peers were forced to take positions as curates, and stood, at Mr. Bennet's death, to inherit Longbourn. Yet before her was clearly a man who, despite all of his accomplishments and good fortune, had managed to remain estranged from all common sense.

She recognized him at once as the man she had seen Mr. Bingley leading away from the carriage earlier in the day. He was dressed in black though he was now bareheaded, but of more concern to her was his clumsy attempt to dismount. While one foot hovered a few inches above the ground, the other was still firmly tucked up into a stirrup. He was trying to steady himself by grasping the saddle but it slipped a bit. The horse was turning in tight circles protesting this mistreatment, neatly avoiding the stable boy's increasingly desperate grabs with increasingly harried tosses of his head. When the horse began skittering to one side, Elizabeth nearly dashed forward to take the reins. She was not certain whether she was more concerned about the man or the horse, but in any case, her forward movement was stilled by a hand placed lightly on her arm.

"Fitzwilliam knows what he is about, Miss Elizabeth," Mr. Darcy said gently. "Best let him handle it."

As if he had heard his cousin, Mr. Fitzwilliam smoothly pulled his own mount astride the harried horse and quickly took control of the reins. "You are fortunate I am here, Collins," he declared in a booming voice. "Another minute, and you and your horse would be parting company." He shook his head in disgust and gestured at Collins's foot in the stirrup. "Though not as soon as you might hope, I daresay." He barked out a few instructions, and with the stable boy's assistance, Mr. Collins soon had both feet on the ground.

Once he was assured that the horse would not run off with Mr. Collins still attached to the stirrup, Mr. Fitzwilliam realized he had an audience. A wicked smile grew upon his face, and, still atop his horse, he pointed directly at Mr. Darcy. This rude gesture surprised Elizabeth until she recalled they had grown up together and must often take such liberties with one another.

"Dun territory, Darcy," Mr. Fitzwilliam called as his horse pranced to the side. His expression was playful and yet promised some form of retribution would be forthcoming. "Deep, deep dun."

Both Mr. Darcy and Mr. Bingley began to laugh. This also was not proper. It was not a mild break in decorum, a chuckle, brief and stifled. It was a full, deep, body-shaking laughter that only close friends shared. Mr. Bingley bent at the waist, hands resting on his thighs to support him as he gasped for breath. Elizabeth met Jane's eyes over the man's back and saw that her sister wore the same bemused smile that she knew graced her own face. They did not know exactly why the men were in such a state, but their laughter was infectious. It made her think that there was yet another advantage to marrying Mr. Darcy should their courtship lead to what she was now fully expecting to be its logical conclusion. He and Mr. Bingley were on such easy terms that she and Jane were sure to spend a good deal of time together, at least when they were both in town.

This made her very cheerful indeed until Mr. Collins scampered over to their small group. He immediately made a ridiculously deep bow so close to her that she was required to take a step back to avoid being struck by his head. Mr. Darcy's hand on the small of her back steadied her; his face was no longer wreathed in humor, and it was this more than the man before her that dampened her pleasant mood.

"Miss Elizabeth," Mr. Collins said, then repeated the process in Jane's general direction. "Miss Bennet." He finally straightened. "I am Mr. Collins, your cousin."

"Mr. Collins," Elizabeth replied with a shallow curtsey once he was a safe distance from her. She intended to take some pity on him. He was family, after all, no matter how distant, and perhaps nobody had taught him the importance or order of a proper introduction. *You cannot be pleased by a lack of propriety in Mr. Darcy and then displeased by it in Mr. Collins*, she told herself sternly, though she knew the situations were different. It would be better for everyone if she could hide her distaste; it was not Mr. Collins's fault, after all, that Mama had given him expectations.

Then Mr. Collins opened his mouth to speak. In an instant, every charitable thought dissolved.

"My dear cousin," he began, and there was a smoothness to his speech that made her vaguely ill, "I have been most particularly anxious to meet you. Your excellent mother has explained why you were not here to meet me, and I must say that your dedication to nursing your ill sister back to health has only increased my esteem." He took her arm to lead her away and was startled to find that she had not moved. He tugged again, not hard, but as though she was unaware of his intent, and Elizabeth was forced to take a shuffling step forward. She did not need to see Mr. Darcy's expression to know that it was darkening.

"Mr. Collins," she said to him, hoping to avoid a physical response from Mr. Darcy. "You will kindly remove your hand."

He laughed as though she had told him a very good joke. "But how are we to get to know one another, Cousin Elizabeth, if we do not spend time together?" He addressed Mr. Darcy. "I am certain Mr. Darcy will not mind. He cannot mean to remain here long."

"Why would that be, Mr. Collins?" Mr. Darcy all but growled, staring at the man.

Mr. Collins was undaunted. "Because as lovely as Longbourn might be, sir, my cousins and I are not of your sphere. Quite beneath it. I assure you, I am not insensible to the requirements of rank and precedence." He smiled, then, his lips twisting into a pained half-grimace. "I understand that you are to have Rosings when you marry, an estimable estate indeed."

Mr. Darcy stepped up next to her and Elizabeth saw that Mr. Fitzwilliam was approaching Mr. Collins silently from behind. Mr. Fitzwilliam lifted an eyebrow at his cousin. As she watched with great interest, Mr. Darcy and his cousin held a conversation with nothing more than a few exchanged looks and a smug expression on the part of her suitor.

While grateful for the show of strength, she worried that the situation might get out of hand. She cleared her throat, and the attention of all three men turned to her while Bingley stepped around them to usher Jane away from the confrontation and into the house. Jane did not appear pleased to be rushed away, but she allowed it. Elizabeth returned her gaze to the strange man in black who stood expectantly before her.

"A gentleman does not *take* the arm of a woman, he *requests* it." Elizabeth straightened her shoulders. "You will remove your hand, Mr. Collins."

But it was clear he had not understood at all. "Oh, of course, Cousin Elizabeth," he crowed. He let his hand drop and then smirked. "May I take your arm?"

She sighed. "No, Mr. Collins, you may not."

The pastor tilted his head slightly to one side, confused. "But I have requested it, as is proper."

"Which is not the same as Miss Elizabeth granting that request," Mr. Darcy replied. He spoke evenly, and Elizabeth thought he had recovered his equanimity, but after a fleeting glance at the frost in his eyes, it was clear he had not. She offered him a little smile and turned back to her cousin.

"Mr. Collins," she said, trying to speak softly, "I know my mother has told you I would have no objection to receiving your addresses, but she is not possessed of all the facts. I am not available for marriage to you, sir, and I must ask you to desist in your attentions."

Mr. Collins waved his hand. "But I am sure you could have no objections to my suit, madam. Not when approved by your excellent mother."

Despite the insult to her own understanding, Elizabeth could not help feeling a tickle in her throat accompanying the pique. She had seen that Mr. Collins was rather dim but now he was displaying a tendency for pomposity that was wonderfully absurd. She could not help but ask, "And why is that, sir? What about you is so entirely splendid that no woman dare say nay?" Mr. Fitzwilliam's lips quirked upward but he otherwise maintained a straight face.

"Elizabeth," Mr. Darcy growled, and she was startled enough at his use of her Christian name to press her lips together. "You are not helping matters."

I should stop. I cannot stop. "No, I should truly wish to know, Mr. Collins," Elizabeth continued. "What could possibly negate my very clear refusal of your attentions?"

He entirely missed the set-down. Instead, Mr. Collins's chest puffed a little as he began to lay out his accomplishments in a well-rehearsed speech. He had a fine living and a lovely home. He was a man of the cloth, much respected; his wife would have purpose in life and leadership in her community. "Not to mention that I enjoy the great condescension of Lady Catherine de Bourgh." He paused to take a deep breath.

"I thank you for laying out all the advantages of the match so completely, Mr. Collins," Elizabeth said hurriedly at this juncture, meaning to end the monologue. *You did this to yourself. Mr. Darcy tried to warn you.* "You must speak with my father, sir," she said, trying to be gentle but not so gentle as to be misunderstood. "I say again that I am not available as the object of your matrimonial aspirations."

She turned back to the house and saw that Mr. Bingley had returned, standing a little further away, but observing them carefully. Mr. Darcy offered his arm and she took it. Elizabeth felt as she believed a queen might as he led her away and Mr. Fitzwilliam and Mr. Bingley fell in behind them. She laughed softly. The duke and marquess could not have handled it better.

"What is it precisely that you find humorous, Miss Elizabeth?" Mr. Darcy asked. She could see that while he was somewhat more relaxed now, he had very much wished to have words with Mr. Collins.

"Oh," she replied lightly, with one shake of her head. "I was just wondering how you would respond to an *actual* threat. Would you call out the militia, do you think?"

They entered the front hall in a knot, and as Elizabeth watched, Mr. Fitzwilliam bowed to her smartly and gave her a wink. "If necessary, madam."

She eyed him warily. "I hardly think . . ."

He shook his head, and her thought trailed off. "We take care of our own, Miss Elizabeth," he said.

Elizabeth had been prepared to treat the entire ridiculous event with good humor and banish it from her thoughts entirely, but the notion brought her up short. It made her heart leap and ache at the same time. *One of our own.*

"After he took the stairs, checked every room in the guest wing, the entire first floor, was served tea . . ." Richard paused to issue a heated glare at his cousin and host. "And I will have you know the man does not stop speaking even when he is eating . . ."

Darcy and Bingley grimaced.

"Then I had him check the gardens, after which he required a sit-down of half an hour to catch his breath. Unfortunately, that merely restored his voice."

Bingley's eyes were twinkling, but Darcy knew they dare not laugh while his cousin was still complaining. He bit the inside of his cheek.

Richard continued outlining his efforts. "We were then off to the stables where he was nearly kicked in the head more than once." He tossed back the rest of his brandy. "I almost drew his cork myself, but the stable hands finally shoved him atop a horse just to ensure he would depart." He shuddered at the memory. "It was," he closed his eyes, "ugly." His eyes popped open and he fixed them on Darcy. "You owe those boys some coin."

"Richard," Darcy said apologetically, "I am in your debt." *More than you know.*

"More than one bottle of cognac, no matter how fine," was his cousin's sour reply. "I am done to a cow's thumb. Have not faced so obtuse a man since the army."

Bingley spoke up then. "I will match Darcy's offer with a few bottles of my best brandy, Fitzwilliam," he said. "It was as much in my service as his that we sent Mr. Collins on to Netherfield."

"You are already hosting me," Richard replied, and stood to pour himself a drink. "You took me in when I needed refuge from my matchmaking mother. You and I are square."

Darcy's head shot up. *Oh, dear Lord.* "Richard," he said, drawing his cousin's name out uncertainly. Richard's eyes narrowed.

"What?" he almost barked, drink forgotten. "I am not taking that man out again, Darcy. There is not enough cognac in the world that can tempt me to it."

"I learned something a few days ago, but I did not think . . . "

"Something you have been surprisingly good at since we have been at Netherfield," Bingley goaded him.

Darcy rolled his eyes. "No defense is being mounted, Bingley."

Richard waited silently.

"Miss Bennet . . ." Darcy began.

"Miss *Elizabeth* Bennet," Bingley interrupted, and Darcy frowned at him. "Do not look at me like that, Darce," Bingley scoffed. "I simply wish to be clear that Miss Bennet is my future bride, not yours."

"Well, the confusion should not last long, Bingley," he said stiffly. "For Bennet is not Elizabeth's only surname."

"What?" Bingley asked, puzzled.

At least he did not withhold that from me, Darcy thought. Bingley and Richard waited impatiently for him to finish. *They saved me from making a huge mistake. Elizabeth would not have remained unattached for long.*

"Richard," he said again, and plowed forward. "Miss Elizabeth Bennet is, in truth, Miss Elizabeth Bennet . . . Russell."

"Russell?" Bingley blurted out. "The Miss Russell Fitzwilliam was hiding from?"

Darcy nodded slowly. "The very one."

Richard was dangerously silent for a long moment. "So she is *not* Georgie's age."

"No," Darcy confirmed.

"In fact," Richard said slowly, "she is of an appropriate age and quite handsome."

Darcy's face began to grow warm. "Quite."

"And," Richard mused aloud, "connected to the Duke of Bedford, which my mother was certain to mention." He cocked his head to one side. "My mother hand-selected her for me." Darcy could not decide whether his cousin was indeed upset or whether Richard merely wanted him to squirm. *Perhaps both?*

"I do not believe she spoke for Miss Russell, cousin," Darcy warned.

Richard fell back into his chair and said nothing, and Darcy felt guilty, though he knew none of it was his fault. Bingley—Bingley was grinning from ear to ear.

"She told me when I proposed," Darcy said. "I swear I did not know until then. And then I was so . . . ."

His cousin gave him a sidelong glance. "So?"

Darcy closed his eyes. He might as well be honest. The two men in this room could be trusted, though he knew he would forever be the source of their jests. "Happy. I was so happy, I did not even think about the name, not until later."

Richard harrumphed, and lapsed again into a brooding silence. He sat and sipped at his brandy. Eventually his eyes closed and he leaned his head against the back of the chair.

"Speaking of not saying anything, Bingley . . ." Darcy asked, truly interested but also eager to change the subject. "You made me appear a complete fool in front of Mr. Bennet today."

Bingley's expression was smug. "It seems things went well enough."

Darcy pressed his point. "You knew they were comfortable, Charles, that they will require no more than trifling assistance when Mr. Bennet passes. You are my friend. You might have hinted, at least." *I might have proposed earlier. But would it have helped?* He had to admit to himself that it probably would not have. He had already uttered those stupid words at the assembly.

Bingley settled into a comfortable chair next to Richard, entirely unrepentant. Darcy took the chair opposite.

"There are two reasons I did not, Darcy." Bingley lifted his feet onto the ottoman and observed Darcy closely. "First, I had promised Mr. Bennet that I would not betray his confidence." He frowned, deep in thought.

Darcy grudgingly allowed that once having given his word, Bingley could not have broken it. "And the second?" he prompted his friend.

He watched Bingley's face. Charles was by far the youngest of them and had always been the most easy-going, willing to acquiesce to the other, stronger personalities that surrounded him. But something had changed in Hertfordshire, although whether it was being the temporary master of Netherfield, finally coming to terms with his sisters, or falling in love with Miss Bennet, Darcy could not say. He had a sense that Bingley was coming into his own, that he would not be easily guided from here on out. It made him simultaneously irritated at Bingley for choosing this particular time to grow stubborn and proud of him for becoming his own man. Darcy's conflict was confirmed when Bingley raised his head and stared straight into his eyes without flinching.

"The second reason, Darcy," Bingley said decisively, "was that you did not yet deserve her."

As that statement hung in the air, Richard pushed himself to a standing position. "An Arabian," he said, leaning over his cousin, his entire posture daring Darcy to decline. "I want the next Arabian from your stables."

CHAPTER TWO

Elizabeth took a deep breath of the frigid November air. It was early on Monday morning and she was out walking the estate with her younger sisters. She had been inside all day on Sunday, remaining with Jane instead of venturing out to church with the rest of the family. While it had provided a respite from Mr. Collins's unwanted attentions, she was sorely in need of some time outdoors.

Although Jane now seemed fully recovered, the girls had let her sleep, not wishing her to venture into the cold just yet. They *had* rousted Lydia from her bed to allow Mrs. Grover an opportunity to sleep a bit later, but Elizabeth was currently questioning that decision. Lydia had complained nearly the entire hour. She was not pleased with being forced from her warm bed on a chilly morning and had made certain her grievances were heard.

"Lydia," Kitty had finally said, exasperated, "kindly cease. Nobody cares that you are cold. We are all cold."

"We should have left her at home to face Mr. Collins alone over the breakfast table," Mary groused.

Lydia's eyes opened wide, her mouth snapped shut, and she shook her head in short, sharp movements.

"Elizabeth is expecting Mr. Darcy this morning, but you do not see her crying about taking a walk instead of picking out a gown and fixing her hair," Kitty pointed out. Elizabeth tried not to laugh. It would not have mattered if royalty was coming to visit, she was unlikely to spend her morning in such a way. Mary gave her a skeptical look and Elizabeth returned it with a mock glare. *Mr. Darcy will have to take me as I am. He does not seem to mind.* Her heart warmed at the thought.

"I cannot believe Mama put Mr. Collins in the room across from yours, Lizzy," Kitty said in her cautious way. "He is so . . . "

"Unctuous?" Mary finished. She shuddered dramatically. "It is difficult to believe he is a man of the cloth."

"A man of the cloth is still a man," Lydia retorted, and they all stopped and turned to her. Her face flushed red. "Well, he is! And he is not a gentleman at all. I saw how he brushed your arm at dinner, Lizzy. Twice."

Elizabeth crinkled her nose. "You saw it? The first time I thought it might have been in error, but then he did it again."

Mary's eyes narrowed. "How *dare* he!" Her face darkened like a storm cloud. "I shall pinch him," she declared.

"No, let me!" Lydia cried. "All Papa will do is send me upstairs and I have to be there for lessons regardless." Even Kitty laughed at that. "No, really!" Lydia insisted. "I do not wish to be downstairs when *he* is a visitor at Longbourn. Besides, I am the best pincher of us all."

Elizabeth smiled at the three of them. "I appreciate your defense of me," she said. "But I am already spoken for. It is better he wastes his time with me than turn his sights to any of you." She glanced at Mary, whose face grew solemn. Kitty paled. Lydia's face screwed up defiantly. "His visit will soon be over," Elizabeth continued, "and Lady Catherine de Bourgh will recall him to Kent. From Mr. Collins' descriptions of his patroness, I suspect that his leave is unlikely to be extended."

"No doubt," Mary scoffed. "Back to Rosings he will go, the palace with a thousand windows, the glazing on which originally cost in excess of fifty pounds apiece," she said, placing the back of her hand against her forehead and striking a pose. "Oh, but Mr. Collin does not actually *live* there. He never has much to say about his *own* home."

Kitty placed a thin hand on Elizabeth's arm. "Lizzy," she said, "you should tell Mr. Darcy."

Mr. Collins is just incredibly awkward and a little self-involved. Perhaps more than a little. She shook her head. *I do not require help to handle things with Mr.*

Collins. "No," Elizabeth said firmly. "We will let things go for now, and none of you shall say anything to Mr. Darcy."

Mary and Lydia loudly expressed their dissent, but eventually Elizabeth secured the agreement of all her younger sisters. They then decided that they had been out in the cold long enough and returned to the house.

Elizabeth left her sisters at the top of the stairs as they turned one way to their rooms and she went in the opposite direction to her own. She stopped short in the hall when she saw Mr. Collins lingering outside the door to her chambers. He ran a finger along the tabletop in the hallway, clearly loitering.

"Mr. Collins!" she snapped, not caring if her voice carried. "What are you about, sir?"

"Cousin Elizabeth!" he cried, one hand flying to his mouth. "I thought perhaps you were readying yourself for breakfast. I did not know you had already been out." He smiled at her crookedly and her ire rose. "Your habits coincide with my own," he continued. "I always rise early to tend to my duties." He clasped his hands behind his back and rocked back on his heels.

"My sisters wished to walk, sir," she replied. *My habits have naught to do with you.*

"You are uniformly charming," he told her abruptly.

He is thick, Elizabeth thought. She took a moment to consider. He was a sensible distance away and was not moving towards her. *He is just awkward and not terribly sensible. That is all.* She hoped that was all.

No sooner had she decided this than Mr. Collins scuttled forward and beamed down at her. He was neither as tall nor were his shoulders as broad as Mr. Darcy's, but he was still physically imposing. "May I escort you to breakfast?" He suddenly remembered to hold out his arm.

Elizabeth was nearly overpowered by a floral scent mixed with stale sweat and something that smelled like a tallow candle. *Animal fat?* Was he styling his hair with it? She swallowed hard.

"No, sir," she replied, brushing past him to open her door and enter her room. "I am not hungry."

Mr. Collins shook his head at her as though she were a misbehaving child, but thankfully did not attempt to follow her. "Your mother . . . " he began.

Any sympathy she held for him evaporated entirely. "Mr. Collins, surely you *must* understand by now," she said. "My mother does not speak for my father, sir. Or for me. I am being courted by Mr. Darcy."

His forehead furrowed, and Elizabeth shut the door. Safely behind it, she located the key, turned the lock, and dropped the key into her pocket. *He will soon be gone.* She stood still until she heard his heavy footsteps leading away. Only then did she lay on her bed and close her eyes. His odor had turned her stomach, but now that he was gone, her appetite had returned. It mattered not. She could not go down to breakfast now—she would simply change her clothes and begin her day.

Darcy ate a hearty breakfast, relaxed in the absence of Bingley's sisters. When he was nearly finished, Richard appeared, setting down a plate and flinging himself into the chair opposite, stuffing his mouth with eggs and ham. He completed his meal with several rolls smothered in butter and preserves. He waved at a footman who came over to serve him a cup of steaming coffee. When he finished, he wiped his mouth with the napkin.

"What are your plans for today, Darcy?" he asked. He tossed the napkin on the table. "Off to Longbourn to court my wife?"

Bingley chose that moment to enter. He headed directly for the coffee. "You have a wife, Fitzwilliam?" he inquired. "I could have sworn you were a confirmed bachelor."

"I *might* have had a wife," Richard replied, "if Darcy had not stolen her from me." He raised an eyebrow. "Had I not played the loyal fool and withdrawn from the field, I am certain I would have won the lovely Miss Russell." His eyes were alight with challenge.

He will not goad me, Darcy thought. *Not today.* "I suppose we shall never know, cousin." He offered his cousin a smug smile. "For she has accepted *me.*"

"A courtship," Richard said, waving a hand. "A courtship is not a betrothal."

Bingley sat at the table. He placed the napkin on his lap and picked up his fork. "It matters little, Fitzwilliam," he said. "Anyone can see how besotted she is with the man, little though he deserves her."

Darcy's head swung to Bingley. "Truly?"

Richard snorted. "Insecure lovers. Makes me so ill I can barely eat."

"You just ate half a pig, Richard," Darcy observed with a grin. *She is besotted.*

"You see?" his cousin fired back. "I am used to eating an *entire* pig at breakfast." He patted his stomach and eyed his cousin. "I am quite wasting away."

Bingley shook his head. "We shall head to Longbourn after breakfast, Darcy."

"I have a letter from Mrs. White in town," Darcy said. "I must answer, but I shall be quick about it." He stood, but before turning from the table, plucked a flower from the centerpiece and stared at it. He looked at Bingley inquiringly. "Bingley, might I impose . . . "

This time Bingley laughed. "I should make you grovel, but I am too happy myself to require it. Go ahead to the conservatory. I already have a bouquet for Jane."

"Thank you, my friend," Darcy responded.

The letter from his London housekeeper Mrs. White mentioned that she had set a servant to polishing the silver, and when she counted everything before beginning, two silver spoons were missing from the set. She had counted the spoons several times to be certain. He sent back a letter suggesting she have the house searched thoroughly. If that did not resolve the problem, she should gather the staff and question them. He sealed his reply and set it on the salver for outgoing post before heading to the conservatory.

Later, as he waited for his coat, he heard Bingley, still in the breakfast room, inviting Richard to join them.

"You had best believe I am coming along," Richard replied, still put out. "You two are never leaving me alone again."

Elizabeth left her room only when Lydia knocked on the door to inform her that Mr. Bingley's carriage was approaching. When she stepped into the hall, Lydia pushed a seed cake into her hand.

"Bless you," Elizabeth whispered, breaking it into small pieces and making short work of it. It was terrible behavior, she knew, to eat in such a manner, but it would be worse if her stomach rumbled during Mr. Darcy's call. She waved Lydia off to the school-room before heading downstairs.

When she arrived in the drawing room, there was thankfully no sign of Mr. Collins. Mr. Bingley and Jane were seated in one corner, Mary was reading, Kitty was at her needlework, and Mr. Darcy was standing by a window waiting for her. She was struck, again, by how very tall he was, and how handsome. His dark curls just touched the collar of his shirt, and his eyes followed her as she approached. He was holding a small, tightly bound nosegay of white roses with deep green leaves, bound by a red ribbon. Her heart began to beat a little faster, a little harder.

"Good day, Mr. Darcy," she said, feeling unaccountably bashful.

"Good day, Miss Elizabeth," he replied. She let the deep, smooth tone of his voice wash over her. She glanced over at Jane and saw that Mr. Bingley had given her red roses in full bloom. She wondered why Mr. Darcy had chosen white, though she appreciated that each was an exquisite, only slightly-opened bud. They would last longer, blooming in her room and filling it with scent. He smiled as he offered them to her, and she knew from that smile he had noticed her comparing her sister's flowers to these. *Nothing I do escapes his notice*, she thought, embarrassed. Then she was struck by the truth of her observation. *Oh. Nothing I do escapes his notice.*

He waited for her to take them and then said in a voice only she could hear, "I saw the white roses and could not resist." He brushed his fingers lightly over hers. "Greek mythology tells us that Aphrodite, the goddess of love, was born from the foam of the sea."

She nodded. She had read that myth, too. She raised the flowers and bent her head to inhale their fragrance. It was crisp and sharp, like lemons. *I love them,* she thought.

He lowered his voice. "The Greek poet Anacreon claimed that the foam which fell from her as she emerged from the ocean transformed into white roses." He touched one of the buds tenderly. "When I think of Aphrodite, I think of you."

Elizabeth was certain her cheeks were bright red. His words were both innocent and daring. Her impulse was to tease him but could not find the words—he had struck her speechless. She found she did not mind.

When she glanced shyly up at him, his small smile grew into a wider one. "Would you like to take a short walk? The day is growing a little warmer."

"I would love to," she told him, despite having already been out. She glanced over at her sisters. "Mary," she asked, "would you care to accompany us outside?"

Mary agreed immediately, and Mr. Fitzwilliam rose from his seat near Kitty. "I will escort you, Miss Mary, if you will allow me." He cocked a challenging eyebrow at his cousin, and Darcy almost rolled his eyes. Mary seemed pleased, and Elizabeth worried her sister might have taken the request the wrong way. There was nothing for it, however, and the four of them walked out together. Elizabeth and Mr. Darcy had soon outpaced their chaperones.

"You are very bold this morning, Mr. Darcy," she said as he placed his free hand over hers where it rested in the crook of his arm.

"I promised myself when you agreed to be courted, I should be entirely open with you," he replied. "It is not easy for me, but I have caused misunderstandings enough with my behavior." He gazed at her, his expression troubled. "I have not been *too* bold, have I?"

Elizabeth paused a moment, then lifted her head. "No," she assured him. "You have been precisely the proper amount of bold."

The worry lines around his mouth disappeared. "Good," he said, lifting her hand to bestow a light kiss. "Good."

Elizabeth could not have related much of what they spoke of on their walk. Mr. Darcy, true to his word, demonstrated his care through numerous small gestures that assailed her senses: offering steady assistance over a stile, plucking a fallen leaf from the brim of her bonnet, gazing at her face as though nothing else mattered when she was speaking. It was necessary, she thought, to have *some* weightier conversation, to learn the things about one another that might ensure the felicity she was currently experiencing would last beyond their first argument as husband and wife. But he had entirely discomposed her. What topic might they possibly broach?

"Tell me about your childhood," she said at last, thinking that an exchange of personal stories might help them know one another better. "Why do you call your cousin by his Christian name while he calls you Darcy?"

"Habit, I suppose," Mr. Darcy said. "He called me by my Christian name as well until he returned from his first year at Eton. I call him Fitzwilliam in company, but not when we are in private." He smiled at her. "I suppose I have slipped a bit on this visit or you would not have heard it, but he has always been Richard to me."

Elizabeth smiled. "Have you and Mr. Fitzwilliam always been close, then?"

He looked over his shoulder at his cousin and Mary, who trailed a good distance behind them. "We have," he said, returning his attention to her. "I was, of course, the perfect child, but my cousin was constantly drawing me into trouble."

"I see," Elizabeth replied, "and should I ask Mr. Fitzwilliam, would he agree?"

"Of course," Mr. Darcy replied glibly. She only caught the quirk of his lips by the merest chance as she glanced up at him.

"Yes, it is just as I thought," she scoffed, triumphant. "It is always the quiet ones that must be watched, Mr. Darcy."

He laughed, then, with a sort of pleased surprise. "You have caught me out, Miss Elizabeth," he told her. "I was generally the instigator. Richard was older, and it was he who figured out how to make my wild plans work. It was no surprise to me when he chose the army over the church." He smiled, his eyes faraway for a moment. "When I was ten, we spent the entire summer training my dog to steal biscuits from the kitchen."

She smiled. *I can picture that so easily.* And she could, two young boys hiding in the woods as they trained their dog to fetch. "And were you successful?"

"Yes and no," he replied, with a shrug. "Jericho stole the biscuits and absconded cleanly, but we found him disinclined to share."

She smiled. "No honor among thieves, then?"

He shook his head mournfully. "Not at all. We were completely betrayed."

Elizabeth laughed gaily, but stopped abruptly when he patted her hand and said, "And you?"

"Me?" she asked, pretending not to understand, instead mimicking his words. "I was the perfect child, Mr. Darcy."

"Oh, come now, Miss Elizabeth," he chided her. "Do not think me so generous as to reveal my own criminal trespass without recompense. I imagine you made a good deal of mischief of your own."

"I would not say I had grand plans," she admitted, "though I did have a great many questions and a very fertile imagination. My aunt and I traipsed all over the grounds at Weymouth House, particularly the long stream that cuts through the property and the woods beyond. I think my uncle quite despaired of us at first."

"How old were you then?" he inquired. There was a soft smile on his face.

"Oh, ten or eleven, I should imagine. Far too old to be scaling trees with my sketchbook or removing my shoes and stockings to capture frogs in the creek."

"Were you so interested in frogs, then?" he asked with interest.

"I wanted to draw them, so I needed to see them," she explained. "The texture of their skin, the way their legs fold up, their large eyes—they were wonderful subjects, if a bit unwilling to sit for their portraits." She smiled at the memory. "My Aunt Olivia was the only adult I knew who would help me."

"What did she do, precisely?" Mr. Darcy asked.

"Why, she perched on a boulder and held the frog while I drew it," Elizabeth laughed. "It did not seem at all odd to me at the time, Aunt Olivia sitting cross-legged on a boulder above the creek in her best walking dress with a handful of frog. Uncle Phillip simply laughed at us both. But it was a good laugh," she hastened to add. "A happy laugh." She cast her eyes straight ahead and blinked rapidly until she was once again composed. "I had a lovely childhood, Mr. Darcy."

Darcy was charmed by Elizabeth's story about the frog, but he noted several things as they took turns reminiscing. One was that most of her happy memories were from Weymouth House, with a few from the trips she and the Russells had taken together. Another was that her departure from Longbourn had been painful. And the third was that she still deeply missed her uncle and was eager to see her aunt again.

She fit in with her sisters so well it was sometimes difficult to recall that she had only been a resident here for less than half a year. It was as if she had never been away, at least to his eyes. He was pleased to hear in her stories a rather profound attachment to each of them; he had not spent much time with her sisters, but they seemed pleasant enough. Miss Bennet was all that was proper and lovely and would make Charles an excellent wife. Miss Bingley might choke on her own bonnet, but she could not deny that even the tangential connection Miss Bennet had to the Duke of Bedford through the Russells was a substantial coup for her brother.

There was something else in her conversation, though, that struck him. She was not as close with her parents, and he suspected that it bothered her. Mrs. Bennet he found flighty and impolitic, but while he would not wish to escort her to a London soirée, there seemed to be little real harm in her. At least, he had thought so until he met Collins. However, Elizabeth's relationship with her mother seemed fraught and complicated. He would need to tread carefully there.

He rather liked Mr. Bennet. The man was witty and clever, much like his second daughter. But as she spoke, he considered that once they were no longer small, Mr. Bennet had not spent a great deal of time even with the daughters who remained at home. Elizabeth seemed concerned that he did not pay as much attention to them as he might. It was not uncommon among fathers to leave daughters to their mothers, to be sure, but the hurt he detected in Elizabeth's descriptions, even as she made excuses for his behavior—it touched him. He would never be that kind of father, he determined. He would *know* his children, boys and girls alike. Unfortunately, in what was becoming an annoying habit, his mind drifted away to a troop of little dark-haired children. Before he knew it, they had taken a fork in the road and were hidden from view by a stand of trees. Miss Elizabeth was standing in the middle of the path, her hands on her hips.

"Distracted so soon, Mr. Darcy?" she asked, her pert expression nearly undoing him right there on a public pathway. How had they walked so far?

"Thoughts of you *are* incredibly distracting, Miss Elizabeth," he said honestly. "My apologies, madam."

"Do you expect me to believe that you were thinking of me and not of the spring planting or your holiday plans, sir?" she inquired.

She was trying to remain stern and offended, but Miss Elizabeth was not made for unhappiness. *She cannot even hold a proper grudge*, he thought. *Thank God for that. She is the perfect woman for a man who cannot help but offend.* He reached out for one of her hands, which she obligingly offered. "I humbly beg your forgiveness, my dear," he said playfully, glancing around to be sure they were alone before crouching down in front of her in mock supplication. "I was only imagining what it would be like to have our children racing about the grounds at Pemberley, catching frogs and drawing them."

She slapped his shoulder lightly, her face a beautiful shade of light pink. "Get up, Mr. Darcy, before someone thinks you are proposing."

He released her hand, standing as she asked but leaning in, close but not touching, making her cheeks flush even pinker. "But I *am*, Elizabeth."

She shivered as he spoke her Christian name. She bit her lip and looked up at him.

"When I bring you flowers," he said, only now articulating the thought even for himself, "I am proposing. When we walk, I am proposing." He took a half-step back, extending his hand, palm out, waiting for her to accept it. When she did, he continued. "When we exchange tales of wayward youth, I am proposing." He smiled at her and saw her free hand lift, then drop.

She wants to touch me, he thought, elated. He made small circles on the back of her hand with his thumb. "*You* are the one who asked for a courtship, and I am happy to give you the time you need. But make no mistake, Miss Elizabeth," he said, his eyes gazing steadily into her own. "With my every action, I am proposing marriage to you. It is my deepest desire, and I hope to soon make it yours."

When they all returned to the house, Richard placed a hand on Darcy's shoulder and allowed the women to precede them into the drawing room.

"Miss Mary spoke to me about Collins," he said, once the women were gone.

"Tell me," Darcy said sharply.

Richard slapped his gloves lightly against his palm, speaking as he swept the room with his eyes to be sure they had privacy. "He has apparently made Miss Elizabeth uncomfortable enough that she missed breakfast with her family this morning rather than sit next to him."

Darcy's stony expression never wavered, but his back stiffened.

"We will take care of it, Darce, but discreetly," Richard said. "Miss Mary says her sister is mortified but also determined to put up with the man so he does not turn his attentions to her younger sisters. Miss Elizabeth seems to think him awkward and perhaps petty, but ultimately harmless. She extracted a promise from them not to mention anything about it."

"Then why did Miss Mary tell you?" Darcy inquired.

Richard smiled. "Apparently the promise was rather specific—Miss Mary promised only that she would not speak to *you*. The promise did not mention *me*. She felt that in this case, the spirit of the promise should give way to the letter of it."

"Clever girl," Darcy said approvingly.

Richard nodded and then grinned. "Miss Mary suggested we would be wise to act before Miss Lydia does."

Darcy's mask remained intact, but his words were warm. "I like these Bennet girls, Richard," he said. "I like them very much."

As he strode towards the entry to the drawing room, he could have sworn he heard his cousin mutter, "I like them, too."

When he entered the room, Darcy saw, to his displeasure, that while Miss Elizabeth had taken a chair, Collins had drawn a chair up beside hers. She could not move her own chair away without appearing rude, but her arms were drawn in tight against her sides, her hands resting on her lap, her body tilted slightly away from the reverend. She was the very picture of discomfort. Darcy made his greetings quickly and moved to the pair.

"Mr. Collins," he said quietly. Elizabeth's chin came up. He could feel the heat of her gaze.

Mr. Collins stood to make a bow. "Mr. Darcy," he said. "How kind of you to visit with my poor cousins."

He might have laughed in Collins's face were it not for the sight of Elizabeth's misery. Instead, he said, "Mr. Collins, would you be so kind as to request more water be brought for tea?"

It was not Collins's position, either as a man or a guest, to make such a request, but he scurried off, pleased to be of service to a nephew of his benefactress. Darcy grasped the back of the chair with one hand to move it to a more respectable distance from Miss Elizabeth. Then he sat in it.

He leaned towards her. "I thought he would never leave," he said in a conspiratorial whisper.

She closed her eyes and took a deep breath. Her posture relaxed. "Thank you, Mr. Darcy. You are once again my knight in tarnished armor."

"Is Mr. Collins bothering you, Miss Elizabeth?" he asked seriously. "More than . . .?" he gestured to the space between them.

She wanted to deny it. He could read the expressions warring for precedence on her expressive face. "He is not . . . but . . . yes," she finally whispered back. She appeared embarrassed.

He nodded.

"What will you do?" she asked, pulling at her sleeve. "He will remain nearly a fortnight more."

"I shall tell him we are courting, and he will desist," Darcy replied simply.

Miss Elizabeth frowned. "I have told him so myself. I have also asked him to speak with my father, but evidently Mr. Collins cannot be bothered to do so."

He will listen to me, Elizabeth. "Then we shall not offer him a choice," he told her. "It is past time he turned his attentions elsewhere, wherever that might be."

"He will look to Mary next," she said anxiously. "I would not wish that. Perhaps we should allow things to remain as they are. He is embarrassing, but he is not vicious."

She was more anxious than he expected, and it made him angry. Having Collins in such close quarters even for a few days had unsettled her. "Will you trust me?" he asked, shifting very slightly towards her, and rejoicing silently when she unconsciously mirrored his movement.

She smoothed her skirt and glanced up at him. His breath caught at the faith he saw shining in her eyes. "Yes," she said simply, and that was all.

"Mr. Collins," Darcy said quietly as the Netherfield party rose to take their leave, "might I have the honor of a conference outdoors before we depart?" Mr. Collins's chest puffed up a little, and though he heard Richard scoff and saw Bingley's eyes shoot up the ceiling, he was determined to show no emotion at all.

Mr. Bennet had just finished giving his steward a set of instructions and was dismounting a stout Cleveland Bay in the drive when the men walked out. He raised an eyebrow as Mr. Collins followed Mr. Darcy out of the house, Mr. Bingley and Mr. Fitzwilliam not far behind.

Darcy nodded at him. "You are more than welcome to join us should you wish, Mr. Bennet," he said politely. "I have a message to relay to Mr. Collins you might wish to hear."

Mr. Bennet's eyes cut over to his cousin, and he nodded. "Very well," he replied. He handed his horse off to a stable boy and joined them.

They gathered together near a pair of trees that marked the beginning of the crescent-shaped approach to the house.

"Collins," Darcy said, "I understand you have been ignoring Miss Elizabeth's requests that you speak to her father before approaching her."

Mr. Bennet's face grew stormy.

"I hope I do not speak out of turn, sir," Darcy said, with a small bow to Elizabeth's father, "but from what Miss Elizabeth says, Mr. Collins has ignored her reasonable request, though she has made it more than once."

"He has not spoken to me," Mr. Bennet said, scowling.

"I presumed as much." Darcy turned to Collins. "Mr. Collins, you cannot court Miss Elizabeth, because I am already courting her. It is a formal arrangement, sanctioned by her father." *And her aunt, which might be more important.* "You will cease your attentions to the woman I intend to make my wife."

"Mr. Darcy," Collins began, making an inelegant half-bow, "your gracious condescension to my cousins brings to mind your most excellent aunt. She sent me here to heal the breach between our families.

A marriage would ensure Longbourn remains in the Bennet family, after a fashion, of course. Lady Catherine de Bourgh," here he let out an affected sigh, "is never wrong, and she has said, many times, that you are to wed her daughter, sir, that it has been planned so since you were in your cradles." He pressed his fleshy hands together. "Her ladyship has not yet informed me when you and Miss de Bourgh are to be wed, but it would be my great honor to perform the ceremony, indeed, most . . .'"

Darcy simply stared at the man as he continued to babble, trying to make him out. *The man is not sensible.* He cocked his head to one side, feeling as though he was listening to the squeaking of a rather tall, rather heavy rodent. He must have had a peculiar expression on his face, for Richard placed a hand on his shoulder.

"We could just drag him into the woods, Darce," his cousin said nonchalantly, not even trying to keep his voice down. "There is a deceptively deep bog on the northern edge of Netherfield's lands. Between the mud and the animals, nobody would ever find the body."

Bingley sighed dramatically. "Why do your plans always include so much extra work, Fitzwilliam?" he grumbled. "Why must we drag him miles into the woods? Just bring Mr. Bennet's horse back and let him try to ride it. Nature would surely take its course."

The clergyman's face paled alarmingly, and he looked to his cousin for some sort of reassurance. Mr. Bennet's lips twitched. "I cannot be a party to murder, Mr. Fitzwilliam."

Collins began to regain a little color, until Mr. Bennet spoke again. "I shall therefore remove to the house. If Mr. Collins does not return, I will understand that he followed you gentlemen back to Netherfield on foot." He smiled at Richard. "Perhaps he became disoriented."

"But, but . . . cousin," sputtered Collins. "I am here to heal the breach. Surely . . ."

Mr. Bennet's detached amusement disappeared suddenly and he stepped up to the younger, taller man. "Collins," he said, and icicles nearly formed upon his words, so cold were they, "I have spent nearly my entire life trying to bring this estate back to its former glory. You have showed not the slightest interest in riding the property with me. I have no doubt that within ten years of your stewardship, decades of constant, painstaking work will be undone." He glared at his cousin and shook his head slowly. "Do not test me. I more than anyone would profit from your disappearance." He gave the parson a cold once-over. "You will not speak to any of my daughters about courtship or marriage, do you understand? They are unavailable to you, no matter what wild scheme their mother has cooked up."

Darcy was a little startled at the quiet vehemence Mr. Bennet was displaying. *I did not know the man had it in him.* He heartily approved.

Mr. Bennet narrowed his eyes. "I will allow you to remain here, for now, dependent upon your good behavior. I should not protest a local woman becoming the mistress of Longbourn, for such a woman may care more for its history than you have demonstrated." His face hovered inches from Collins's. "But listen well: the next mistress of Longbourn will not be a Bennet." He stepped back, and Darcy noted the shocked delight on the faces of Richard and Bingley.

Mr. Bennet turned to face them, his countenance again relaxed. "Gentlemen," he said. He gave them a shallow bow, and strode away.

CHAPTER THREE

"Where is your mother, girls?" their father asked from the doorway of the drawing room.

Jane stood. "I believe she is in conference with Mrs. Hill, Papa." She cast a concerned glance at Elizabeth, who lifted her shoulders minutely.

"Thank you." He turned to leave, but suddenly stopped and turned back. "Elizabeth," he said cautiously.

"Yes, Papa?"

"You were not home when my cousin arrived, and I am sorry to say I have not been paying him much mind." He cleared his throat. "Where has your mother put Mr. Collins?"

Elizabeth looked up at him. "Across the hall from my chamber."

A muscle twitched in her father's cheek. "You will remove to one of your sister's rooms while he is with us, Lizzy."

She nodded, and then he was gone.

Mr. Collins did not appear for dinner that evening. Elizabeth ate enthusiastically while her mother complained. He did appear for breakfast the following morning, albeit briefly, sitting next to Kitty and not making any conversation at all. When he rose and took his leave, no one was sorry to see him go.

"You shared with Jane last night, Lizzy," Lydia said immediately. "Share with me tonight, please?"

Elizabeth smiled. "You snore, Lydia. I should have no sleep at all."

"I do not!" Lydia exclaimed indignantly, looking around the table for support. "I do not!"

"Yes," Kitty said firmly, "you do. You practically make the paint peel."

Mr. Bennet lifted his paper higher, though it did shake a little. Mrs. Bennet seemed not to hear the conversation at all, and wandered out to the hall, presumably to watch Mr. Collins leaving.

Jane, Elizabeth, and Mary stifled their laughter, but Jane finally cracked, setting her elbow on the table and leaning her forehead against her hand. "Oh," she said between laughs. "Oh dear." Then she drew in a breath—and snorted.

The girls all stopped. The edge of the newspaper turned down to revel one brown eye. There was complete silence as Jane's hand flew over her mouth and she flushed a deep pink, which only had the effect of making her lovelier than ever.

And then there was laughter enough to rattle the windowpanes.

It was not long after the noise died down that the mistress of the house could be seen through the breakfast room's open door. She was pacing the hall, complaining of ill use on the part of her husband and second daughter to the long-suffering Mrs. Hill. When the front door closed behind Mr. Collins, she began to wring her hands as she walked. One by one, the girls excused themselves, cast a glance at their mother, and fled upstairs. At last, only Elizabeth was left in the dining room, as she intended to show her father the same support he had offered her the day before.

"Mrs. *Bennet*," Mr. Bennet said harshly, rubbing his forehead. "Come inside."

She did, still in a flutter.

Mr. Bennet sighed, folding his newspaper neatly and placing it next to his plate. He folded his hands together and laid them on the table. "Sit down, Mrs. Bennet."

Elizabeth's mother took a seat at the table.

"I will not say this again. Mr. Collins will not receive my permission to court Lizzy. He will not receive my permission to court *any* of my girls, and I have told him so. Mr. Darcy is courting Lizzy, and he is disinclined to give her up." He watched her pulling at her sleeves. "I would have thought you would see the very great advantages of such a match."

"It is only . . ." Mrs. Bennet said in a small voice, glancing over at Elizabeth. "It is only that Derbyshire is so far away, Thomas. Hunsford is much closer. And then, Lizzy would be mistress *here* one day."

"Mama," Elizabeth said, her patience fraying, "please try to understand. I will not marry for the sole purpose of maintaining a tie to Longbourn." *Nor will I ever marry an idiot.*

"But," her mother began.

Elizabeth moved to the chair next to her mother. *Be patient*, she told herself. *She is vexing, but she does love me. And I love her, too.* She took Mrs. Bennet's hands and held them still. "Mama," she said quietly, "It is not the *house* to which I am attached. You will always have me, whether I am in town or elsewhere."

Her mother was silent. Elizabeth thought she might be holding her breath, though she could not say why. At last, she patted Elizabeth's cheek and nodded before exiting the room.

Elizabeth and her father exchanged glances; Mr. Bennet shrugged his shoulders and was about to return to his paper and his coffee when they both heard a sob coming from outside the door. Mr. Bennet gave his breakfast a wistful glance and, with a half-hearted smile at Elizabeth, left the room to tend to his wife.

Mrs. Bennet was still in her room upstairs when Mr. Bingley, Mr. Fitzwilliam, and Mr. Darcy came to call.

"We wished to come here first," Mr. Bingley said, "to issue a personal invitation to you all. To a ball, at Netherfield, on November the twenty-sixth."

Elizabeth let out a breath before meeting Darcy's gaze. If the ball was going forward, that could only mean one thing.

"My sister Caroline will be returning tomorrow," Mr. Bingley announced, before smiling at Jane. "She is bringing my Aunt Cleopatra Bingley with her."

Cleopatra? Elizabeth's lips formed the name silently as she observed Darcy's somber mien. Except it was not truly somber. She could see his good humor in the slight press of his lips and barely discernable squint of his eyes. He gave her a small nod and closed the space between them.

"I would ask something terribly impertinent about whether Aunt Bingley lived up to her Christian name," Elizabeth said, "but every possibility turns dangerous."

A small burst of air escaped Mr. Darcy's nose. "Indeed. From liaisons with powerful men to retain her kingdom to committing suicide by asp, it is difficult to find a jest suitable for mixed company."

"An opportunity lost, then," Elizabeth conceded, and changed the subject. "How are you this morning, Mr. Darcy?"

"Wishing for an answer about the first set at Bingley's ball, Miss Elizabeth. I realize it is not the done thing to ask before the event, but as we are courting, I believe an exception might be made."

"Oh," she said, frowning. "I would enjoy that, Mr. Darcy, very much. But I do not dance the first."

His eyebrows lowered. "Why is that, if I may ask?"

Elizabeth gazed around the room and moved to a relatively isolated corner, indicating he should follow her. Then she fidgeted with her fingers until Mr. Darcy laid a single warm hand over them.

"Just tell me, Elizabeth," he said, in a repeat of his words in her father's study. "You will feel better when you do."

"I missed dancing the first dance of my first season with Uncle Phillip," she said in a rush, nearly before he had finished speaking. "And I just . . . until I dance the first with Cousin John in town, I . . ." She peeked up at him. "I know it is silly."

His disappointment was clear, but he only nodded. "It is perfectly understandable," Mr. Darcy assured her. "You feel it would dishonor your uncle, whom you loved very much."

She nodded. "Cousin John was his best friend. I feel that once we have our dance . . ." She caught her bottom lip between her teeth.

"That you will then have paid your respects to your uncle." His expression had not changed, and she hoped he was not upset.

"Yes." She turned her palm up to capture his hand and smiled weakly. "How can you make this sound so reasonable? It does not sound rational even in my own mind."

"Miss Elizabeth," he replied, something close to mirth in his tone, "I have made a study of you almost from the first moment of our acquaintance."

Elizabeth stared at him askance.

"I said *almost* from the beginning," he said in response to her unasked question. With a quiet chuckle and a shake of his head, he asked, "May I finish?"

She nodded regally.

"I mean this in the best sense, you understand," he stopped until she nodded again, more like herself this time, and he continued with a small grin. "You are not that complicated."

"I see." She lifted an eyebrow. "Very well then, sir, is our business completed?" she asked, enjoying being teased by this serious man.

He was unperturbed by her flippant response. "Not at all. I have yet to secure a set. Let us say I shall keep you company during the first, dance the second, and . . ." he pretended to think, "I should like the supper dance as payment for my trouble."

"Trouble?" she asked, feigning pique. "I think you are trouble, sir, tying up my sets."

"Trouble," he confirmed. "A great deal of rather wonderful trouble." He ran his thumb up and down her forefinger and it was all she could do not to shiver. "Please, accept my hand for these dances, Miss Elizabeth," he said, "or I shall have to insist on having the last as well.

He leaned in just a bit and said emphatically. "Which might cause a great deal of *talk*."

"Very well, sir," she responded, pretending his proximity did not affect her. "The second and the supper dance are yours, as you have forced me to it."

"Forced you?" he exclaimed, keeping his volume low but casting his eyes swiftly about the room anyway. His attention returned to her. "I have charmed you, and you know it."

He was so very sure of himself that she wished to deny it merely to provoke him. Then she recalled how easily he had understood her desire to honor Uncle Phillip. *It is far from the first such consideration he has shown me.*

The pretense fell away, and Elizabeth softened. "Indeed," she said. Her eyes met Mr. Darcy's, and she saw he was surprised at her capitulation. "There is no charm equal to tenderness of heart."

In the end, Longbourn was the only home the men visited to issue an invitation in person. Bingley was sure his sister would wish to make the rounds with them to the other principal families and so they awaited her arrival.

The following morning arrived with gray clouds hanging heavy in the sky. An expensive but old-fashioned coach came to a stop before the house a few hours after breakfast. Bingley stepped smartly up to the door while Darcy and Richard remained on the steps.

"Tell me again, Darcy. Why are we a part of this welcoming party?" Richard asked.

Darcy sighed. "Because Bingley asked us to greet his aunt." He had never met Bingley's Aunt Cleopatra, but he had heard enough to surmise that Bingley was fond of her.

Bingley was now handing an elderly lady out of the coach. Darcy evaluated her. She hardly seemed capable of bearing the weight of the tremendous bonnet she wore, precariously affixed by a single ribbon tied beneath her chin. He worried, for a moment, that the weight of it might topple her, but she raised her head to greet Charles without incident. The woman was barely tall enough to reach even Caroline's shoulder, and despite her heavy coat, he could see her frame was slight. Bingley's smile as he returned her greetings was tender and kind, and Darcy was so engaged with watching his friend that he almost missed the consternation on Miss Bingley's face as she stood by herself, waiting to be acknowledged. He nudged the reluctant Richard and they stepped to Bingley for the introductions.

Within a few minutes, the introductions had been made, greetings exchanged, and they were all standing in the entry hall.

"Goodness," Aunt Bingley sighed, untying her bonnet and removing it. Darcy was certain, now, that it was half the size of the diminutive woman who wore it. There was a wide yellow ribbon wrapped around the crown and . . .was that a bird's nest on the brim? "I do so enjoy visiting you, Charlie, but I do not enjoy long rides."

Charlie? Richard made a sort of choking, stifled sound. Darcy knew it was impolite, but he was compelled to steal another look at Mrs. Bingley's hat. Yes. Definitely a bird's nest. With eggs glued inside. As Aunt Bingley handed it off to a perplexed maid, who turned it all about before making off with it, he spied a stuffed bird affixed to the other side.

"I do not know why you insist on wearing that monstrosity," Miss Bingley said to her aunt.

Darcy tried not to react to the unusual sound of Miss Bingley . . . whining. For all her faults, she rarely showed petulance, at least in company. In fact, he could not recall another instance of it.

"Because the brim is large, dear, and keeps off the weather," came her aunt's mild reply.

Miss Bingley's pained smile was accompanied by closed eyes and a minute shake of her head. She would not point out, Darcy knew, that they had been in a closed coach. *But she wants to,* he thought, amused.

"May I, Mrs. Bingley?" Richard asked genially, offering his arm. The older woman gazed up at him and gave him a brilliant smile.

"Oh, you are a gallant one," she replied with a genuine smile. "You most certainly may." She accepted his arm and was led into the drawing room.

"Charles," Miss Bingley said, resigned, "I shall repair to my rooms and then seek out Mrs. Nicholls. I presume you can show our aunt her rooms when she is ready?"

"Of course, Caroline," Bingley said seriously. "Leave her to me."

"Mr. Darcy," she said, and then turned to the stairs. Bingley grinned and clapped his hands together. "Come, Darcy, let us have some conversation with our dear Auntie Cleopatra."

Our? "I cannot call her that, Bingley," Darcy remonstrated.

"Oh," Bingley said with a laugh, "you will. She will insist upon it."

Outside, the rain began to fall.

That night, Miss Bingley chose to bring up the invitations for the ball, most of which she had written while still in Northamptonshire.

"With this rain," she said, "it will be best to send a servant around."

Charles nodded. "We have already invited the Bennets, Caroline, but they should also receive formal notice."

Miss Bingley's face grew sour. "I plan to invite a number of our friends from London as well, Charles. We certainly have the room, and it would considerably elevate the ball's consequence."

Richard opened his mouth. Darcy stared at his cousin, unnerved. He tried to communicate without speaking. *Do not mention Elizabeth's consequence. It is not Miss Bingley's business and nothing good shall come of it.* His cousin rewarded him with a scowl but remained silent. Fortunately, Miss Bingley was too irritated with her brother to pay them any mind.

"Choose a few favorites, Caroline. This ball is being held for my Meryton neighbors, a thank you for their kind welcome into the neighborhood."

Darcy speared his fish and focused on chewing carefully. It would not do to choke on any bones, after all. Not that Mrs. Thistlewaite would allow bones in her fish. The sauce tonight was something light, lemon in chicken stock? And . . . sweet, too? He was going to miss Bingley's cook when he left for town in a few weeks. He wondered, suddenly, whether Hurst was mourning the loss.

With his head now turned to his plate, Darcy could not see Richard, but suspected he was also hiding as well as he was able. Neither could help but hear Miss Bingley's exasperated reply to her brother.

"You *cannot* be serious, Charles," she said haughtily, and Darcy winced. He recognized some of his own attitude in that phrase. *Not anymore,* he promised himself. *Elizabeth would never allow it.* He found comfort in the idea that she would help him keep his pride under good regulation. She was proud, too, but never arrogant.

Bingley was not in the least affected by his sister's scorn. "I am perfectly serious, Caroline. Any time you wish, Auntie Cleopatra can take over the preparations for the ball. It would be a shame, though. You have already done so much work."

"Charles, I—" Miss Bingley started to say, but was cut off by her aunt.

"Oh, that would be marvelous," Mrs. Bingley said, clapping her hands together. "I have such lovely ideas."

"*Charles,*" Miss Bingley said, sounding dismayed. "I have already written several of my friends that I am to be hostess. If they were to arrive to dead birds littering the ballroom, they would think it was by my design."

"Stuffed, my dear," the older lady said good-naturedly. "They are stuffed."

Darcy and Richard looked at one another. Richard's face was a study. Darcy willed himself not to laugh. Miss Bingley's reply was strangled and undecipherable.

"The answer is simple, Caroline," Bingley replied, as though he had understood her. "Do not invite anyone from town."

"We could place the parrot on the punch bowl," Mrs. Bingley remarked cheerfully. "So colorful."

Miss Bingley's face paled. "Charles, *stop* her," she insisted.

"It would appear to be drinking!" Mrs. Bingley said gleefully. "How charming." She speared a roasted turnip and popped it in her mouth.

Bingley just lifted his shoulders and addressed his sister. "What is wrong with putting the parrot on the punch bowl, Caroline?" he asked, a picture of befuddled innocence.

"Very well. Have your way," Miss Bingley hissed, tossing her napkin angrily on the table. "I shall not invite any of my friends from London." She turned away from her brother. "Mr. Fitzwilliam, Mr. Darcy," she said, her voice tight and strained. Then she left the room.

Bingley gave his aunt a small smile. "Perhaps we should allow Caroline to decorate, Auntie," he told her gently. "She has been waiting for an opportunity to be hostess for a very long time."

The old woman reached over to pat her nephew's hand. "Of course, my dear." Then she picked up her fork and tucked into her fish as though nothing had happened.

"I say, Bingley," Richard said, his smile bright and his cheeks returning to their normal color, "your family dinners must have been exceedingly entertaining."

Bingley glanced at his aunt, who appeared not to be paying any attention to the men at all. "You have no idea, Fitzwilliam," he said, the remaining trace of his smile at odds with his words. "No idea."

※

The next morning, Darcy and Richard were sitting in Netherfield's library while Darcy attempted to calculate precisely how muddy the roads were. If they were sound enough to support the carriage, he intended to make a visit to Longbourn. He felt sure Elizabeth was warming to the idea of marrying him and he did not wish to lose any ground with her. Still, trying to ride through the weather and becoming ill would only make it worse. He could not risk missing his opportunity to dance with her.

"No," he said impatiently, watching the rain coming down. "It is not going to improve if I just sit here and watch." He stood. "I shall take the carriage to Longbourn." He addressed his cousin. "Would you care to join me?"

"We may find ourselves pushing the carriage instead of being conveyed by it," Richard warned. "The roads in the country can be . . ."

"Richard," Darcy said sardonically. "Do you mean to tell *me* about country roads?" He strode for the door. "It is only one day of rain, and at this time of year, who knows how long this storm will last. It may be our final opportunity to leave the house before the ball."

Richard frowned at that and followed him out of the room. "The ball is four days away, Darcy. I cannot be confined to the same house as Miss Bingley for four days."

Darcy shrugged. "You barely see her now, she is so busy with the arrangements."

"And arguing with her aunt." Richard smiled wickedly. "Have you seen Auntie Cleopatra pretend to be hard of hearing when Miss Bingley says something she does not wish to acknowledge?"

Darcy's lips tugged up. He motioned to a footman and relayed that he would like his carriage brought around. He waved another down and asked that Mr. Bingley be informed. Those errands complete, he turned his head towards his cousin. "Yes."

"Would that I had thought of it the first time I met the girl," Richard said thoughtfully. "I suppose it is too late to claim deafness from cannon shot now."

"Rather late, yes." Darcy replied wryly. "Perhaps we can arrange a hunting accident." He spied Hanson coming down the stairs with his greatcoat cleaned, brushed, and folded over one arm. *How did he know?*

"I suspected you might require this today, Mr. Darcy," Hanson intoned as he helped Darcy into his outerwear.

The men all glanced to the window where the rain was still coming down steadily.

Hanson retrieved Darcy's hat and gloves and handed them to his master. "Have you need of anything else, sir?" he asked.

"No, Hanson, that will be all," he replied, but gave the man a warm nod. Hanson bowed stiffly before returning to his duties above stairs.

Richard was sliding on his own greatcoat and motioned to the retreating valet. "You always get the good ones."

Before Darcy could answer, the sharp click of boots on marble alerted them to Bingley's approach.

"May I accompany you, gentlemen?" he asked. "I cannot listen to ball preparations any longer, particularly when Caroline and Auntie Cleopatra can agree on none of it." Without waiting for an answer, he spoke a few words to a servant and was soon in his coat. Word came that the carriage would be around momentarily—evidently the request had been anticipated.

Richard chuckled. "You are becoming predictable, Darcy."

It did bother Darcy that his comings and goings had evidently been discussed among the servants, but if it got him on his way more expeditiously, he would not dwell on it. After all, was not anticipating his needs the sign of an excellent staff? Of course it was.

Richard shook his head. "He is congratulating himself, Bingley." He gestured to Darcy's face. "Do you see how the left eye narrows while the right eye does not?"

Bingley laughed. "I see it." He nodded at his butler, who had motioned to the door. "Gentlemen," he said, still chuckling, "our carriage awaits."

Elizabeth and her sisters were happily ensconced in the family parlor, located near the rear of the house. It was only half the size of Longbourn's formal drawing room and less formally decorated yet housed a larger fireplace. This allowed for a generously sized coal basket, and a large, thick fireback that kept the room pleasantly warm. It was therefore the ideal place to congregate on rainy days when no visitors were expected.

Lydia and Kitty were holding a conversation in French while Mrs. Grover offered gentle correction, Jane was seated in the corner practicing her harp, and Elizabeth was reading the newspaper, making notes and carefully explaining in a low voice to Mary what generally caught her eye and how she categorized her notes for future use. Pencils, paper, watercolors, brushes, and a small canvas on an easel were temporarily abandoned a table set snugly into a corner nearest the window. Mrs. Bennet had just stepped out to speak to Mrs. Hill and the cook about the butcher's order.

Mr. Hill knocked on the door and the girls all looked at one another. *Surely,* Elizabeth thought, *nobody would be out in this weather.*

"Mr. Bingley, Mr. Darcy, and Mr. Fitzwilliam," Mr. Hill said tonelessly, as though it was perfectly natural to announce visitors when it was pouring down rain. The women all stood.

"Mr. Hill, will you please inform my mother that we have guests?" Jane asked. Mr. Hill nodded and removed himself from the room. They all greeted one another.

Mr. Darcy immediately approached Elizabeth. "Good day, Miss Elizabeth," he said, with a satisfied air. "I see we find you in the family rooms this morning."

She nearly laughed at him but held it back. "You look suspiciously smug, Mr. Darcy," she said, extraordinarily pleased to see him.

"No," he retorted, "just a man who made his way through the pouring rain and is delighted to find himself in very good company."

"And this you do not find at Netherfield?" she asked. "I am all astonishment."

"Miss Bingley and *Auntie Cleopatra* arrived yesterday," he told her, his unease with the informal address still full in force. "Bingley's aunt is . . ."

"Eccentric?" Elizabeth asked quietly. "Mr. Bingley mentioned that to Jane. She told me and Mary, but I promise it shall go no further."

Darcy shook his head. "I may even begin to feel sorry for Miss Bingley."

"I cannot imagine that," Elizabeth replied with a low laugh.

"What are the two of you doing here, Miss Mary?" Mr. Fitzwilliam asked as he joined them.

"Lizzy is teaching me to watch for opportunities," Mary said softly. Elizabeth glanced at her sister, puzzled. Mary never said anything softly. Brusquely, firmly, with great irritation or conviction—but never softly.

"Oh?" Mr. Fitzwilliam asked. "Are you teaching Miss Mary to play the horses, madam?" he teased Elizabeth.

"I suppose it is not that far a reach, Mr. Fitzwilliam," she said cordially. "My uncle's interests include a number of investments. He began teaching me how to apply his methods when I was barely thirteen; I daresay I have improved since."

"I should like to hear more of that myself, Miss Elizabeth." Mr. Fitzwilliam reached for the paper, asking permission with his eyes and receiving it. Elizabeth saw Mr. Darcy's chest puffing up and shook her head. *As if he had anything to do with it,* she thought fondly. But it felt good to have someone be proud of her. It felt exceptionally good to have *him* feel proud of her.

"Why did you gentlemen brave the flooded roads to make a visit?" she asked impertinently. "I should think you would have been better served to stay at home today."

Mr. Fitzwilliam tapped the corner of the paper against his lips. "I cannot recall . . . oh, yes. Darcy was sitting in the library being angry at the weather. He decided he was impervious to the rain and that he should come despite it. Oh," he added as an afterthought, "and he invited me along in case we were required to give the carriage a shove."

Mary laughed. Elizabeth gave her sister a teasing look, and Mary's laugh stopped abruptly.

"I am sure," Elizabeth replied, "Mr. Darcy was wise enough to lash a rowboat to the top of your coach. He is always very prepared, I find."

It was Mr. Darcy's turn to laugh. "I must admit I did not think quite that far ahead."

"For shame, Mr. Darcy," Elizabeth scolded. "One must always think through all the possibilities. Otherwise you might forget the oars."

Mr. Darcy's tender look halted her banter as suddenly as she had stopped Mary's laugh. "I promise," he said, "to do better in future." He stood. "Would you show me your artwork?" he asked, nodding at the southern wall.

A number of youthful efforts from all the sisters were hanging in a line, but in the center were two more recent portraits done in thin-lined crayon, something between a drawing and a watercolor. The first was of Miss Mary, with great attention paid to her eyes. The next depicted four blond-haired girls, three in a circle around the fourth. The perspective of the rendering came from a fifth position, where another person would have been standing. As he moved closer to examine it, he was impressed by the fine detail in the faces. It was clear that these were her sisters; Miss Bennet's profile showed her to be in the center, and her younger sisters crowded around, holding hands, smiling, dancing.

"These are yours," he said, and she nodded. He gestured to the second drawing where the sisters' skirts appeared to drift on the breeze. "There is such movement here. How do you do it?"

She tipped her head to one side and lifted a shoulder. "My aunt drilled the basics into me and then I drew what I felt. Later, I had a drawing master."

It was not precisely what he was asking, but he accepted the answer. Darcy saw writing at the bottom of the picture. It intrigued him that she did this; he was glad to see it was not only his own dreadful portrait that had driven her to it. He peered at the words, half-hidden by the frame, and read, "A host of dancing Daffodils." He smiled to himself. "You enjoy Wordsworth, Miss Elizabeth?"

"You recognize it?" she inquired, with a smile. "I do." She touched the frame gently. "My sisters reminded me so much of that poem. Do you know it?"

He recited the second stanza so that only she would hear: "The Waves beside them danced, but they / Outdid the sparkling Waves in glee:-- / A Poet could not but be gay / In such a laughing company. . ." He faltered. "I am afraid my memory fails at that point."

She was staring at him, a light in her eyes like glowing embers. She nodded. "Well done, Mr. Darcy." She touched his arm. "Shall we join the others?"

Her words were all that was polite, but he was sure the fire in her gaze was for him. *If only I had memorized the whole blasted poem.* He nodded. "Of course, Miss Elizabeth."

The rain continued for all four days preceding the ball. Only on the fourth were the men from Netherfield unable to safely traverse the roads. Darcy was irritated, but it would only be one more day before the ball. Perhaps the women would not wish to have callers today in any case. He had already spent a great deal of time with Elizabeth, far more than a typical courting couple—after the conversation in Mr. Bennet's study, her father had not once protested Darcy's continual presence in his home. Darcy was a determined man. He had used the week and a half to great advantage, spending all day and many evenings at Longbourn.

He sat in a chair near the library's large window. The rain had stopped before dinner, but the roads were a mess. They would have time to dry out somewhat if they had no more poor weather before the ball; as everyone invited lived nearby, he expected all who had accepted would show.

He began to review the progress he had made in his suit. Elizabeth was always very pleased to see him, and the family had not removed to the drawing room to accept their calls even when Mrs. Bennet knew to expect them. There was something cozy, even intimate about being shown into that little room at the back of the house, where the most personal of family items were displayed. Elizabeth's excellent drawings, of course, but also etchings from the other girls, first samplers, childish watercolors of dubious skill but a great deal of charm, dog-eared picture books, and several work baskets that always seemed full, no matter how much work was done. Curious, he had asked Elizabeth yesterday why she did not sew like her sisters, and the women had all laughed heartily while she blushed.

"Aptitude, Mr. Darcy," she had told him plainly, when the noise died down. "I have none. I am afraid you shall have to pay a seamstress to make your shirts after we are married. That is, unless you wish to wear one with a crooked hem or a third arm."

"Thank goodness, Lizzy," Lydia had chimed in happily. "I should hate it were you good at everything. It would be very difficult to like you then."

"Lizzy is very helpful in the stillroom," Kitty admonished her younger sister.

Miss Elizabeth had only smiled. "Thank you, Lyddie," she had said. "Thank you, Kitty."

Darcy had not heard much from the final exchange between Elizabeth and Miss Lydia. All he could hear—all he could still hear—was "after we are married."

The ball, he decided. *It is perfect. I shall ask her again at the ball.*

CHAPTER FOUR

Thanks to Hanson, Darcy was ready early, but remained in his rooms until the final moment. Were he to do as he wished and stand by the window over the drive, Richard would have had great sport with him.

The first carriages were arriving when he finally made his way downstairs. Bingley had invited both him and his cousin to stand with them in the receiving line, but they had politely declined. He was especially relieved by his decision when he spied Auntie Cleopatra descending the stairs. Protruding from her Turkish turban were no fewer than seven long feathers in a variety of colors. Bingley had done his sister a favor discouraging the expansion of her guest list to London.

Instead of greeting all and sundry, he waited anxiously for the one guest he most wished to see. There seemed to be an interminable number of other people entering the house who greeted him and required return civilities, but in fact, the Bennet carriage was among the first to arrive. He could hear Mrs. Bennet's shrill exclamations preceding them up the staircase: the beauty of the house, the number of torches already lit outside despite the bright night, the large number of guests, the superior supper they might expect. Darcy cringed a little; Mrs. Bennet was correct about it all, but when she had joined them in the family parlor over the past week, she had mostly spoken with Miss Bennet and Bingley. This was the first time he had heard her in full voice.

Then Miss Elizabeth reached the top of the stairs, stepping lightly to the side to await the rest of her family. Her dark hair was swept into an intricately woven knot sitting low on the back of her head. As she turned to greet her sisters, he spied several curled tendrils arranged upon the bare skin of her slender neck. His fingers twitched.

As she faced forward again, he took in her gown. It was snow-white, with a thin, golden-colored net overskirt fashioned like lace. Gold embroidery along the neckline and long sleeves picked up the color of the skirt. *She favors yellow*, he thought, recalling the dress she had worn to the first dinner at Netherfield. This gown, like the one she had worn before, was meant to take advantage of the candlelight. His eyes traced the dipping neckline that suggested but did not reveal what lay beneath the rich silk.

When the women had made their way past the Bingley family, Elizabeth stopped before him. Her cheeks were a little flushed and Darcy suspected her mother's continued exuberance was the cause.

"Where is your father?" he asked.

"Although I suspect you have a large carriage, Mr. Darcy, I doubt that it accommodates eight," she said cheerfully. "Particularly when six of the occupants are women in ballgowns." She smiled. "My father offered to wait with Mr. Collins. The carriage will return to Longbourn for them."

Six? Darcy glanced to the side where the Bennet ladies were congregating with the Lucas family. Miss Lydia was indeed there in a soft pink gown, standing with Miss Bennet. He had not thought she was out, but truthfully, he had not spoken with her much. However, if her presence had kept the parson from riding in the carriage with Elizabeth, he could only be pleased.

"I have not seen Mr. Collins all week," he said. If there was a touch of self-satisfaction in his tone, she would surely forgive him. "Has your cousin behaved himself, Miss Elizabeth?"

She nodded, and Darcy indicated they should walk to the ballroom. "Papa has exerted himself to keep Mr. Collins much occupied in his study, trying to teach him something about the estate."

"How does he get on?" Darcy asked, picturing Mr. Bennet tossing Collins out the window.

"Not well at all, I am afraid," Miss Elizabeth said, lifting her sparkling eyes to his. "It is now more an entertainment for my father than a serious task." Her joy faded, replaced by an air of solemnity, and he mourned the change. "I believe I must thank you for intervening."

"Not at all, Miss Elizabeth," he replied. "I did speak with the man, but it was your father who finally convinced him to cease."

Her brows knit together. "Is that true, Mr. Darcy?" she asked. He thought he detected some hope in her question.

"It is," he said simply.

Darcy was repaid for his honesty with a small, sweet smile. "Thank you for telling me," she said quietly. "Papa has not said a thing about it."

"You are very welcome," he said. He noted her locket, the one he had meant to examine before. "Now, I have a question for you. Is that a lion on your locket?"

The smile grew. "Indeed," she said, her hand rising to touch it. "It is a part of the Russell coat of arms. A gift from my aunt."

Darcy nearly rolled his eyes. *Of course it is. How many other clues did I miss?*

He wondered if she knew what he was thinking, for her smile turned suddenly amused. She opened the locket for him. "These are pictures of my aunt and uncle when they first married."

Be a gentleman, Darcy, he reminded himself before dropping his eyes to her chest. *Look only at the locket.* Inside were painted two very small miniatures. Unexpectedly, he was drawn to the painting of the woman. "This is your aunt, Miss Elizabeth?"

"Yes, Mr. Darcy," Elizabeth told him.

"I only ever met her later," he said. "I recall thinking her handsome when I was a boy, but she was older than my father." The hair, the skin, the shape of her face . . . "You resemble her a great deal."

She nodded and closed the locket with some satisfaction. "I know." Apparently, he was not the first to note the similarity.

"She was a beautiful woman, Miss Elizabeth," he replied softly, and she glanced away modestly, but, he thought, pleased by the implication.

"May I say, Miss Elizabeth," he said, "you look enchanting this evening."

"Thank you, sir," she replied and gave him a saucy little curtsey. "You are rather dashing yourself." Her eyes met his.

Darcy swallowed. *Oh, this will never do. I have an entire evening to get through.*

He changed the subject to her lessons with Miss Mary. Elizabeth was excited about her sister's progress, and they conversed for a time. When they at last entered the ballroom, it was nearly time for the dancing to begin. The crowd had increased significantly. All the local gentry had been invited as had the militia's officers.

"There must be nearly two hundred people here," Miss Elizabeth said. Darcy nodded. The ballroom was made up of several rooms opened to one another by sliding back walls. The rooms had been scrubbed and the floor waxed lightly in preparation. Scores of fresh, colorful flower arrangements, each one precisely the same, were placed along the walls of the room in tall porcelain vases. In one corner of the largest room sat a table with an immense crystal punch bowl and cups. Several servants stood behind it, waiting to serve the guests. The musicians sat in the corner farthest from the refreshments, on a platform that spanned the back wall of two rooms.

Darcy was only a bit disappointed that there were no stuffed birds perched in the alcoves, no nests on display. *To be fair*, he thought, *Miss Bingley has done well.*

"The quality of the instruments is very fine," Miss Elizabeth noted. "The musicians must be from town."

"The flowers as well," he pointed out. "The hothouse at Netherfield could not produce

so many."

Miss Elizabeth nodded. "I must credit Miss Bingley," she said, as though she could read his thoughts. "She has done a splendid job."

Elizabeth stood on her toes to try to see around the room. She was eventually able to locate her sister Jane standing just inside the entryway with Mr. Bingley. Jane was beaming, but before Elizabeth could approach, Jane took Mr. Bingley's arm and allowed herself to be led away. She spied Mama and Lydia near the refreshments and was relieved when she spotted her father walking through the crowd to join them.

"I was surprised to see Miss Lydia here tonight," Mr. Darcy said. She glanced up at him, but there was no censure in his expression.

"She begged to be allowed to attend," Elizabeth explained, "and none of us had the heart to deny her. She is to dance the first with Papa, but otherwise must remain with a family member."

"Georgiana is the same," Mr. Darcy replied. "Perhaps when we are in Derbyshire, I might allow her to attend a private ball under the same strictures. Will Miss Lydia be able to stay up so late, do you think?"

Elizabeth shook her head. "Papa will escort her home after supper." *Kitty may wish to go as well.* The hum of voices was increasing in volume, and it was becoming difficult to hear. "I believe," she said, speaking a little louder, "offering a little freedom when a girl has proven she is worthy of it is the best way to ensure her continued good behavior." She thought of Georgiana, flattered by the attentions of a handsome older man but reaching out for help anyway. "I think Georgie would be very pleased if you demonstrated that sort of trust in her."

Mr. Darcy appeared as though he was about to reply, but people began shushing one another. Mr. Bingley had stepped up on the dais where the musicians sat. He began his welcome to all the guests, thanking his sister, then his aunt for their hard work. Then he held out a hand to assist Mr. Bennet to the platform and stepped down himself. The buzz of voices increased in volume.

Elizabeth clapped her hands together and beamed up at Mr. Darcy. She spun back to view her father. "Oh, Jane," she whispered. "Oh, how wonderful."

Mr. Darcy scratched the back of his neck. "Bingley could not even wait until the ball began, I see," he told Elizabeth with a grin. "Shall we try to make our way over?"

Elizabeth nodded her head enthusiastically. "Please, Mr. Darcy," she said, her face glowing with happiness. "You are sure to clear a path more quickly than I."

"Ladies and gentlemen," her father said, his voice intentionally raised above the excited babble, "I am very pleased to announce that Mr. Charles Bingley has proposed marriage to my eldest daughter, Miss Jane Bennet, and she has accepted him."

The murmuring nearly exploded into congratulations and well wishes. Mr. Bennet held up his hands and finished his announcement. Elizabeth and Mr. Darcy arrived at the side of the happy couple just as her father's speech was complete. Elizabeth gasped Jane's hands and bounced up on her toes. "Oh, Jane!" she exclaimed. "I am so happy!"

Mr. Darcy was already shaking Mr. Bingley's hand and clapping him on the back, so Elizabeth waited her turn, taking him by the hands and warmly expressing her delight. He smiled widely at her and accepted her good wishes.

Miss Bingley stood slightly to the side, a pained expression on her face. Once Elizabeth stepped back, she stepped up to her brother and Jane.

"Congratulations," she said, her voice strained but polite. "Charles, if you meant this to be an engagement ball, you ought to have told me. I would have done things a little differently."

"Oh," Jane replied, reaching out to take Miss Bingley's hand, "please do not worry about that, Miss Bingley. Everything is very elegant. It is beautiful just as it is."

Miss Bingley offered her brother's betrothed a wan smile. The musicians indicated they were ready to begin, and suddenly Mr. Fitzwilliam appeared.

"Congratulations, Bingley, Miss Bennet," he said enthusiastically. He held his hand out. "Shall we, Miss Bingley?" he asked, rather more formally than was his wont. Elizabeth remembered that he was the man of highest rank in the room; he would lead the first dance of the ball with the hostess. She wondered idly whether Miss Bingley might not have preferred a different partner, and the thought made her stomach harden and a flash of heat burn in her chest. The flame grew hotter when Miss Bingley smiled coyly at Mr. Darcy.

"As hostess, I will not dance often tonight, Mr. Darcy," she told him, "but I shall save a dance for you."

Brazen woman! Elizabeth thought before she could stop herself. She schooled her features a moment too late; Miss Bingley raised a perfectly shaped eyebrow at her and gracefully took Mr. Fitzwilliam's arm. Elizabeth was darkly pleased to see her led away. The farther Miss Bingley was from Mr. Darcy, the better. When he held his arm out to her to lead her to a chair where they might watch the first set, she held it more tightly than normal, and he gave her a curious look.

"Are you well, Miss Elizabeth?" he asked quietly.

She looked over at Miss Bingley before turning her face up to his. "I am perfectly well, Mr. Darcy."

His gaze dropped to her hand, tucked tightly in the crook of his arm, and then back out to the dance floor. "Whom do you seek?"

"No one, Mr. Darcy," she replied tartly. "Why do you ask?"

He turned his face in the direction of her glance, and his forehead creased. "Were you searching for Mr. Fitzwilliam?"

Elizabeth pursed her lips and met his inquiry with the truth. "No." She knew her cheeks were pink; he had found her out *again*. Insufferable man.

Mr. Darcy's expression suddenly brightened. He turned his face to the floor, but she could still see the bright smile that was breaking across it and her tender heart expanded at the sight. Mr. Darcy helped her to sit. She folded her hands primly in her lap and stared straight ahead. He lowered himself to the chair beside her and raised his head, also staring straight ahead.

"Were you shooting daggers at Miss Bingley, Miss Elizabeth?"

She released a barely audible huff. She would prefer to cross her arms over her chest, but it would give too much away. "I possess no daggers, Mr. Darcy."

"Do you wish *you* were dancing with Mr. Fitzwilliam, Miss Elizabeth?" he asked, his voice low but the tone light. "As hostess, you know, it *is* Miss Bingley's place to lead the first dance."

She frowned. "I do not wish to dance the first at all, Mr. Darcy, as I believe you are aware."

Mr. Darcy leaned just an inch towards her without moving his head. "Miss Elizabeth," he whispered so close to her that it sent a little shiver down her spine. "Are you jealous?"

"Jealousy is a base emotion," she replied succinctly. "Of course I am not jealous." She tipped her head to one side. "Are not the musicians wonderful?"

Darcy's heart leapt in his chest. *She is jealous.* He was uncharacteristically joyful at the thought, but then, he was always happy in Elizabeth's company. The only question was whether she could be happy in his; it had been a little less than a fortnight they had been courting. *But we have been in company nearly every day for many hours at a time.* He was grateful yet again that they were in the country and the Bennets were in favor of the match. A courtship in London would have been far more restrictive. He glanced at Elizabeth, whose cheeks were flushed pink. *She already knows my intentions,* he told himself. *Thanks to Georgie, she already thought well of me, and I have made my intentions clear. A proposal will not come as a surprise to her.*

"Indeed," he replied politely, as though he did not wish to kiss her senseless. "The musicians are excellent." *Pay attention to her, Darcy,* he warned himself. *If she appears at all skittish, you must not push it.* But she did not seem skittish. She seemed possessive. *Perhaps I should just test . . .* He patted her hand. "I suppose I ought to dance with Miss Bingley this evening. She is my hostess, after all."

Miss Elizabeth frowned, and his smile reappeared.

After a few minutes, Kitty and Mary came to sit with them, and all private conversation was at an end. Darcy spoke with them both, but had he been asked, he could not have repeated the topic. He was anticipating a dance as he never had before, and when at last the couples began to form a serpentine line, he held out his hand to Miss Elizabeth, reveling in the warmth he felt even through their gloves as she slid her hand into his.

Darcy could feel Mr. Bennet watching them even as his youngest daughter continued to chatter excitedly next to him and his other daughters were led to the floor. He imagined the older man's dark eyes twinkling merrily; he had not made any attempt to disguise how diverting they were for him. Darcy simply could not bring himself to care. Let the man have his fun, so long as he was willing to give official permission to a second engagement tonight. He escorted Miss Elizabeth to her place and then stepped to his. He met her gaze as they stood across from one another, and this time, when he found himself staring at her, Miss Elizabeth was staring right back.

Mr. Darcy was staring at her. *That* stare, the one that conveyed a burning disapproval, the one he had first fixed upon her at Netherfield, the one she had captured in her drawing, the one she drew still. He did not seem to disapprove of her now. He had been embarrassed by the drawing. He had said it was not disapprobation. But then . . . Elizabeth met his gaze and felt as though she was trapped in it, pulled in by it. Drowning in it.

You have been such a fool, she scoffed, as the realization broke over her, leaving her breathless. *That is not disapproval. It is love. Not polite love. What did he call it? Ardent love . . .* Her mind was awash with light and color, but everything else around her melted away. She lacked the words to describe it, the images to draw it. It was to be felt, not described.

There was only him.

Darcy could not pull his eyes from Elizabeth. She was striking. The candlelight reflected from her overskirt created both a warm glow that seemed to emanate from her skin and sparks that flickered like tiny stars in her dark hair. She was ethereal. He tried to show her his heart in his gaze.

The music began, and she stepped towards him, then, as she retreated, he followed suit. Then they stepped together, just inches apart, and he took her hand. A powerful shock traveled up his arm. They moved in a tight circle, then changed hands and circled the opposite way, their eyes never wavering, their steps never faltering. Even when they were forced apart by the dance, the longing remained, each return a homecoming. She was seeing him as he had hoped she might. She was seeing the depth of his love for her, and she was returning it in full measure. Some things were simply beyond words. He could not articulate it, but he could feel it.

The ballroom fell away, the music faded to a low murmur. He fought to catch his breath, but it was not the exertion of the dance that was stealing it away.

There was only her.

They stood together perhaps a moment too long at the end of the dance, eyes still locked together in complete and perfect understanding. Then Elizabeth blinked and the rest of the world rushed back in a cacophonous rush. Mr. Darcy offered his arm.

"Might we step out to the balcony, Miss Elizabeth?" he asked her. "It is rather warm in here." She felt the warmth only between them but nodded.

I would go anywhere with you, she thought, and knew.

There was a voice calling Mr. Darcy's name from behind them, but they ignored it, stepping outside instead. She watched as Mr. Darcy gave the balcony a cursory once-over, and, assured they were alone, began to speak.

"Miss Elizabeth, if it is too soon . . ."

She placed her gloved hand gently over his mouth and his breathing hitched. "You said you have been proposing all along," she said pensively, lowering her hand.

His words were tender, but direct. "I have."

"I will never have a proposal as exquisite as that dance, Mr. Darcy," she said quietly.

Mr. Darcy took her hand and bowed over it to bestow a kiss. His eyes lifted to hers, and in them she saw love, anticipation, even desire. It was lovely and discomforting at the same time.

She touched his face, and his eyes closed as he leaned his cheek against her palm.

"Yes," she said.

Mr. Darcy's eyes flew open. "Yes?"

She smiled broadly, then. "This is an unfortunate time to lose your hearing, Mr. Darcy."

He grasped her hand, reverently turning her palm up, sliding her long glove down, and placing a feather-light kiss on the inside of her wrist. She placed a hand on his arm and leaned against him as her legs weakened. Her lips parted slightly, and she sighed involuntarily.

"Please do not tease me, dearest, I beg of you." He straightened, pulling her glove carefully back into place while still providing her a steady arm. Then he placed a hand beneath her chin and carefully lifted it. His eyes burned into hers. "Tell me truly. Will you marry me?"

Without moving her eyes, she wrapped both of her hands around his. "I will."

"You are fortunate it was Bingley and me who made up your set," Richard hissed in his ear as Darcy entered the ballroom with Elizabeth on his arm. "I do not think anyone else was paying attention."

Darcy recalled, vaguely, that Richard had partnered Miss Mary and that Bingley had danced with Miss Kitty. They watched as Elizabeth was hurried away by her three younger sisters. He physically felt the loss.

"After a display like that, you had best be on your way to see her father," his cousin growled in Darcy's ear.

Already protective of her, Darcy thought, pleased. Elizabeth did inspire that sort of loyalty. He could not help but smile stupidly at his cousin.

Richard cocked his head, then half-grunted, half-laughed. "Of course you are, you old mooncalf. It seems all the crack tonight." He clapped Darcy on the back. "Go get yourself riveted." He strode away to seek his next partner, good humor restored.

Mr. Bennet was easy to locate. He was waiting near the first row of chairs, most of them still empty this early in the evening. He motioned silently to the door; Darcy made to follow him.

He was detained by a hand on his arm. "Mr. Darcy," Miss Bingley crooned, "I am ready for my dance, sir." She said it loudly enough that he could not refuse her without appearing churlish. His duty fought with his honor, but the struggle was short-lived.

"I must apologize, Miss Bingley," he replied, for the benefit of the crowd around them. "I had not intended to dance the third, and I shall not be free again until after supper. Shall we say the dance following?"

Her face froze. "Mr. Darcy," she said urgently, though she spoke more quietly now, "you need not offer for her out of some misguided sense of . . ."

"Miss Bingley," he chided her, also lowering his own voice. "I have been courting Miss Elizabeth since before you departed Netherfield. This is the logical conclusion." He indicated her hand. "Please release my arm, madam. I have business with Mr. Bennet."

Miss Bingley's eyes opened wide and she pulled her hand back as though she had been burned. "I do not understand," she said, and her expression was indeed uncomprehending. "I did not think that you would ever consider . . ."

"I am not certain why you would believe my private affairs open for your review, Miss Bingley," he replied, shaking his head and making every effort to mask his offense. Bingley did not deserve his ire, even if his sister did. Besides, he had a more pressing concern. "Pardon me."

He had lost sight of Mr. Bennet, but he knew just where to find him.

Elizabeth was irritated with her sisters for dragging her away from Mr. Darcy the very moment they stepped inside. They rushed her to the retiring room, were they had her all to themselves.

"La, Lizzy!" exclaimed Lydia, "I thought Mr. Darcy would eat you alive, the way he was watching you."

"Or the reverse," Mary added teasingly. "Lydia is watching, Lizzy. A *little* decorum, if you please."

Lydia rolled her eyes. "It could not be so very bad. Papa was watching, too."

Elizabeth considered that this knowledge ought to make her blush, but it did not.

"I thought it was romantic," added Kitty, sitting demurely next to Elizabeth. "Like something out of a dream."

"Has he gone to Papa?" Lydia asked abruptly, pale pink ribbons flying as she bounced up and down in her chair. "Oh, this is so exciting!" She gave each sister a short glare. "I would never have forgiven you all if I had to remain home tonight. I would have missed everything! Two sisters engaged!"

"Please do not say anything," Elizabeth begged. "Papa should have that pleasure." Her sisters agreed, though Lydia was not best pleased.

"Congratulations, Miss Elizabeth," said Miss Bingley from the doorway.

Even Lydia stopped speaking as all the air seemed to leave the room. Mary made a face and lifted a questioning eyebrow at Elizabeth, who nodded. Mary held out her hands to her younger sisters and the three Bennet girls slipped back to the ballroom.

"I thank you," Elizabeth replied to Miss Bingley as Mary shut the door behind her.

Miss Bingley sat on a chair opposite Elizabeth and closed her eyes. She took a deep breath and swallowed before clasping her hands together. "I know enough to know when I am beaten, Miss Elizabeth. Be assured that I shall pay off every arrear of courtesy to you as Mrs. Darcy. As to my advice before I removed to my aunt's, it was kindly meant." Her face was pale with the effort of her good grace.

"Oh, come now, Miss Bingley," Elizabeth said with a small smile. "*Kindly* meant?"

Miss Bingley's eyes opened in surprise. "Yes indeed. I was direct with my intentions so that you would not be embarrassed in public. I truly had no idea you and Mr. Darcy were already courting, or I should not have felt the need to say anything."

She would have known it was not in her best interest to say anything. "So now that you know I am *somebody*," Elizabeth replied, "you will deign to accept me?"

Miss Bingley pursed her lips. "It may not be the world I would wish, Miss Elizabeth," she said tightly, "but it is the world in which we live." She frowned. "Perhaps I should say that it is the world in which *I* live, as you seem to flout every rule and yet . . ." She touched a spool of thread that sat in a basket on the table next to her. "If I might ask, how did you manage to secure him?"

"Secure who?" Elizabeth asked even as she realized that Miss Bingley meant Mr. Darcy. She was a little offended to hear their courtship described in such a way. He had pursued *her*, not the other way around. Not that she considered his pursuit a hardship.

Miss Bingley pulled a face, which amused Elizabeth no end. She had never seen Miss Bingley behave so authentically.

She laughed a little. "Forgive me. I did *not* secure him, Miss Bingley. I entirely misunderstood his attentions for some time. Eventually, we had a quarrel over that, and came away with a better understanding of one another." She paused. "We were simply our own imperfect selves."

"Well," said Miss Bingley with a disbelieving huff, "that is hardly a strategy I can employ. When my family behaves like themselves, I wind up dealing with outrageously uncouth accusations and stuffed parrots on the punch bowl."

The statement was so utterly asinine that Elizabeth began to giggle. Miss Bingley watched her with one perfectly arched eyebrow, which only made her laugh harder.

"Quite right, Miss Bingley," she said, and feeling almost giddy, leaned forward and whispered, "My mother thought Mr. Collins would make me a good husband."

Miss Bingley's mouth fell open before she snapped it shut.

Elizabeth nodded, still giggling. "Can you imagine?"

Despite Miss Bingley's typical iron control, a laugh escaped her lips. Then another. One more bubbled up before she cleared her throat and ran her hands over her skirt.

"Well," Miss Bingley said, and stood, "we must simply do what we can to keep your mother and my aunt from ever meeting." She evaluated Elizabeth, resigned. "I still do not like you, Miss Elizabeth," she said, though her lips tugged upward, and Elizabeth thought perhaps the ice had at last begun to crack. "However, I think we shall get on as best we are able."

Elizabeth smiled. "I shall look forward to it, Miss Bingley."

Caroline Bingley squared her shoulders and left the room in a swish of silk.

"Mr. Darcy," Mr. Bennet drawled from his relaxed seat in the library, a glass of wine sitting on the table next to him. "I was wondering whether you had perhaps lost your way."

"No, sir," he replied. "Just a small delay."

Mr. Bennet then surprised him by laughing heartily. "That was some dance, my boy. Mrs. Russell would have dragged you out by your hair had she seen it."

Darcy's cheeks warmed. "I did not intend any insult, sir."

Mr. Bennet waved his hand. "Never mind, son," he said. "And you are fortunate you are courting Lizzy, for my son you must be after *that* performance." He reached to the side table for his glass of wine. "We shall remain here a suitable amount of time, for appearances' sake, you know." He shook his head and grinned. "As my aunt has already given her permission and all of Hertfordshire will shortly be made aware that you are in love with my daughter and she with you, I think we can call this business concluded." His nose wrinkled and he scratched the back of his head. "Unless you wish to make your speech. Did you spend much time preparing it?"

Could it be this simple? "No, sir," he stammered. "Truthfully, I was more concerned about my speech for your daughter."

"Was it a good one?" Mr. Bennet asked, a faint smile lingering on his lips.

Darcy shrugged. "Not particularly, no. It matters little, as she did not require that I deliver it."

"Then she spared you both." Mr. Bennet sipped his wine. "Of course, you will need to present the marriage contract to His Grace. I do not envy you that." He relaxed against a cushion. "I suspect Olivia has him working on Elizabeth's already."

Darcy sat on the nearest chair, astonished Mr. Bennet was not more hesitant to hand off the duty of arranging Elizabeth's settlement, but upon reflection, he supposed the decision had been made some years ago. Frankly, he was overwhelmed at how the evening had progressed and was thankful for the brief respite. He felt completely content. Here the ball was only just beginning and both he and Bingley were engaged.

His attention drifted, wondering when they might wed. Would she make him wait for the season? He hoped not, though he felt secure now that he knew she would be his. He closed his eyes and remembered the look in her eyes as they danced together. He could wait. He could.

Mr. Bennet's voice broke through his reverie. "You should know, Mr. Darcy, that asking for a woman's hand is not the same as being married to her. The asking is easy. Facing everything together—that is hard."

"I believe we will do very well together," Darcy replied stiffly.

"I believe that, too," Mr. Bennet replied solemnly. "I would not be so sanguine about offering my permission did I not."

Darcy felt some of the tension leave his shoulders.

"All I am saying, son," the older man continued, "is that you must never forget that she is the first person you must consider in everything you do—and she will have to consider you first as well." His face clouded over. "Life is much more difficult when you do not have this agreement between you."

Darcy nodded. "I will remember." He held out his hand. "Would you call me Darcy?"

"If you call me Bennet." Mr. Bennet shook Darcy's hand and held up his wineglass. "Let me finish this and then we should head back. Shall we make it official with another announcement?"

Darcy leaned back and crossed his legs. "Are you trying to catch me out already, Bennet?"

Elizabeth's father laughed again. "Ah, well done, my boy. Let us ask Lizzy what she desires."

"I think it might actually do Miss Bingley in at her own ball," Elizabeth said contritely. "Besides, I should hate to make Jane share her night." She gave Mr. Darcy an apologetic look. "Would you mind very much if we waited? It does not make the engagement any less real."

Mr. Darcy took her hand. "I am just happy you said yes, Miss Elizabeth."

"A politic answer!" cried Mr. Bennet with a chuckle. "You are a quick study, Darcy."

"I do my best, Bennet," Darcy replied, his eyes never leaving his betrothed.

"Now, the both of you—it is time for other partners," Mr. Bennet said, shooing them away. "I believe you are meant to be dancing with another of my daughters, Darcy," he said. "And you, miss," he said fondly, taking Elizabeth's hand and giving it a squeeze, "are with me."

"I should be very pleased to dance the next with you, Papa," Elizabeth said, hugging his arm to her side.

The next hour passed agreeably enough. She danced with Papa and then with Mr. Fitzwilliam, who welcomed her into the family with his usual good cheer.

Then it was halfway through the evening and time for the supper dance. Mr. Darcy collected her and they lined up for what would be a form of quadrille.

This dance was different than the first. The eye contact was still continuous throughout the set, but it was tender rather than heated. *There are many different facets to love,* she thought, *and I shall experience them all.* She was anxious to begin.

Before she knew it, the second dance was ending. Elizabeth released Mr. Darcy's hand and curtseyed. He bowed and offered her his arm. Their side of the room was near the end of the line and Darcy realized, to his chagrin, that they would be fortunate to even reach the food before the supper break was over. He ought to have paid more attention to their position. They stood together, the rest of the crowd pressing through the doorways and out of the now-stifling ballroom. The musicians stood, setting down their instruments, wiping their brows with large handkerchiefs and shaking their jackets to cool themselves; several made for the balcony and the cold night air.

Despite being rather hungry, Darcy was content to stand with Elizabeth and slowly make forward progress toward the food. Being at the very end of the line offered some privacy, and he thrilled each time the back of her gloved hand brushed his own. "Perhaps we would be better served to head directly to the kitchens," Elizabeth said drolly. "Mrs. Thistlewaite will be sure to feed us, and the food will still be hot."

To their right, Mr. Collins was speaking with Miss Lucas, something about beekeeping and rendering wax for candles. Darcy thought the young woman unusually interested in the discourse, or he would have inquired of Elizabeth whether he should intervene. Collins pointed at one of the candles to demonstrate something to his companion. Darcy turned away, hoping not to hear any more of the parson's intricately detailed lecture on—*did he say slumgum?*

"Oh!" Elizabeth gasped, and grabbed her skirt before scurrying away.

Darcy turned back to see Collins gesticulating wildly with a lit candle as he continued to speak. It took several seconds before the pastor realized he had lost his student. He glanced around, oblivious to the blue flame that now licked up the curtain beside him. When he at last noticed it, he twisted awkwardly this way and that, blowing at the fire frantically and apparently seeking help.

Miss Lucas had already hurried to a table by the opposite wall, where a pitcher of water sat. She was joined by Elizabeth, who had retrieved a pitcher from another table. Before either could reach the spot where Collins remained, uselessly flapping his arms, candle even yet clutched in one waving fist, Darcy had taken advantage of his long legs to quickly cover the thirty feet or so to the curtain, pull it off the wall, and stamp the flames out as the heavy brass rod clattered to the floor. Elizabeth handed him her pitcher, and he poured the water over the burnt cloth.

"Collins," he snarled, grabbing the man by the front of his jacket, "what the *devil* are you about? Have you any idea the panic that would ensue were there a fire in the ballroom?" He looked over his shoulder; only one or two people other than the musicians seemed to have noticed. Everyone else was finally at supper.

Darcy released Collins, bending to slide the ruined curtain from the rod and pick up the cloth. He shook it at the man, trying to contain his fury. "There are hundreds of people in this house tonight. Even were nobody hurt by the fire, there would certainly be injuries as a result of the inevitable flight outdoors." He rolled up the heavy fabric, hoping to secret it downstairs and get the servants to air out the room as well as they could before the dancing resumed.

He felt a small hand on his arm. "Mr. Darcy," he heard Elizabeth say, "we will see to things here. Just take the curtain away."

He closed his eyes and brought his anger under control. He nodded once and moved towards the servant's entrance. At that moment, several footmen entered from the adjoining room, bearing jugs of fresh punch to refill the bowl. When they saw the mess the first man set his jug down and hurried over.

"Fisk," Miss Elizabeth said, "thank goodness you are here. There has been a mishap, and Mr. Darcy has taken care of it. Would you be so good as to remove that curtain?"

Fisk's eyes went first to the burnt material in Darcy's hands and then shot briefly over to Collins. Without a word, he accepted the material and disappeared through the servant's door. He reappeared to heft the brass rod up in his hands and place it inside the servants' hallway before closing the door firmly.

Darcy pinched the bridge of his nose and prayed for patience. Collins, to his credit, did appear embarrassed as he shoved the beeswax candle back in its holder.

"I was only explaining the many benefits of keeping bees," he muttered. "I thank you for your assistance, Mr. Darcy. Your aunt has always extolled your ability to think well under duress, and I believe she has been proven correct this evening. She is extraordinarily . . ."

"No more, Collins," he said gruffly. Miss Lucas had approached the remaining footmen and was speaking quietly to them.

"Come, Mr. Darcy," Elizabeth said softly. "Let us go to supper. Charlotte has things well in hand, and Mr. Collins will help her. Is not that the case, cousin?" she asked.

"Of course, of course," Collins mumbled, his face and neck flushed. Darcy allowed himself to be led off.

He took a deep breath. "Thank you, Elizabeth."

"You know," she teased, "I do not recall you ever asking to use my Christian name, sir, yet you are making rather free with it. It is rather a presumption on your part." She gazed up at him, humor sparkling in her eyes. "Should I be concerned about this flaw in your character?"

He frowned at her, but he could not hold it, and she laughed and pressed her cheek briefly against his shoulder. "You know," he responded, "I was going to ask you when we were on the balcony, but you stopped my lips."

"Truly?" she asked pertly. "Then my interruption caused you to propose?"

"As I recall," he said confidently, "you answered before I could ask."

"Arrogant man," she laughed. "Come, you must feed your impertinent betrothed."

They stepped into the hallway that separated the ballroom from the supper rooms, and Elizabeth suddenly stopped walking, forcing him to pause mid-stride.

"What is it?" he asked, then followed her line of sight. A man with thin, reddish-brown hair stood at the end of the hall, closest to the front entry, Mrs. Nicholls beside him. He was unwinding a long woolen scarf and handing it over to the housekeeper. His expensive greatcoat and highly polished Hessians indicated that he had not come to dance. Darcy took a second look.

"Tavistock?" he asked aloud. He glanced down at Elizabeth, who had not moved and whose face had paled to a sickly white.

"Francis?" she whispered.

CHAPTER FIVE

Darcy reached to steady Elizabeth, concerned by her sudden pallor, but before he could touch her, she was off, nearly running in the direction of her cousin, slippered feet sliding slightly with the force of each step. Darcy started after her, his gait more deliberate. Tavistock's posture relaxed when he saw Elizabeth, and the marquess held out his arms. She launched herself into them, though by the time Darcy had reached them both, she had pulled away.

"Aunt Olivia?" she asked, her voice pinched and tight. Darcy's heart broke a little, hearing in Elizabeth's question an echo of a young Georgiana. *Papa will recover, will he not?*

"Lizzy, Olivia is fine," Francis reassured her, but his expression remained serious. "She has had a bit of a fright."

"Tavistock," Darcy replied, wishing he could embrace Elizabeth as her cousin had. "What brings you to Hertfordshire so late?"

The marquess eyed him cautiously. "Darcy. I was told you would be here. Has your business with Elizabeth been concluded?"

"Yes, yes," Elizabeth said impatiently. "We are betrothed, though it has not been formally announced."

"Excellent. Congratulations," Tavistock said brusquely. "Darcy, would you ask your friend if we might use his study? I need to speak with Mr. Bennet right away." He paused before adding, "You should join us."

"Francis," Miss Elizabeth said, balling her hands into fists. "What is going *on?*"

"Not here, Lizzy," her cousin said firmly. "Let us collect your father and then we can discuss this in private."

Darcy nodded. "Of course. I presume you do not wish your presence noted?"

Tavistock nodded.

Darcy turned to Elizabeth. "Let us find your father and Bingley," he said gently.

"Oh," Tavistock said suddenly, "Is your Fitzwilliam cousin here? Not the viscount, the soldier?"

Darcy's stomach clenched, and he felt his stoicism returning for the first time in over a month. His mask dropped into place. "He is."

A fleeting grimace appeared on his face before Tavistock issued an order. "Bring him."

When they entered the room, Elizabeth slipped into the crowd to search for her father. From a distance, she saw him seated at a table with her mother, Mrs. Cleopatra Bingley, Lydia, Jane, and Mr. Bingley. Mrs. Bingley had plucked a vibrantly green feather from her turban and was examining it with her mother. As she watched, Mrs. Bingley reached up to her turban to pluck another and hold it out for comparison. Not far away, Mr. Fitzwilliam sat at a table with Mr. Goulding, Miss Bingley, Mary, and Kitty.

At that moment, her father happened to glance up and meet her eye. Elizabeth was grateful when his own eyes narrowed and he made his excuses. Nobody seemed to be bothered by his absence, as even over the rather loud hum of conversation she could hear her mother's raptures.

"Oh, I have ever so many plans for the wedding, Cleopatra," she was saying, while Lydia tried to speak with an embarrassed Jane and Mr. Bingley. Only Mrs. Bingley was listening, but it did not dissuade her. "How grand it shall be! Just imagine! The flowers!" She rested her hand lightly on Mrs. Bingley's wrist. "The feathers!"

Mr. Darcy watched her father disappear into the crowd before he made his way over to Mr. Bingley. He leaned over and made his request quietly. Mr. Bingley nodded and stood.

"What is it, Lizzy?" her father asked as he reached her side.

"Francis is here," she said, her heart in her throat. "He wishes to speak with you."

Her father frowned. He briefly laid a hand on her arm and then brushed past her on his way out of the room.

Mr. Bingley said something to his sister, then left through a different door. Mr. Darcy made a small motion with his head to Mr. Fitzwilliam and then tugged at the side of his coat once, where his watch chain normally hung. Mr. Fitzwilliam saw the gesture, she was sure of it, but he did not react. After speaking to a few guests in a bid to waste time, Mr. Darcy turned away and led her back out to the hall.

Elizabeth took a shaky breath as they stepped into the study. Francis, Papa, and Mr. Bingley were already there, waiting.

"Fitzwilliam will be along," Mr. Darcy said in response to a look from Francis. "We could not all remove at once."

"Tavistock," Mr. Bennet said quietly, "this is Mr. Bingley. He is the current master of Netherfield and is betrothed to Jane. Bingley, this is the Marquess of Tavistock."

Mr. Bingley bowed. Francis studied him for a moment, then took a letter from a pocket inside his coat. He held it out to her father. Mr. Bingley joined him.

"Olivia received this today in the post. She was taken ill soon after." He turned his attention to Elizabeth. "She had an attack, but she is well, Lizzy, resting. However, you know she has not been herself, even before this shock, and she needs to see that you are well."

Elizabeth swallowed a growing sense of dread. She had hoped for her few remaining weeks in Hertfordshire to be spent with Mr. Darcy and her sisters, enjoying her engagement. Once she left for London, her life would change in more than one way, and her aunt knew it. Aunt Olivia would never cut her visit short unless there was a very good reason.

She expected to see the message next, but Mr. Bennet handed it to Mr. Darcy, and she watched his stony features turn to granite. He moved to give the letter back to Tavistock. Elizabeth cleared her throat and held out her hand.

"Mr. Darcy, if you please," she said. He hesitated, but her hand remained out. "This directly affects me, sir. Keeping me in ignorance is hardly helpful."

As she watched Mr. Darcy, he seemed to recall something, and he reluctantly passed the letter to her. Behind her, the door opened and shut, but Elizabeth was focused on the handwriting. Masculine hand, tight, angular letters. There was nothing of grace or civility in the hand, and only two lines:

Mrs. Russell,

One will die and one will mourn. Where is your niece?

"What is the plan?" Richard asked, his voice hard, flat, and very close. Elizabeth realized he had read the note over her shoulder.

"My father wants Elizabeth back in London where we can reunite her with Olivia and keep them both safe," Francis replied. "The moon is bright. We have lanterns on the coach and fresh horses. We should be on our way shortly."

"Are you sure that is safe?" asked Mr. Bennet. "The note asks for Lizzy's whereabouts. If he does not know where she is, perhaps she should remain in the country."

Francis grimaced. "Lizzy's family ties are not widely known in London, Bennet, but they are not a secret, either. If he does not already know about Longbourn, it will not be difficult to discover. I do not mean to offend, but . . ."

"We do not generally require guards, Tavistock," her father said, all traces of humor from earlier in the evening now gone. "I understand."

"I left men at Longbourn when I stopped there, and with your permission, they shall remain." Francis laid a hand on her father's shoulder. "While Lizzy is a Russell, we shall not leave her Bennet family unprotected." He pulled away as Elizabeth offered him the letter. "Both my father and I suspect this is a threat that shall precede a letter of extortion rather than a physical confrontation. But we do not intend to take any chances."

Mr. Bennet nodded, brow furrowed. He turned to Elizabeth with regret, took her by her hands and kissed her forehead. "I have very much enjoyed having you home with us, Lizzy," he said. "I will tell your mother and sisters when we return home." He gave her a sad smile. "Lydia will be pleased to stay at Netherfield a little later." In a rare show of affection, he rested his forehead against hers. "Goodbye, Elizabeth. Go with God, my love, and write us when you are safely at St. James's."

"Thank you, Papa, I shall," she whispered, breathing in the comforting scent of wine and pipe tobacco. "I love you. Please make my farewells to Mama and the girls. Tell them I shall write."

Mr. Bennet nodded, misty-eyed, and left the room.

"I shall remain and assist Mr. Bennet at Longbourn, unless you have another task for me," Mr. Bingley stated.

Tavistock shook his head. "That would ease my mind considerably, Mr. Bingley."

Mr. Bingley nodded. "Take all the time you need here. I must return to my guests before my absence is noted." He smiled encouragingly at Elizabeth. "I will take care of your sisters, Miss Elizabeth."

"I thank you, sir," she said, grateful. Mr. Bingley gave Darcy a stare that conveyed something—she was not certain what—and then was gone.

As Mr. Bingley closed the door behind him, Tavistock turned to Darcy. "I assume you will wish to ride in the carriage with Elizabeth?"

Darcy nodded. "I will. I require but a short time to change."

"Mr. Fitzwilliam," Tavistock said, "I should like you to join the outriders, if you would be willing. My best man remained in London with the family. You were in the rearguard, were you not?"

"I was, my lord," Richard replied with a small bow. "It would be my honor to help escort Miss Russell."

Elizabeth's head began to swim with everything that was happening. She wanted to ask the men to stop, to give her an opportunity to think, but competing with that desire was an overwhelming need to reach her aunt.

Francis stepped to her. "Lizzy," he said gently, "I have read your letters. I know how much you came to enjoy being anonymous here in Hertfordshire, particularly this autumn. But that time is done." He looked in her eyes. "You are a Russell. It is time to take back your name and all it demands of you."

Darcy's eyes were on Elizabeth as she blinked. He could almost see the weight of duty and responsibility settling over her shoulders like a cloak. It was a feeling he knew intimately, and impulsively, he reached out his hand to hers. She looked up at him, and there was no fear or weakness there, only anger and worry and determination. A deep and abiding love for her surged through him, and he tried to give her a little smile as he felt her fingers curl around his.

"You are a Russell, Elizabeth, but you will soon be a Darcy as well," he told her. "You will not face any of this alone."

"Will you meet us at Longbourn?" she asked, still holding his hand, but indicating her ball gown and slippers. "I cannot travel like this, and I should like to be back to Aunt Olivia by morning."

"Of course," he said. "Richard?"

"With you," Richard said, his words tight and clipped. He gave a short bow to Elizabeth. "Miss Russell, we shall see you shortly."

Elizabeth stood and drew in a deep breath. "Francis," she asked, "shall we go?" She was out the door before her cousin could respond. He watched her depart, a fond smile playing on his lips.

"By all means, Lizzy," he said to her back. He turned to Darcy and indicated the empty doorway. "I hope you have what it takes to be married to a Russell woman."

Darcy's eyes lingered on the last place he had seen her and could not bring himself to smile. "I hope the same."

The small group entered the hall to see their hostess gracefully descending the staircase.

"Mr. Darcy, Mr. Fitzwilliam, Miss Elizabeth," she said graciously, "I noticed you had not returned to the ball and wished to see whether I might offer any assistance."

Mr. Fitzwilliam barely acknowledged Miss Bingley, and Mr. Darcy only offered the woman an irritated glare. Elizabeth, knowing the quickest way out was to directly address the woman standing in their way, took over. She glanced at Francis, who gave her a wink, which she took as permission to make the introduction. "Lord Tavistock," she said, "this is Miss Bingley, Mr. Bingley's sister. Miss Bingley, this is the Marquess of Tavistock."

Miss Bingley's hand hovered briefly over her heart, though she trained one eye on Elizabeth. *No doubt wondering why I am the one facilitating the introduction*, Elizabeth thought.

"Lord Tavistock," Miss Bingley intoned, and curtsied deeply.

Elizabeth saw Francis's lips quirk up and nudged him. Hard.

"Hey," he hissed. "Sharp elbow, Lizzy."

Elizabeth opened her eyes quite wide and tipped her head in the direction of Miss Bingley, who was rising, a questioning expression on her face as she fixed her attention on Francis.

"Charmed," her cousin said. Elizabeth frowned, and he shrugged a bit.

"And to what do we owe the pleasure, my lord?" Miss Bingley asked, nonplussed. "Would you care to join us upstairs?"

"No, I thank you, Miss Bingley," he replied. "I am only here to retrieve my cousin."

Miss Bingley paled, her lips parting slightly. She cast a quick, desperate look first at Mr. Darcy, who shook his head once, then did the same with Mr. Fitzwilliam, who rolled his eyes. Her vision then landed on Elizabeth, her face frozen with shock, a red spot appearing on each cheek and beginning to spread.

"You should speak to Jane, Miss Bingley," Elizabeth instructed the stunned woman. "Perhaps your brother's match has hidden benefits."

Thinking that there was simply not enough time for a more complete explanation, she touched Francis's arm. "We really must be leaving." She bobbed a quick, shallow curtsey for Miss Bingley. "I thank you for your hospitality. It was a lovely ball. Good night."

Elizabeth fidgeted as the carriage pulled away from Netherfield, a maid perched next to her. Normally Elizabeth would have held a conversation, even if a brief one, to learn the girl's name and inquire after her family, but she could not. She could sense Francis observing her, but she could not help growing sick with anxiety for Aunt Olivia. *She has had an attack.* Had the night not been so cold, even in Francis's fancy closed carriage and with the heated bricks she knew were likely being readied at her father's house, she might have considered heading to London in her ball gown and dancing slippers. She might even have mounted Kensington and ridden there herself.

"Do not get any wild ideas about riding to London, Lizzy," Francis grumbled from the other bench. "Even after a two-year absence from your company, I know how your mind works. Your aunt would skin me alive, and my father would finish the job. Even my gentle wife might have a go at me." He crossed his arms over his chest. "I should remind you that your betrothed would not be able to ride with you in the carriage if you mounted your mare and rode away like a heroine in one of those terrible novels my wife loves."

"*Your wife* loves them. Truly?" Elizabeth replied, knowing he was attempting to divert her, but willing to allow it.

"Of course," he responded. It was dark in the carriage and she could not see his face. "When *I* read them, it is research."

"Research," Elizabeth scoffed. She was quiet for a moment but could not resist. "I shall be sorry I inquired, I know, but whatever would you be researching?" Her nausea began to ebb.

"The female mind," he parried, and she knew he must be grinning. "It is ever a mystery to me, but I do find that these novels open up an entirely feminine world of intrigue and swooning."

"Intrigue and swooning," she repeated, rubbing her forehead and willing the throbbing to subside. "Francis, you can be such a ninny."

"Thank you, my dear," he said, triumphant.

She laughed softly. "Thank *you*, Francis."

His words were affectionate, though all he said was "Of course."

She leaned forward, now able to see his eyes in a shaft of light from the lanterns outside. "Now I should like to hear about Aunt Olivia. What exactly happened?"

Francis frowned. "I was not there, but His Grace said that Olivia had trouble with her breathing and complained of her heart."

Elizabeth closed her eyes. *Remain calm.* "Was this all?"

"The worst of it, yes. She mentioned a numbness in her fingers, and His Grace mentioned that there were some spasms in her hands."

Elizabeth drew a deep breath and forced her eyelids open. "Yet she is resting now and appears well?"

"When I left her, she was much recovered," Francis reiterated, "but adamant that I retrieve you."

Elizabeth thought of another question to ask but was stopped by a sudden swerve of their carriage to the left. She and Francis hit the side of the coach, and the maid was forced against her. Another carriage, less grand than their own but still rather expensive, swept past without stopping, traveling at a speed that was unsafe even during daylight. The maid immediately began to apologize as she swiftly returned to the other side of the bench, but Elizabeth assured her there was no need.

"This particular stretch of road has become increasingly dangerous in the past weeks," she said, her mind still with her aunt. "Let us hope they arrive at their destination safely."

Francis was indignant. "If we were not in such a hurry, I should catch them up myself and insist on an explanation."

Elizabeth watched the landmarks as they traveled past. "We are nearly to Longbourn, Francis," she said. "Let us not waste any time."

Darcy and Richard made their apologies to Miss Bingley, who remained where she was as they hurried upstairs to change out of their formal attire. Darcy burst into his chambers, where Hanson had already laid out a nightshirt and banyan. His features registered surprise that his master had come upstairs so early; by the time Darcy began rooting about for trousers and grabbed his newly polished boots, the young man's expression had regained its accustomed coolness.

"Sir," the valet asked, "may I assist you?"

"I have received an urgent summons to London, Hanson," Darcy said, removing a clean cravat from a drawer. "My cousin and I are leaving immediately. Get some rest tonight. You should follow with our things tomorrow."

Hanson nodded, but passed a critical eye over the items his master was hurriedly tossing on. He reached into the closet where he had hung Darcy's coats and selected one from the group. Then he chose a waistcoat in just as decisive a manner. He selected a shirt more suited to travel than a ballroom. Then, without further conversation, he helped Darcy dress. He tied his employer's cravat in a simple, neat knot, then disappeared into another room and reappeared with his master's hat and greatcoat, already brushed and ready to be worn.

"Thank you, Hanson," Darcy grumbled, as he shook himself into the warm coat and grabbed the brim of the hat. "You will be expected at Grosvenor Square by the end of the day tomorrow."

"Very good, sir," the young man said, picking up the discarded clothes to put them away properly. Darcy dashed away.

Richard was waiting, already dressed for a cold ride. As Darcy joined him, they heard a single furious howl of frustration from the direction of a family sitting room at the far end of the hall, followed by what sounded like the word *unbelievable*. The men exchanged grimaces, and as they reached the top of the main stairs, they heard a door open. Richard turned to see who it was, and though Darcy was sure he already knew, he remained with his cousin.

Miss Caroline Bingley stepped from the room with a candle in one hand. She lifted the other to pat her coiffure into place. Her expression, lit by the candle's small flame, was serene and pleasant, and she began to stroll down the hallway, presumably to return to the ball. As the family and their guests were expected not to return to their rooms until nearly four, the hallway remained dark. Miss Bingley, her mind clearly on other matters, turned to take a family stairway to the ballrooms without observing them.

When they were sure she had gone, Richard let out an exaggerated sigh. "Say what you will about controlling your emotions, Darcy," he grunted. "It is better to have a wife who cannot help but show what she is feeling. That one might just kill you in your sleep and look none the worse for wear in the morning."

Together, they made their way to the front of the house to await their carriage. There were no further words spoken between them. Darcy's anxiety grew ever sharper with the inactivity, and Richard just stood motionless, vision fixed on a spot over Darcy's shoulder. Darcy knew his cousin's vacant stare hid an analytical mind already reviewing possible risks and potential solutions. It had always been thus. They remained in the front hall, Darcy tapping his foot impatiently as muffled strains of music and laughter from upstairs drifted down to them. He heard the crunch of carriage wheels on gravel and the coachman calling to his horses. He was relieved that his coachmen had been so quick, and he threw open the heavy door himself, eager to get to Longbourn and Elizabeth.

He pulled up short at the sight of the coach. It was not his, though it was familiar. He could just make out the family crest in the light of the torches. *Good God. What in blazes is* she *doing here?*

"Bloody hell . . ." he heard Richard whisper, half in frustration and half in awe, as the steps were lowered and one of Bingley's footmen reached inside.

What else could possibly go awry this evening?

"Nephew!" cried a very familiar, very imperious voice. "You will attend me!"

Elizabeth gave a brief greeting to Mr. Hill and flew up the stairs, Francis's maid behind her.

"Lord Tavistock said to have your trunks sent after, miss, but is there anything you might wish to bring with you tonight?" she asked.

Elizabeth noticed that candles had been lit for her and that there was already warm clothing laid out upon her bed. She stopped for a moment to gather her wits, and then listed a few items and began to move about the room. She never went anywhere without her drawings, sketchbooks, and pencils and she did not trust anyone else to pack them up properly. For the same reason and for privacy's sake, she would need to collect her correspondence and notes. Then she would only require her personal grooming items, which she asked the maid to assemble. The trunks that had accompanied her aunt to London should have everything else she needed.

"Do you know if they have made arrangements for my mare?" she asked.

"No, miss," the girl replied. "But I would guess they have. The master is very thorough, he is."

Elizabeth gave the girl a little smile. "I have been rather distracted, I am afraid. I have not even asked your name."

"Oh, it is of no matter, miss," the girl said with a small smile. "The whole house was in uproar today. I quite understand." Elizabeth waited for a moment until the maid's face lit up. "Oh! Delilah, miss. My name is Delilah." She bobbed a curtsey.

She remembered Francis's words and replied, "I am Miss Russell, Delilah."

"Yes, miss."

She sized the girl up. Delilah was young, perhaps Lydia's age. She was neatly attired and pretty, in a girlish sort of way. She also seemed eager to please.

"Delilah," Elizabeth said, "I am in a great hurry to get to my aunt. Where should we begin?"

Delilah smiled. "Let us take down your hair and make you more comfortable for a carriage ride, miss. The gentlemen will have to take some time to change as well."

Elizabeth nodded and sat down. As Delilah's deft fingers undid her hair, pulling out hairpins and brushing out the tight curls, she gazed into the mirror before her, visually tracing the shadow and light in every plane of her features. A specter stared back at her and she beat back a nearly overwhelming urge to weep. Elizabeth imagined, longingly, the path that crossed the fields between Longbourn and Netherfield. Walking there with her sisters, the ground wet with dew and autumn rain, was already a part of her past. She absorbed the dark reflection of the room behind her, the one that she had all but abandoned since the beginning of Mr. Collins's visit, and knew that however temporary her stay at Longbourn had been, she would miss it. She had been Elizabeth Bennet here. She had not wanted to be, but in the end, it had been good. She thought perhaps Mr. Darcy would agree.

"I am right here, Aunt Catherine," Richard said blithely, stepping forward. "How may I be of assistance?"

Lady Catherine de Bourgh, tall, imposing, and clearly incensed, brushed past him without a word.

"Aunt Catherine," Darcy welcomed her, giving no outward sign of his desperation to be rid of the woman, "I cannot begin to account for your presence in Hertfordshire of all places, and at such an hour. What has happened?"

The old lady leaned in and shook a piece of paper at him. "How can you think to deceive me? Why would you even make the attempt?" She frowned, taking in their clothing. "Where are you going?"

Darcy managed to still an angry reply, though a strangled sound did manage to escape. He would have to forgive himself for that small loss of control. It had been a wonderful evening at the start, but it was becoming increasingly trying. From the corner of his eye, he spied his cousin hovering nearby. *Ready to intervene before I pick the woman up and place her bodily back in her carriage, Richard?*

"What sort of inelegant utterance is that, Fitzwilliam Darcy?" she demanded, so close to him that Darcy could smell the stew that had likely been her ladyship's most recent meal.

"Aunt Catherine," Darcy responded, his jaw nearly too tight to speak, "I resent the implication that I am in any way dishonest."

"I have the proof of it here, nephew," Lady Catherine declared, again holding up a folded sheet of paper in her hand. "A servant of yours in London was so kind as to send it to me. Did you believe you could hide it from me forever?"

None of my servants would send you anything or they would find themselves without a position.

"What proof, Aunt Catherine? Of what do you speak?" Richard asked coolly. "We will get nowhere if you continue to speak in riddles."

"I will not hold this conversation out of doors like a common . . ."

Darcy held up a hand, palm out. "Enough." He gestured toward the house. "Let us enter."

Richard gave orders to the coachman to take the horses around to the stables while Darcy hoped against hope for the appearance of his own equipage. He had a vision of hopping inside and departing while his aunt waited for him indoors. But Richard was already showing Aunt Catherine inside and still had to ride twenty-odd miles tonight. He could not in good conscience leave his cousin on his own to ride another three.

"Best to see what the old girl wants," Richard whispered as Darcy reached his cousin and they reentered the house. "We shall finish with her swiftly and get Bingley to put her up for the night."

The sight of Lady Catherine in Bingley's study was jarring, and whatever she was about to say was certain to aggravate him at a time when he was already dreadfully agitated. Darcy composed himself. It was important never to appear anything other than perfectly calm when in his aunt's presence.

His aunt waved the paper at him, and he could see now that it was a letter.

"Your own father desired it," she said to Darcy. "How you can deny it when it is here in his own hand? For shame, nephew." Her face was turning red and her hand shook.

"May I see that, Aunt Catherine?" Darcy held out his hand.

She gave him a haughty look. "I cannot be sure you will not destroy it."

He did not withdraw his hand. "I will make no response to that. Nor will I reply to your accusations without seeing what you have brought."

She handed the letter to him, and he felt Richard stand at his shoulder. It was a letter from his father, advocating a marriage between himself and his cousin Anne de Bourgh. It was Aunt Catherine's favorite wish, to unite Rosings and Pemberley, even though he had stated unequivocally some years ago that he was not bound in any way to his cousin nor she to him. He had ignored the repetition of her desires afterward. His father had never said anything to him about marrying his cousin, and one declaration of his freedom was all Darcy had stooped to make to his aunt. He did not wish to wed his cousin Anne; Anne had no wish to marry at all.

He studied the letter. The writer could not be clearer. *It is my dying wish, Catherine, to complete this business between Fitzwilliam and Anne. I have not the time for a contract, but you may consider this letter as my binding promise.* It was his father's hand, except . . . He stared closely at it before his aunt tore it away. He shook his head.

"I have never seen that letter before, Aunt Catherine," he said wearily. "I wonder you took the trouble to come all this way on so slight a provocation." His legs fairly trembled with the desire to be on his way.

She sniffed. "I should have waited for your April visit had not the pastor of Hunsford written me. I sent him here to marry. He is the cousin to a family of five daughters who will all be cast out when their father dies." She straightened to her full height. "An entail away from any daughters is a ridiculous thing. A marriage between the heir and one of the daughters would secure them all."

Darcy groaned inwardly, and his cousin put a hand over his eyes. *It might have been a kind gesture,* Darcy admitted to himself, *had the man not been who he is.*

"Mr. Collins had the gall," Aunt Catherine sputtered, "to relate that he had been refused by his choice of bride because you, my own nephew, were already courting the penniless country chit." She straightened her sleeves. "I knew it must be a scandalous falsehood, but I would have you contradict it at once."

Richard ran a hand over his face. "Aunt, I can tell you that Darcy is not courting Miss Elizabeth Bennet." He held out his hand. "May I see the letter?"

The worst of Lady Catherine's pique seemed to melt away. "You may." She proffered the letter to him and sat down in a chair. "I am pleased to hear it, but not surprised. You could not have forgotten your duty so entirely."

I could. I did. And it was that which will save me. Darcy read the letter again. "This is not my father's letter, aunt."

"Despite your willfulness, Fitzwilliam, you cannot deny your duty. It is your father's dying wish!"

Darcy grimaced. "Aunt, have you even read this letter other than the part you most wish to believe?"

The old woman drew herself up, the picture of offense. "I have, many times!"

Darcy took the letter from his cousin and held it out. "The date, madam." He shoved it back at Richard and strode for the door, where he rang for a servant. A harried-looking maid appeared at the summons. "Inform Miss Bingley she has an unexpected visitor who will require a room for one night." She nodded and scurried away.

Richard was scrutinizing the letter. "29 December 1806." He shrugged, bemused. "Your father passed on the last day of the year, Darcy."

"He did. But he was insensible for the entire week preceding, as Aunt Catherine well knows." Darcy met his aunt's gaze and held it. "He was barely awake and spoke not at all. He could not have held a pen, let alone written in such a strong hand." He shook his head. It pained him to speak of his father's passing; it had not been a pleasant or a peaceful one. This reminded him that Elizabeth's aunt might herself be very ill. He needed to end this discussion.

"I am sorry I was not there," murmured Richard.

Darcy acknowledged the sentiment but remained resolute. "I will admit that the letter is well done. But it is a forgery, nonetheless." He pointed at a few sentences. "In addition to the date, Father's 'b' never had a loop quite that wide. I have read enough of his business correspondence to tell the difference."

"You cannot deny this letter, nephew," insisted Lady Catherine, though a great deal of the fire had left her. "It came from your own home."

"I doubt that very much, Aunt," Darcy replied. *Which is another question. Who would send her such a thing?* He heard a knock upon the door. When he opened it, he was surprised to find Cleopatra Bingley standing outside.

"Darcy, dear," she said sweetly, "I hear we have an additional guest?"

"Yes, Mrs. er . . . Auntie Cleopatra." He bade her enter. "My aunt, Lady Catherine de Bourgh, requires a room." He had not examined the old woman's apparel before this moment, but he was relieved to see it was reasonably tasteful. That is, it was until she walked past him and he saw an enormous, garish peacock embroidered in bright colors on the back of her skirt. He held in a sigh.

"Who is this woman you address as an aunt?" fumed Lady Catherine, but Darcy was already in the hallway.

"Aunt Catherine, your hostess, Mrs. Cleopatra Bingley," he said.

"Good evening, your Ladyship," he heard Bingley's aunt say. "I am ever so glad to meet you!" He could imagine Aunt Catherine's horrified countenance, but she had made the journey of her own free will, and she could damn well suffer the consequences of her interference. He left the women to it and escaped outside.

The carriage was waiting, and he nearly dove into it head first. *Hurry, Richard,* he thought anxiously. *We must be away before any other relations appear out of the midnight mist.* Even as he finished the thought, Richard tossed himself into the coach, causing it to rock heavily to one side before it righted itself.

"Leaving without me?" he teased. "Hardly fair to abandon me to the aunts."

Darcy tried to sit still as the carriage began to move, but his foot tapped out a steady rhythm on the floorboards. "What did you tell her, Richard?"

His cousin grinned. "She wanted to know if you had shown the *chit* any particular attention, to which I said that you had."

Darcy groaned. "You did not . . ."

"I did," Richard said with a grin. "It is the truth, is it not?"

He closed his eyes. "It is."

"Then she asked again where we were going."

Why are you stretching this out, Richard? "And you said?"

"I told her I was taking you away to London. Immediately." He leaned back and examined his fingernails.

Darcy felt a warm smile beginning to grow. "You know she will think you are separating us."

His cousin snorted. "She also thinks you have never courted Miss Russell. But I only said you were not courting now—and you are not. Well done, by the by."

Darcy leaned his head back against the squabs. "Thank you, Richard."

Richard's voice grew solemn as he reached into his coat and withdrew the letter. "We shall have to find the scoundrel who has dared to forge your father's signature, Darcy. It could cause a great deal of trouble if this is not the only document." He held the letter out.

Darcy ran a hand through his hair and took it. *I cannot think of it now.* "I know."

Elizabeth paced the hall as the servants rushed about with all manner of tasks to complete. Her trunk had been lashed to the back of the carriage for nearly half an hour and she still awaited the arrival of her betrothed and Mr. Fitzwilliam. But they did not come. She crossed her arms over her stomach and tried to remain still.

Francis poked his head back inside. "We are ready, Lizzy," he said quietly. "We shall just wait a bit longer for Darcy and Mr. Fitzwilliam."

She touched her ear. "What could be keeping them?" she asked, knowing she sounded peevish but unable to prevent it. Surely Miss Bingley had not found some way to delay them?

It was another ten minutes before Mr. Darcy's carriage rolled into the drive and she rushed outside. Darcy barely waited for the steps before he burst out of the carriage to meet her.

"My apologies, love," he said. "Unexpected and unavoidable."

"Is that all you plan to tell me?" she asked, her anger flaring.

"No," he replied, drawing close enough to look her in the eye. "But the tale can wait until we are on our way."

Elizabeth shook her head. "Of course. I am just . . . "

"You are afraid for your aunt," he said, with a comforting squeeze of her hand. "Come." He led her to the larger coach that was waiting in front of his own and handed her up into it. "I shall join you shortly."

She watched out the window as he spoke to his own coachman, relieved when he returned quickly. Delilah entered the carriage and sat next to her while the men climbed in and took the rear-facing seat. Mr. Fitzwilliam rode past their window to take a position at the back of the coach, and she tried to ignore the rifle hanging from his saddle. Then she felt the welcome sway of the carriage as it began to move, and they finally began the long, dark journey to London.

CHAPTER SIX

It was a good night for traveling. The moon shone clear and bright and there had been no rain for nearly two days. The roads were still damp enough not to toss up dust but firm enough to support even the duke's substantial coach. Darcy's eyes rarely left an unusually silent Elizabeth. He wished heartily that they were alone so that he could offer her some comfort. It was increasingly difficult to witness her suffering and be unable to sit next to her, to draw her into his lap, to allow her to rest her head under his chin. He did not wish to rush her to marriage, but he longed for the right to hold her.

His eyes strayed to the window from time to time. The outriders regularly rotated positions, no doubt to remain alert. He was beginning to feel drowsy but would not sleep until they had all made it safely to St. James and he had seen Elizabeth restored to her aunt. It was not terribly far to his own home from there.

Before they turned onto the Great North Road, he related the story of his aunt and the letter. He had already denied Collins's claims that he had an understanding with Anne but wanted there to be no misunderstandings. Tavistock demonstrated an interest in the forgery, but Elizabeth only nodded sympathetically as she worried the hem of her glove into unraveling. His own hands curled as he tried to keep himself from moving to her side.

Darcy withdrew his gold watch and opened the cover. In the light of the lanterns, he could see that it was nearing half-past three in the morning; they should reach St. James's Square by five. He placed the timepiece back and glanced at Elizabeth again. Her pallor was returning.

Damn it. Ignoring Tavistock, he leaned forward and reached out to Elizabeth with one hand. She leaned towards him and took it, her now gloved fingers cold in his, a stark contrast to the warmth of their first dance only a few hours earlier. Her troubled gaze lifted to his and she tried to give him a smile.

A loud *crack* split the air.

Darcy's fingers closed convulsively around Elizabeth's wrist and he tugged her forward. In one fluid movement, they were both kneeling on the floor, Darcy's body shielding hers, his back to the direction of the sound, his hand holding her head to his chest. There were shouts and the pounding of hooves outside as several riders raced off to pursue the threat. The carriage horses sped up, and Darcy braced his bent arm against the bench to hold them both steady. The carriage rattled wildly for a few minutes before the coachman brought the team back to a steady gait. There were no more shots.

Darcy loosened his grip, placed a hand on her cheek, and stared into her eyes. "Are you well?" he asked Elizabeth, his voice rough with fear for her. She gazed back, frightened and weary.

"I am uninjured, sir," she said quietly, moving to rest her forehead against his chest. "I thank you."

Tavistock had moved to their side of the coach and already had a pistol in his hand. He handed another to Darcy, who helped Elizabeth back to her seat before accepting it. He then bade Elizabeth to slide to the center of the bench as he took up the place next to her and nearest the window where she had been sitting.

Darcy heard the riders calling out their return—his cousin among them. Even with the moonlight, it was too dark to take the horses over unknown terrain, and although he knew instinctively that Richard had given chase, he also knew his cousin would not want the carriage to travel too far ahead without him. Whoever it was had likely taken a random shot and then run off into the brush before their outriders could respond.

Richard maneuvered his mount to the side of the carriage where the men were now sitting. "Is everyone well?" he inquired, his voice raised a bit.

"We are," Tavistock assured him.

Behind him, Darcy heard a small sniffle that briefly took his attention away from the window. The maid was trying not to cry, her face collapsing in on itself in the attempt. She was very young. Elizabeth put her arm around the girl and pull her into a comforting embrace.

"There now, Delilah," she said. "It is just someone trying to frighten us."

"Pardon me, miss," the girl replied, beginning to hiccup, "but he is succeeding."

"He can only succeed if we allow it, my girl," Elizabeth said soothingly. "And we never shall. Come, dear, dry your tears." She pulled a handkerchief from her sleeve and handed it over. Darcy turned back to the window.

"Oh, no, miss," Delilah protested behind him. "'Tis too fine a cloth."

"The material *is* lovely, Delilah, but I am sorry to say that I have already ruined it," Elizabeth said with what he recognized as an intentionally dramatic sigh. "My embroidery is dreadful but my aunt was determined that practice was all I required. Would that it were true."

Darcy recalled his Aunt Catherine's similar refrain and smiled a little to himself. A very little. Tavistock snorted.

"There now," Elizabeth said gently as Delilah wiped her eyes. "Look how well protected we are, Delilah. Do you think these men will allow anything to happen to us?"

A few more tears tracked down her cheeks, but the girl shook her head. "No, miss."

Elizabeth focused on comforting Delilah, grateful for the excuse to turn her attention away from what was happening outside. When Mr. Darcy came to sit in her place by the window, she purposely did not move entirely away. The occasional touch of his hip or leg against hers made her feel safer, stronger.

She was aware that the duke and marquess received many letters like the one Francis had carried to Netherfield; only very rarely did they amount to anything tangible. Her concern had primarily been the effect of the threat on her aunt. It was typical of the family to travel with a small army—the number of outriders had never alarmed her, nor the use of a coach and six, one that could outrun any other it might encounter. She had learned long ago that with a title such as John's came many enemies, earned or not. It was yet another reason her Uncle Phillip had been content simply to remain a gentleman.

In the long months immediately following her Uncle Phillip's passing, her aunt had trouble sleeping. Many nights, Elizabeth would read or sing to her, and when she could at last see her aunt's eyes beginning to close, she would hum. It had helped her aunt relax into slumber and caring for Aunt Olivia had helped her make her own way though that terrible time.

She closed her eyes and began to hum softly, hoping it might work to calm Delilah as well as still her own wildly beating heart.

They traveled on that way for close to ten minutes, nothing being said, the only sound in the dark of the carriage her gentle humming, when the horses began to slow. She wondered why, whether the rain had opened a hole in the road they would need to move around or one of the horses had thrown a shoe.

Then they stopped completely. The men tensed, alert. Elizabeth stiffened. *What now?* Delilah's eyes were wide with fright, and she wrung her hands. Fortunately, the girl remained silent and still—she did not give in to tears again.

Elizabeth stopped humming and for a second it was silent as the men peered out into the night. Francis slid across the bench to the other side of the carriage, where he had originally been seated, and moved to open the door.

"Tavistock," Mr. Darcy said with quiet urgency, "let the escort come to us. Our place is here."

Francis frowned, but removed his hand from the door. "Quite right, Darcy."

It was not long before Mr. Fitzwilliam was again at the window. "There is a large branch blocking the road," he called. "We have men removing it." He did not join those men, though, instead remaining where he was. Elizabeth noted that a second outrider had taken up a similar position on their other side, and that both men were holding their rifles.

It is a branch, she reassured herself. *It might just as well have been knocked down by the rains. There is no reason to fear.* But sitting still in the middle of the road, not far from where someone had fired a gun as they passed and where anyone might engage them—it was a daunting prospect.

She could feel the tension building inside the coach and thought she ought to do what she could to ease it. So she began to sing softly, choosing a popular folk song they might all know. "Believe me, if all those endearing young charms, which I gaze on so fondly to-day."

Delilah turned her face up, and Elizabeth nodded encouragingly. Delilah added her voice, and they sang together softly. "Were to change by to-morrow and flee from my arms / Like fairy-gifts, fading away!"

They continued the song, and Elizabeth did not fail to note that both Francis and Mr. Darcy seemed to benefit too, the tautness in their shoulders loosening just a bit. In a few minutes, she and Delilah were singing the final line, "The same look which he turn'd when he rose!"

She was considering what they might sing next when several shouts rose from the front of the carriage, and Mr. Fitzwilliam leaned in to tell them that the road had been cleared. Francis gave her an approving smile, and Mr. Darcy reached over to squeeze her hand. He removed his hand directly, though she wished he would not. She understood. He was eloquent and romantic when they were alone or had some expectation of privacy, but like many men, he did not appreciate an audience. *Nor would it be proper,* she chastised herself. *He is showing you the respect you have always demanded.*

Elizabeth took a deep breath and let it out slowly, reclining against the squabs and allowing her mind to wander back to Netherfield. The ball would be breaking up now, and her family standing in the front hall awaiting their carriage. She imagined Mr. Bingley arranging for it to be brought around last, stealing a few extra moments with Jane, and the picture made her smile. She wanted to draw them; it could be a wedding gift.

"Well done, Elizabeth," Darcy praised her, as the coach picked up speed. "You have kept us all calmer than I would have thought possible."

"But I have no *need* to be concerned," she replied impertinently, though she had been worried, terribly worried, to own the truth. She feared for herself, but even more for the men protecting her. "I have all of you to do that for me." *Perhaps that was said too airily,* she thought. *I should not like him to think me unaware of the danger.* She placed a hand over his. "It was the only thing I had to offer."

He raised her hand to kiss it. "It worked." Elizabeth felt her own muscles begin to relax. He caught her gaze and held it. Too long, evidently, for Francis cleared his throat, and she saw him scowling at Darcy. Irritation flared up inside her, and she snapped at her cousin. "Leave it, Francis," she said firmly. "This is no ordinary night and we are not at a society gathering."

Francis sat back, glowering long after Mr. Darcy had released her hand.

It was in this state, Francis in a temper, Mr. Darcy studiously ignoring him, and her arm once again around Delilah, that they crossed over the city limits and into London.

※

For all the difficulty of the journey, they arrived not long past the time they had been expected, though with their nerves more than a little frayed. They filed into the entryway of the expansive home, every one of them exhausted. Though Richard was with them, the other outriders had accompanied the coachmen to the stables a few blocks away. Delilah hung back.

Unsurprisingly, the Duke of Bedford was awaiting them. He entered the front hall shortly after they did, smiling at Elizabeth and holding his arms out wide in the same manner as his son. Darcy noted that the two men resembled one another in additional ways—both had the same coloring, were roughly the same height, and while Tavistock still had most of his hair, it was already thinning. His father was entirely bald.

Elizabeth embraced the duke, holding on a little longer and a little tighter than he must have expected. Darcy rubbed his eyes wearily but did not miss His Grace raising his eyebrows as he looked at his son, and the frown signaling that what he saw there, he did not like. Richard had dismounted and came to join them, his left leg dragging just a little.

"Thank you for sending for me, John," Elizabeth said gratefully. "May I introduce Mr. Darcy and Mr. Fitzwilliam to you?" Darcy was pleased with the smile she gave him. "Mr. Darcy is my betrothed."

His Grace gave Darcy a once-over. "Indeed."

Elizabeth shook her head at His Grace. "None of that, sir. You gave your approval."

He grunted. "Under great pressure from your aunt and without a proper interview."

Darcy thought Elizabeth would chide His Grace for being ruled by an elderly woman, but she did not.

"Nonetheless," was her only response. Darcy could not see her face, but he thought he knew the look—pert, laughing, knowing. There was nothing the great man could do in the face of his young cousin's tease.

"May I see Aunt Olivia now?" Elizabeth asked. "I should like to go to her directly."

"She is sleeping, Lizzy," His Grace told her. "Why do you not refresh yourself first?"

"I will be very quiet, John," Elizabeth said. "But I cannot wait. I promise not to remain should she still be asleep."

The older man nodded and took her hands. "It is good to see you, Lizzy. We have missed you, my dear."

"It is good to be back, Your Grace," she replied playfully, then sobered. "I am only sorry it is for such a reason. Shall I see you at breakfast?"

He nodded. "Certainly, my dear."

Elizabeth approached Darcy and held out her hand. He bowed over it but did not attempt another kiss. She appraised him with those dark eyes and he offered a soft smile.

"You should sleep today, Fitzwilliam," she said, and his heart flipped in his chest. It was the first time she had used his Christian name. "Will you come see me tomorrow?"

He nodded.

Elizabeth turned to face Tavistock and the former Captain Fitzwilliam. "Gentlemen," she said, "I thank you for your excellent care. I will go to my aunt now."

They all waved her off pleasantly, and she gave Darcy another very particular smile before she walked out of sight down a hallway, trailed by Delilah and flanked by two other maids. He could hear her speaking to them but not what she was saying.

"Francis, gentlemen," His Grace said grimly, "let us all repair to the study. I should like to know what has happened."

Elizabeth arranged for the gentlemen to be brought tea and coffee as well as some food. She knew that, like herself, Mr. Darcy had not eaten supper and was likely famished. She had noticed Mr. Fitzwilliam favoring his leg and gave orders about that as well. Her Grace was not in residence so could not be hostess; Aunt Olivia had mentioned in her letters that she had departed some weeks ago for Woburn Abbey. It was left to Elizabeth, then, to make the arrangements.

"Alice," she asked one of the maids who was typically assigned to her when she resided in the Bedford home, "would you send word to Parker? He should offer his services to Mr. Darcy and Mr. Fitzwilliam as well, once they are finished with His Grace. They traveled through the night to deliver me to my aunt; I wish for them to feel presentable before they depart." It had occurred to her that Mr. Darcy and Mr. Fitzwilliam might need to repair their appearances before arriving at Darcy House unkempt and unshaven. She had no desire to begin any rumors or ignite any fears among Mr. Darcy's staff, but she knew both men were stubborn. Well, Parker would offer, and she would leave it to the men to sort it out between them.

When they finally reached her aunt's chambers at the back of the house, she did not pause to knock. Instead, she carefully opened the door and peered inside. Aunt Olivia was propped up against a mound of pillows, her eyes closed, thin hands clasped and resting on her stomach. In her sleep, her right thumb stroked her wedding band, now so large on her finger that it twisted in circles. Her face was thin, almost gaunt, her skin waxy and more heavily lined than it had been when they said goodbye. One gray plait fell over her shoulder. Aunt Olivia would not like to be seen this way, Elizabeth knew, but she entered the room in any case. Her aunt had been insistent that Elizabeth be removed from Longbourn and would want to know that she had arrived. She motioned for the maid to remain seated when she saw her aunt's eyes flicker open and stepped to the side of the bed to take one fragile hand in her own.

"My girl," Aunt Olivia mumbled, still half-asleep. "Are you really here?"

"Of course I am," Elizabeth chided softly. "You called, and I came."

Her aunt smiled brightly then, and Elizabeth felt her spirits lift. Aunt Olivia's smile was unaltered.

"If only that were true," Aunt Olivia replied archly. "I seem to recall many afternoons when you could not be persuaded to come in to dinner." She reached for the water on her nightstand and the maid handed it to her.

Elizabeth laughed softly. "You have worn me down, Aunt," she teased. "I am more compliant now."

Her aunt shook her head, her eyes sparkling, and handed the water back to the maid. She pushed herself up into a sitting position before anyone could assist her.

"Did Francis tell you why I wanted you here?"

"I insisted on reading the note," Elizabeth replied.

Aunt Olivia's lips twitched upwards. "Good, good. The men should know not to keep you in the dark. I would not have had it either."

"Aunt," Elizabeth asked seriously, "do you know who might have written it?"

Aunt Olivia sighed. "I have been thinking about that, Lizzy, and I cannot fathom it. Phillip was no saint, but he was fair in all his dealings. He had disagreements over business with several men over the years, but nothing that would result in such a violent message. Truly, it might be anyone." She raised a hand to her forehead.

"You should rest, Aunt Olivia," Elizabeth said firmly. "I only wished to present myself for your inspection, and now I shall refresh myself and take something to eat. We missed supper last night, and I am very hungry."

"Oh, what a shame," Olivia murmured, settling back into her pillows. "You were so looking forward to Mrs. Thistlewaite's white soup."

"I was greatly anticipating everything Mrs. Thistlewaite sent to the table, in fact," Elizabeth said, smiling. "Alas, I shall have to return another time." She raised an eyebrow. "However, this will be made easier by the fact that Jane is now engaged to Mr. Bingley."

"That is wonderful news." Her aunt met her gaze, and Elizabeth had a strange sense of seeing her own face looking back at her. "What of your Mr. Darcy?" Aunt Olivia asked.

"Fitzwilliam? Oh, he is very much *my* Mr. Darcy," Elizabeth replied cheerfully.

"Oh," her aunt breathed. "Oh, my dear, that is the best of news. He was a dear boy and has grown up well. When did he propose?"

"Last night, after we danced." *While we danced.*

"And then we pulled you away?" Her aunt appeared distressed.

Elizabeth patted her aunt's hand. "He attended me in the carriage with Francis and Delilah."

Olivia rolled her eyes. "Whoever named that child ought to be flogged."

Elizabeth laughed. "Be that as it may, Mr. Darcy and his cousin are in conference now with John and Francis. I have every confidence they will put an end to this nonsense. Have no fear."

"I *was* afraid," Aunt Olivia said, searching Elizabeth's face. "I have never *been* so afraid." She held Elizabeth's hand in both of hers. "I am ashamed to admit that I was entirely undone."

"It shows your love for me, Aunt," Elizabeth said solemnly, "for which I have ever been grateful." She straightened the blankets and tucked her aunt in. "Now you must rest. I need you strong."

Aunt Olivia smiled again and patted Elizabeth's cheek. "I will sleep a little more, dear. You should as well. We shall speak more this evening."

Elizabeth bent to kiss her aunt's cheek, and then impulsively kissed her hand as well. "I will see you then. In the meantime, I shall try not to disgrace you by invading the kitchens."

"See that you do not," Aunt Olivia scolded, but Elizabeth just smiled.

Darcy watched Richard surreptitiously as they lowered themselves into the richly upholstered chairs in His Grace's study. His cousin was limping ever so slightly, a remnant of his wounds two years ago at Corunna. Darcy knew Richard would cut the offending leg off himself before turning down such a duty as Tavistock had requested, but the ride from Hertfordshire had been long and cold. Darcy felt some guilt over having ridden in the carriage, but he knew his cousin was the better shot from atop a horse. He dared not mention it now, but when they were alone, he would insist that Richard return to Darcy House where he could recover without his mother making a fuss.

"First order of business, gentlemen," the duke said heavily. "You have my thanks. Please call me Bedford." Darcy and Richard tipped their heads in an approximation of a polite bow.

"Second order of business," he said, waving them all to chairs and turning to his son, "is the story. Clearly something of a serious nature has occurred."

As Francis was explaining, there was a knock at the door. Bedford held up his hand and his son stopped speaking. "Enter," he called.

One maid and an older woman Darcy thought must be the housekeeper entered with tea, coffee, and food. Darcy's stomach grumbled.

"Miss Russell ordered a small meal, Your Grace," the older woman said. "Mr. Darcy missed supper last night and she thought you all might appreciate refreshments."

Richard turned his attention to Darcy. "You missed supper?"

He did his best not to color under the scrutiny. "I did."

"Thank you, Mrs. Unger," Bedford said.

"You are very welcome, Your Grace."

Richard was sitting farthest from the duke, yet the younger maid walked to him directly to hand him a cup already filled with tea, and told him, quietly, "This has willow bark in it. Miss Russell says to tell you it will help."

Darcy saw his cousin frown. "Thank you," Richard replied, "but I do not require it."

The maid continued to hold the cup while the housekeeper schooled her features and took over. "Miss Russell thought you might say as much, sir. I am now authorized to say, on her behalf, that you are to stop acting like a child and drink the tea."

Bedford rubbed his mouth with one hand and turned to the window, while Tavistock just chuckled and shook his head. Darcy shrugged when Richard glared at him.

"You wait until she is dosing you, cousin. It will not be a joke then."

"I did not laugh, Richard," Darcy responded. He paused. "But you should probably drink the tea."

The men remained in Bedford's study for an hour. The duke wanted to compare the forged Darcy letter with the one that had so panicked Olivia Russell. Richard had concluded, and they had all agreed, the hand was not the same. Still, it was not beyond the scope of possibility that they might have been written by the same man. If the writer could forge

George Darcy's hand so well, he might be adept at composing letters that appeared to be from different people entirely.

"I remain convinced that these are two different issues," Bedford stated, in the end, "but I suppose we have not enough evidence to entirely rule out a connection. You say your aunt held the letter for a time?"

Darcy nodded. "She did not say how long, but she meant to hold it until I came to her in April."

"Then her parson wrote to tell her that you were courting Lizzy and she came immediately from Kent?" Tavistock asked.

"Evidently." Darcy wished his head was clearer, his fatigue was weighing him down. "It is not news she would spread about." But it did not sit well with him. The letter purporting to be from his father was likely sent recently—Lady Catherine was not *that* patient. However, her delay might have frustrated the writer's plans. His aunt's seeming inaction could have prompted the writer to pen another missive—one with a message that could not be mistaken. Why? Who, outside of her friends and family in Meryton would know Elizabeth was a Russell? Who would make the connection between Elizabeth and himself and wish to drive them apart?

"I believe we are finished for the moment, gentlemen," Bedford said with a sigh. "We will think on it further. Lizzy has invited you back tomorrow, Darcy. Perhaps we can speak then, if you have any other ideas."

Darcy stood and offered the duke a bow. He said his farewell to Tavistock, but when they emerged from the study, there was an older man waiting for them, his face lined but his manner of dress flawless.

"Sirs," he said, bowing crisply, "Miss Russell thought you might appreciate an opportunity to refresh yourselves."

Richard opened his mouth, but Darcy placed a warning hand on his cousin's arm and leaned in. "Do not even think about saying whatever it is you have rolling around in your mouth right now, Richard," Darcy said darkly.

"My orders were simply to extend the offer, Mr. Darcy," the man explained, his offense not so carefully hidden as to remain unnoted. "I believe Miss Russell's words were 'They might not wish to appear at Darcy House in such a state as to frighten the staff.'"

Richard grimaced and rubbed his jaw. "I suppose I would not be averse to a shave . . ." he let the sentence trail off.

"Parker, sir. I presume you are Mr. Fitzwilliam."

Richard narrowed his eyes. "Why would you say that?"

The valet pursed his lips. "No reason, sir."

Darcy was too weary to smile, but he inclined his head. "Lead on, Parker."

Darcy had nearly fallen asleep during his shave—a dangerous business. As Miss Russell had already seen fit to order water heated, both men were also treated to a bath, their clothing brushed out carefully before they finished. Had they waited until they arrived at Darcy House, it would have been another hour to heat the water and carry it to the bathing room. By then, he would certainly have been asleep. He had to own that seeing Elizabeth walk into the duke's London home and assume, at least in part, the duties of its mistress had made him very proud. Neither of her cousins seemed to think her command of the servants unusual in the absence of Her Grace, and to tell the truth, he had never felt so well cared for in another's home. Despite his cousin's grumbling about being alternately ordered about and coddled, and his own concern about the night's events, he was a very happy man.

"How is it that you are still awake, Richard?" he asked his cousin blearily as they made their way back to the entry of the grand townhome.

"Training," Richard replied. "It never entirely leaves you."

Darcy said nothing but gave his cousin a look that had Richard shaking his head.

"I know you are exhausted when you get that mawkish expression on your handsome face, cousin," he said. "Do not say anything that either of us will regret. Old woman." Darcy pressed his lips together and was silent.

Although neither man remarked upon it, they were both grateful to find a smaller carriage better suited to the crowded London streets waiting for them at the front of the house. They had not wished to take a hackney after such a night, and the walk on London streets would take them through at least one rather uncertain neighborhood.

"You have lost your limp," Darcy said innocently as they stepped outside.

"Shut your bone-box," was his cousin's sullen reply.

After breaking her fast with her cousins, Elizabeth composed a brief letter to her father and made certain it would be sent with the morning post. Then she drew a rough outline of her portrait of Jane and Mr. Bingley. Once that was complete, she was finally able to sink into bed. She turned on her side, pulled the blankets up around her ears, and closed her eyes. She tried to make the spinning of her thoughts slow down, but it was difficult to stop them. *Who would send such a note?*

She had spent the past two years taking care of her uncle's business and while there had at times been tense negotiations, it was always John who had conducted those interviews face-to-face. She had herself not initiated new business other than with Uncle Gardiner and, more recently, the steam engine patent, which had required no negotiations. To her rather exact knowledge, there had not been any bargains struck by her Uncle Phillip that had not been beneficial to both parties, though there had been opportunities he had not taken because he did not trust the men in charge.

She rubbed her forehead with the heel of her hand. If she could just stop gnawing on this puzzle like a dog with a bone, she might be able to sleep. She felt safe at St. James's Square. All she required was some rest to help her think more clearly.

She tossed the blankets back. From experience, she knew that putting her mind on something else entirely would help her sleep, so she sat at her escritoire and drew out several sheets of paper. As disappointed as she was to have left Hertfordshire early, London also held its pleasures, not least among them being able to renew old acquaintances.

Dipping her pen in the bottle of ink, she quickly composed notes to Amanda Cooke, Penelope Finch, and Lady Sophia Cecil, her closest friends from school. They had exchanged monthly letters nearly without fail during Elizabeth's time in the north, and Amanda had made the long trip to Weymouth House once the official year of mourning for Uncle Phillip was over. During the six weeks Amanda was in residence, Aunt Olivia had roused herself to play hostess, but the moment her friend's carriage had rumbled down the drive on its way back to London, her aunt had kissed Elizabeth's cheek and returned to her rooms. Elizabeth had made the decision to put off any further visits until her aunt was more fully recovered.

Amanda resided in town most of the year. Penelope had written to tell her that she would be visiting family in Berkeley Square for the festive season; she planned to arrive the week before Christmas. Sophia was likely to be with her younger brother at Burghley House, but Elizabeth thought her note might be forwarded. The scratching sound of the pen on paper, the satisfaction of watching the ink forming words, and the anticipation of many happy visits calmed her racing mind. The business complete, Elizabeth was able, at last, to rest.

CHAPTER SEVEN

The townhomes on three sides of Grosvenor Square were large, even palatial, but on the fourth, where Darcy resided, most measured a sensible twenty-five feet across. They were narrow enough that more than one occupant had fled for more commodious residences, but the house was sufficiently grand for him. Not overly large, but well kept and richly furnished. After all, he was a bachelor, primarily in town only for the season each year. He felt no need to waste money keeping a legion of servants on board-pay.

The location had become fashionable over the years it had been in the family, and he secretly delighted in the disappointment of avaricious women and their matchmaking parents who had heard his address and expected his London home to be expansive. For one glorious season a few years back, there had been rumors that he was not as wealthy as previously believed, but his uncle had effectively quashed them. The next rumor was that he was cheap and grasping, which his relations and friends, led by his aunt, Lady Matlock, had also successfully countered. He was grateful to them all for caring so assiduously for his reputation, but in some ways, he regretted its restoration. For almost one entire season, he had mercifully been left alone to speak with people who did not believe he could provide them with anything other than reasonable connections; it had been as close to comfortable as Darcy had ever been in London society.

As he entered Darcy House, Richard on his heels, he handed his hat to the butler and faced his short, stout, very surprised housekeeper, who had bustled out to greet him.

"Mr. Darcy, sir!" she said between gasps, her snowy hair escaping its pins in tufts and her face aflame. "I must apologize, have I missed a letter?"

"No, Mrs. White," he reassured her. "I was called to town unexpectedly, and there was no time to write. Please do not distress yourself." He gave her a smile. "Hanson will be following with our trunks sometime today; I suspect he is already well into the journey."

"Oh, and Mr. Fitzwilliam with you!" the woman exclaimed as Darcy moved to one side. "Have you boys eaten?"

Darcy nodded. "At the moment, we are most in need of sleep, Mrs. White."

Mrs. White nodded vigorously, her cap perilously close to flying from her head. Obviously relieved, she asked, "When would you like dinner, sir?"

Darcy glanced back at his cousin. "Seven, Richard?"

Richard nodded, but said nothing. Darcy could see his cousin was finally beginning to flag.

"Very good, Mr. Darcy." Mrs. White trundled away, and Darcy heard her muttering, "The list, the list. Must speak to cook, send John out—at least the rooms are in readiness."

He smiled to himself. Mrs. White was considered a peculiar woman by his family, but she held a warm place in his heart. She had been housekeeper here since he was a boy. She was not ambitious, so he was not concerned about her searching for a larger, more prestigious household to serve. She seemed content to provide for him and his guests, and she performed her job admirably.

Mr. Pattuck was impassive as ever, waiting patiently, his hand still out to receive Darcy's coat. He then gathered Richard's outerwear and disappeared, leaving the two men to make their way upstairs and collapse into bed.

Elizabeth slept deep into the afternoon. When she rose, it was nearly time for dinner. She sent word that she would take a tray in Aunt Olivia's room, and threw open the doors of her closet to select a gown. It was as if she had an entirely new wardrobe, nearly all of them finer than those she had taken with her to Longbourn. In fact, some of them *were* new, for she had never worn them. For a private meal with Aunt Olivia, however, she did not require a fancy gown.

Elizabeth selected a delicate rose muslin she knew her aunt favored, and when Alice arrived, she pointed it out. Alice helped Elizabeth dress and put her hair up in an easy but elegant style suited to a family dinner. Elizabeth then made the short trip across the hall to her aunt's chambers.

"Enter," her aunt called in response to her knock.

"Good evening, Aunt," Elizabeth said, smiling to see Aunt Olivia on the settee, a tray from the kitchen set up before her. "Are you feeling well?"

"As well as can be, my dear," her aunt replied, waving her over. "Sit down, Lizzy, and let us eat before it gets cold."

Elizabeth served them both. They supped together, her aunt asking questions about her family and her time at Longbourn. When Elizabeth finished telling stories about her sisters, she found that Aunt Olivia was gazing at her affectionately.

"Aunt?" she asked, but there was no reply. She leaned forward. "Is there something on my face?"

"Lizzy," her aunt complained, "you know very well there is nothing on your face." She turned her face to the window. They were eating early, but the days were short now, and it was already dark outside. "I was merely commending myself for the decision to leave you at Longbourn. You needed your sisters, Lizzy, and now you have them back again."

"I did enjoy my time with them, Aunt," Elizabeth confirmed. "I hope to invite Mary to visit if she is not already to come with Jane for the season. I think Kitty should wait a little longer." She moved her empty plate back to the tray and reached for her aunt's.

"Thank you, my dear," her aunt said softly. Once Elizabeth was done, Olivia patted the settee. "Come sit with me."

Elizabeth did as her aunt requested, and found her hand taken up in Aunt Olivia's.

"I want you to tell me about your young man. I know from your very descriptive letters that it was not love at first sight," she said with a delighted laugh.

"No, it was not," Elizabeth agreed, resting her head on her aunt's shoulder. "He had my enmity, then my sympathy, then my ire." She sat up and placed their joined hands on her knee. "Then he had me utterly baffled and not a little intimidated."

"Nonsense, Lizzy," her aunt said dismissively. "Nobody intimidates a Russell woman."

Elizabeth shook her head. "Mr. Darcy did. He had . . . has this way of staring at me . . . ." She paused.

Her aunt smiled mischievously. "Have you only just realized that he was admiring you?"

Elizabeth let out an exasperated half-laugh and shook her head. "No, but I am ashamed to say it was not as long ago as it ought to have been." She felt a light pressure on her hand where her aunt had squeezed it.

"And now," Aunt Olivia pressed, "he has your love?"

"He does," Elizabeth confirmed. "I love him so much, Aunt Olivia, I cannot even put words to it." She gazed directly into her aunt's eyes. "I cannot even draw it."

Aunt Olivia's face was graced by a smile so tender, Elizabeth thought the older woman might weep. "Aunt?" she asked. "Is everything all right?"

Her aunt touched Elizabeth's cheek. "Everything is precisely as it should be, my dear."

Darcy made his way downstairs for dinner but halted suddenly near an empty alcove in the wall between two windows. He studied it, running his fingers over the empty space.

Richard found him there, tapping his fingertips on the stone pedestal.

"Is something wrong?" he asked.

Darcy nodded slowly. "There should be a small bronze of Apollo here."

Richard's eyebrows rose. "Perhaps Mrs. White removed it for cleaning, or it was sent out for repair?"

"Unless it happened recently, she would have written." He recalled, suddenly, the report of two missing silver spoons.

"Well, let us not linger on the stairs, Darcy. I am starving. Let us go down to dinner and ask her."

Darcy and Richard made their way to the small dining room. There was room for six at the round table here; the formal dining room had space for as many as fourteen, were it required. This suited Darcy perfectly, for it limited his guests by necessity, allowing him to choose only those friends he truly wished to invite. His mind was not on the satisfaction of his arrangements, however, but on the mystery that lay before him. Mysteries.

Mrs. White answered his summons promptly, arriving in a flutter of dark skirts, chatelaine bouncing against her hip.

"You asked to see me, Mr. Darcy?" she asked. She was clutching a piece of paper.

"I was wondering where the bronze of Apollo has gone, Mrs. White," he inquired.

Mrs. White huffed. "I am *not* going mad, then," she said. "At least there is that piece of good news." She handed him the paper. On it was a list of seven items.

"These are all things we have discovered missing since I wrote you, Mr. Darcy. I was making this list to send on. At first, I put it down to forgetfulness, but so many items? It is not possible." She frowned. "The art on the stairway is usually dusted by Susan."

Richard's face was stormy. "Susan?" he asked roughly.

Mrs. White nodded. "I must say, she has always been a good girl, a hard worker."

"Does Susan know I am here?" Darcy asked.

"No, sir, she left not a quarter-hour before you arrived. She works a half-day on Wednesdays when you are not in residence and returns late at night. She has a mother and sister she sometimes visits. Near St. Bart's, I believe."

Darcy felt a headache beginning behind his eyes. "Tomorrow, Mrs. White, you shall take the inventory books through the house. Check every room. Move whatever staff you need from their duties to assist."

"Very good, sir," Mrs. White replied.

"As for Susan, please tell her I shall wish to speak with her in the morning," Darcy said, picking up his napkin and settling it on his lap.

"You may wish to defer that, cousin," Richard warned.

Darcy blinked, but quickly worked out why his cousin would say such a thing. "You may go, Mrs. White, I thank you. Please do not mention either the inventory or our presence to anyone else."

"Yes, Mr. Darcy," Mrs. White promised.

When the housekeeper had excused herself, Darcy addressed his cousin. "You think Susan involved."

"We might be able to catch her in the act if she is," Richard replied. "What if she is connected to your letter writer? Her night off would be the best time to meet with him."

Darcy rubbed the back of his neck but removed his hand when the food arrived. Until everything had been set out and the footman had departed, the men were silent.

The moment the door was shut, Darcy addressed his cousin. "You think whoever this is wanted me to be called to Kent so he could continue to steal from me in my absence?"

Richard snapped his napkin out before laying it across his legs. "I think he wanted you gone to Kent; for what reason, I cannot say."

They began to eat, but neither was much interested in the food on their plates. After a time, Richard spoke quite abruptly. "I have great respect for Bedford, but I do not think the letters are unrelated."

Darcy shook his head. "I have been thinking the same thing. The question is, who has access to and a grievance with both myself and the Russell family?"

"There is one obvious answer to that, you know," Richard said, spearing a piece of fish and popping it in his mouth. He chewed slowly, then swallowed. "I cannot speak to access, but as to grievance? Miss Russell corresponded with Georgiana this summer; you told me yourself it was on her insistence that Georgie reveal all to you."

Darcy set his fork down. He had believed Ramsgate was the dastard's final play—he had made it clear that the man was to stay far away from the Darcy family or he would call in every last debt. He had perhaps been too complacent where his father's former favorite was concerned. But his cousin was correct—*novacula occami* could be successfully applied in this case.

"Wickham," Darcy stated flatly.

Richard nodded sagely. "Wickham."

Elizabeth sat on her aunt's bed, her legs curled up as she worked on Jane's wedding present.

"We must choose a date for your wedding, Lizzy," Aunt Olivia said, placing her book aside and clasping her hands in her lap. "John has put his title to good use for once and has purchased a special license."

Elizabeth paused in her drawing, pencil suspended in air. This was unexpected. John had not seemed overly welcoming of Mr. Darcy, and it was so soon. She had assumed Aunt Olivia would want a large London wedding after her come-out. "Is there a rush, Aunt?" Elizabeth asked.

Aunt Olivia tilted her head at Elizabeth and gave her a searching look. "Dearest, you have *seen* me. Even before yesterday, I have been decidedly unwell. You must know . . ."

Elizabeth shook her head defiantly. "You will rally, Aunt Olivia. You are too difficult a creature to remain ill for long."

Aunt Olivia hesitated. Finally, she kissed Elizabeth's forehead. "Very well, dear, we will not speak of it tonight."

Elizabeth suddenly felt cold, and she wished nothing more than to be wrapped in the arms of her betrothed. She longed for his strength, for she found herself abruptly devoid of it.

"Mr. Darcy will come tomorrow?" her aunt asked, breaking into her ruminations.

"He has said he will." She placed the drawing and pencil aside.

"Bring him to visit me, Lizzy. I have not seen him since he was little more than a boy. I wish to thank him for the letter he sent after Phillip's passing."

"I am sure he will be anxious to see you, Aunt," Elizabeth told her, but the words felt like paste in her mouth.

"Well, I am not sure of *that*," her aunt teased, "but I should like to see him, and I am an old lady. It would be ungentlemanly of him to refuse. You tell him I said that."

Elizabeth swallowed the lump that had formed in her throat. "I shall, Aunt Olivia. I promise."

"I have always thought it was a rather formal name, Fitzwilliam," her aunt said reflectively. "Would you not prefer William? Or Will?"

"I do not mind Fitzwilliam," Elizabeth said, "but I would be happy using whichever name he prefers."

"You might wish to consider it, dear," Olivia said pertly. "Fitzwilliam rather puts one in mind of his cousin."

"No," Elizabeth corrected her immediately. "His cousin is a good man. But he has never put me in mind of Mr. Darcy."

Darcy sat in an armchair in the library, the fire low but still hot, when he heard footsteps in the hallway. Before he could respond, a young maid slipped into the room. He sat up, alarmed that she would so brazenly enter the library when she should be seeking her bed in the servants' quarters. There was a flash of red hair in the candlelight. Susan.

She was facing away from him, the candle held high in one hand, until she reached the shelves where the atlases were kept. His great-grandfather had begun the collection in 1726 to mark the year he had acquired the townhouse. Every ten years, another was added. The original atlas of the collection was bound in leather, the bindings a little loose now, and it was this volume the girl set down her candle to remove. It was a distinctive tome, large, with many hand-colored plates; it was quite valuable and entirely irreplaceable. He stood, intent on blocking her exit.

The sound of his slippers on the floor must have alerted her, for she whirled in his direction, her face pale in the weak light, both thin arms crossed over the book.

"Susan," he greeted her. "May I ask where you are taking that?"

She blinked rapidly, and her words came out haltingly. "I were just going to look at it, Mr. Darcy. I meant no harm."

Darcy sighed. "Susan, you must tell me the truth." Her eyes grew wide, and he pinched the bridge of his nose. She was little more than a child, seventeen at most. He allowed his hand to drop to his side. "If you are in trouble, perhaps I can help. But there are other things missing from the house, and I suspect you are to blame for them all."

Susan carefully set down the book on a reading table. She shook her head and cast her eyes down.

The door to the main hall opened and Richard stepped inside. "I was in your study, Darce, enjoying some of your port, and thought I heard someone returning," he said. "I wondered if Susan might not have someone waiting for her outside."

Darcy kept an eye on Susan. "Did she?"

"She did," Richard said, "but he ran before I could get a decent look. I think he saw your horses in the mews." He approached the girl, and Darcy knew it would not be long before Richard had the entire story.

"Susan, before I allow my cousin to begin this interview, you should know he was an officer in the Army."

Susan's slight body began to quake.

Richard's tone was mild but buried within was a hint of steel. "Things will go far easier for you if you tell us all that you know. Do not make me question you."

Susan kept her face turned resolutely to the floor and began to cry.

For the second time in as many days, Darcy found himself in the Duke of Bedford's study discussing unpleasant news. It was a distinction he would have been happy to forgo, particularly as the man was in a mood to place blame, and Darcy was the focus of his displeasure. At least today he was not also facing Tavistock.

Bedford stood to the side of his desk, toying idly with a stack of papers. "You are telling me that whoever your maid has been dallying with could be the letter writer?" His words were curt—the man was fuming. "And you have brought this wastrel into our lives?"

Darcy held back the angry retort he wished to deliver—if this was Wickham, the Russells *had* been involved, but it was indeed their connection with the Darcys that had repeatedly brought the reprobate back for more. "It is not quite that simple, Bedford. The girl was being threatened." *Romanced, and then threatened.*

"She *says* she was being threatened. The fact remains that she has stolen items worth a great deal of money from your home without detection."

He wished to shout *I was not in residence!* But there was no denying it. "She has," Darcy admitted. "Wickham and I have a long history."

Darcy collected his thoughts. He recalled the days of his youth spent despising George Wickham and being hurt by his father's misguided preference. How Mr. and Mrs. Russell had finally forced George Darcy to see what everyone around him saw: George Wickham was a careless spendthrift with a penchant for wasting other people's money and seducing young women. But he had not considered the man capable of extorting an old woman and a maiden or taking a shot at the carriage of a peer. *After Ramsgate, I should have,* he thought gloomily. *I should have let Richard run the bastard through. Bedford is right to lay this at my feet.*

He took a breath. "My father had a steward . . ."

Elizabeth hurried to the drawing room when she heard that Mr. Darcy had come to call, entering with a bright smile. Her betrothed had his back to her as he gazed out of a window, his hands resting on either side of the casement. His shoulders were hunched. She approached him, touched his arm, and jumped when he startled.

He turned to face her, and she nearly took a step back. He was clearly agitated, for his hair was rumpled as though he had repeatedly run his hand through it—and his expression was grim.

"What has happened?" she exclaimed, grasping his arm. "Are you well?"

He let out a short huff and grimaced. "I am not." He took her hands and lifted his eyes to hers. "Bedford has barred me from the house."

Unspoken but understood was that her cousin had barred him from her company entirely. "What?" she asked, incredulous. "Why?"

He swallowed. "He blames me for what is happening, and I cannot say he is wrong." His thumbs moved in light circles over the back of her hands.

"That is preposterous," she replied heatedly. "How can you take this upon yourself?"

"I believe it is the same man who importuned Georgiana in Ramsgate last summer," he told her solemnly. "I had an opportunity to finish him then, and I did not take it."

"*Finish* him?" Elizabeth asked. "You mean John thought you should end the man's life? Because he was a fortune hunter who tried to woo Georgiana? It was despicable, to be sure, but hardly a hanging offense."

"It is not that I did not kill the man, as much as he might have deserved it. But I let him go, Elizabeth. Told him he would never see a shilling and let him run." He shook his head. "It is more than Ramsgate, love. I would explain it but I do not know how much time I have been given to say goodbye."

"You are not *going* to say goodbye to me, Fitzwilliam. John is not my guardian."

"But he stands in for your uncle," Mr. Darcy reminded her. "I would not wish for there to be a rift between you on my behalf."

"Will there not be a rift between you and your Aunt Catherine on *my* behalf?"

Mr. Darcy smiled sadly. "It hardly compares. You love your cousin, whereas to be severed from my aunt would be a blessing."

"You do not mean that," Elizabeth chided him.

He chuckled without mirth. "I mostly mean that." He kissed her hands. "I promise that I shall do whatever is needed to bring this crisis to its conclusion, so we may wed." He bent to her, his lips hovering near hers for a moment before brushing them softly, then lingeringly.

Elizabeth's entire body tingled even after her betrothed pulled away. "Do not go, Fitzwilliam," she begged as he released her. "Please, do not go."

He kissed the top of her head. "I will not be far, Elizabeth. I will manage this, and then we shall be together."

"Stubborn man," she breathed, both annoyed and saddened. "Do you promise?"

He smiled down at her, but his expression was clouded with regret. "I promise."

❧

Olivia Russell had never seen her niece so distraught. Lizzy was crying too hard to speak coherently. From the little she could make out, it was John's fault. The man had forbidden Fitzwilliam Darcy to return to the house and as a man of honor, Mr. Darcy intended to obey. *Well,* she thought crossly, *leave it to the men to muck it all up.*

"Enough now, Lizzy," she said bluntly. "Nothing will be accomplished with tears. You must tell me what has happened."

As she always did when there was a difficult conversation to be held, Olivia pined for Phillip. His negotiation skills were sharply honed, and he could always effect a compromise. She missed him constantly; it was the refrain of her heart. But it was in these moments that his absence was particularly distressing.

It took several long minutes for the girl to regain her composure and another few to wash her face. Calm at last, Lizzy sat on the side of the bed and began to explain. "Do you recall when Georgiana was having trouble with her companion last summer?"

"Of course," she replied, not having expected this beginning. "We sent a private rider. You told me you received a letter from Lady Matlock afterward confirming Georgiana's safety."

Lizzy nodded. "I did. But I have had nothing from Georgiana since, though she writes to her brother."

Olivia frowned. That was not like the girls, to be out of contact. "The letters all came through me, as we did not wish to publish your whereabouts, dear. Check the stack on my desk before you go. Perhaps I have missed it?"

Lizzy nodded. "I shall, thank you." She plucked at the blanket. "Georgiana never did tell me who the man was, the one who pushed her to accept his hand. Mr. Darcy knew him well. He gave his name to John this morning, and I badgered my cousin until he told me."

It washed over Olivia then, with a sort of absurd clarity. "George Wickham," she said decisively. "That boy was always shockingly loose in the haft."

"Aunt!" Elizabeth exclaimed.

Olivia waved a hand at her. "There are times when polite language will not do the job. This is one of those times."

Lizzy slid her hand under Olivia's where it rested on the sheet. "Evidently you and Uncle Phillip knew him?"

"He was George Darcy's godson, and George favored him." Olivia said with a sigh. "He preferred him, in many ways, to his own son."

"What do you mean, preferred him?" Lizzy asked, indignant. "To *Fitzwilliam*?"

Olivia sighed. "Sometimes," she said, "it is easier to bestow love on a child to whom you do not have any true duty. George treated young

Wickham as he might have treated a second son, and I believe the boy considered himself as holding that position."

Lizzy gave her a hard, shrewd look. "So much so that he believed the line of inheritance would include him?"

Olivia sighed. *That is probably just what he thought, and why not?* "There is no telling what he expected," was what she said out loud. "George did say how angry the boy was to be sent to work after Cambridge."

"What did Mr. Darcy say?"

"I have had this from Phillip, dear, so it is second-hand. Still, if it can help . . ."

"It will help," Lizzy said. "It will."

Olivia reached over and traced the back of her hand along Lizzy's cheek. "Young Wickham barely made it through university. He was intelligent enough, but lacked discipline, and he had certainly never been censured by your Mr. Darcy's father. Phillip and I explained to George that the boy was a threat both to the maids in the house and to Fitzwilliam himself."

"John mentioned an incident near the stables."

Olivia nodded. "After the boys returned from Cambridge, George had a conference with his protégé. He asked what young Wickham's plans were, now that he had completed his education."

"Oh," Lizzy said, understanding. "I cannot believe that was well received."

Olivia shook her head. "It was not. According to Phillip, Wickham was offered a position as a private secretary to a wealthy man in the south of Devonshire who had contacts in the Navy. He was an acquaintance of George's. The salary was excellent. The work was plentiful but not difficult, and there was room for advancement. After some years, he might be recommended for a position at the Admiralty, at which point he could increase his income substantially." She turned Lizzy's hand and traced the girl's palm with her thumb. "George felt he must do as much for the boy since he had promised his steward that he would see young Wickham well settled."

"I assume he did not accept?" Lizzy asked.

Olivia frowned. "He asked George if he might instead be given three thousand pounds to study the law. According to Phillip, the boy thought he would cut a fine figure as a barrister."

She watched Lizzy's brow furrow and knew her clever niece had come to the same conclusion that George Darcy evidently had. *He would have thrown the money away in short order and come back for more.*

"And did Mr. Darcy agree?"

Olivia shook her head. "He had a reason for choosing Devonshire. London would not have suited his purpose."

Lizzy pursed her lips. "It is nearly as far from Derbyshire as one can be and yet remain in England."

"He wanted young Wickham far away from Fitzwilliam," Olivia agreed. "And I believe we now know that he was right to arrange it."

"Did Mr. Wickham know that Uncle was the one who had discredited him?"

"Phillip was sure that he did. However, it was I who prompted the discussion," Olivia said plainly. "Phillip tried to speak with George—Mr. Darcy—on many occasions, but the man was as stubborn as his son seems to be. Your uncle had given it up as a family matter. But I could not let it rest." She smiled at Lizzy's shock. "Do you not think your aunt capable of such a breach in propriety?"

Lizzy's eyes danced, and Olivia thrilled to see it.

"I can imagine it all too well." She kissed Olivia's hand. "You were protecting Fitzwilliam and the maids just as you have always protected me."

"Which is why you were never taken to Pemberley when George Wickham was in residence," Olivia said plainly. She reclined against her pillows. "In any case, Mr. Wickham accepted and was packed off to Devonshire. That was the last I had heard of him, until today."

Lizzy's eyes grew stormy. "John has laid the blame on Fitzwilliam, but there is as much fault on the Russell side as the Darcy. We have all of us stood in the way of the life Mr. Wickham wanted, the life to which he felt entitled."

Olivia pushed herself back up. This was important. "George Darcy did not know what he had set in motion," she said, "but he tried to remedy his mistakes. It is only young Wickham who is to blame here." She drew Lizzy into her embrace. "We shall make them both see that, Lizzy."

"I care not whether John sees it," the girl said, her chin jutting out determinedly. "I have my own home, and if His Grace will not listen to reason, I shall repair there." She took her aunt's hand. "Are you well enough? To accompany me to Kensington?"

Olivia smiled. "Let us hope it does not come to that, dear," she said softly, but her Lizzy was an obstinate girl and very much in love. If John would not listen, to Kensington they would go.

Darcy poured himself a glass of brandy and settled into the chair behind his desk. He tried not to focus on the dull pain behind his eyes as he went over the facts yet again. There was the letter to Mrs. Russell. "One will die and one will mourn," he said to the walls. Wickham had very nearly accomplished that with the threat alone.

He tossed Aunt Catherine's letter on the desk's surface and stared at it. He did not believe it had been sent from Darcy House at all, though there was no way of knowing for sure. Susan could neither read nor write; she had found the atlas last night because she had been given an exact description of it. Another sign pointing to Wickham, who was familiar with the house and could tell the girl what he wanted her to take.

The letter to his aunt—what was the point of it? Even had his father written an actual contract, such marriages would not be approved by the church unless both bride and groom agreed. The most she could have done was demand some sort of remuneration, yet Anne was of age and would have her own solicitor contact him should she wish to pursue it. Lady Catherine had no standing.

He knew Aunt Catherine fretted over Anne—rather excessively, in his opinion. She wanted Anne to marry him to be well cared for as Mrs. Darcy. He had tried to explain that between his Uncle Matlock and himself Anne would be well-cared for regardless, but Aunt Catherine was horrified by the thought of her daughter as a spinster. *Not unlike Mrs. Bennet,* he thought suddenly.

The state of Anne's health meant she would not be able to remain alone at Rosings, nor would the family wish it. Aunt Catherine had long spoken of the humiliation attendant upon Anne were she shuffled between households. His aunt wanted status for her daughter, but there was nobody other than Aunt Catherine who believed a marriage between the master of Pemberley and the heiress of Rosings would ever come to pass. *Perhaps Collins,* he thought, his humor darkening as he worked through the letter again. If Wickham *was* the writer, he knew that all the letter could do was ruffle Lady Catherine's feathers and cause him a little embarrassment; the risk did not seem proportionate to the prize. *Why would he need me in Kent?*

His musings were interrupted by Richard's entrance. His cousin had a pained expression on his face.

"What?" he barked. *I cannot take one more bit of bad news.* "Good God, man, what is it now?"

"I went to the club," Richard said, unperturbed by his cousin's anger. He crossed his legs and unconsciously ran a finger along his boot. Darcy watched it—up and down, up and down.

"There are rumblings."

"About?"

"Phillip Russell," Richard replied. He rubbed his eyes.

Darcy waited.

"Rumors are that Phillip Russell was a smuggler and, among other things, owned slave ships and a plantation in the West Indies." Richard leaned back in his chair. "Not illegal at the time, but certainly morally repugnant and currently unfashionable."

Darcy tipped his head heavenward. Elizabeth was to inherit from Phillip and Olivia Russell. The rumor would taint her inheritance, was obviously meant to taint it. He drew out a piece of paper and began to pen a missive to Bedford. He might not be allowed to contact Elizabeth, but Phillip Russell had been Bedford's best friend. The duke should know what was circulating.

"It is a concerted effort to defame Elizabeth," he growled as he wrote. "Wickham still has friends from university who are probably spreading these lies. But how do we prove it?" He finished writing and sanded the letter. "Was it Hollander? Truscott?"

His cousin shrugged. "I do not know."

Darcy pinched the bridge of his nose. "It is all in bits and pieces, Richard. We have suspicions, but no evidence other than the focus of his malice."

"If it was Wickham last night—and with Susan's description, it very well could be," Richard answered cautiously, "he is still here, lurking about, spewing his poison and waiting for us to make a mistake."

"He is counting on us to act defensively," Darcy concurred.

"So let us do the opposite," his cousin suggested. "In striking out at Miss Russell, he is striking out at Bedford. For some reason, he feels secure in doing so."

"He may have overstepped there," Darcy said. "Why would he be so confident?"

Richard ran a fist along his jaw. "I say we find out."

Darcy eyed his cousin warily. "Tell me what you have in mind."

CHAPTER EIGHT

"It is the grossest falsehood!" Elizabeth spluttered. John had called her and Aunt Olivia to join him in his study. Francis stood to the side of the room.

"Like most gossip," Aunt Olivia said evenly, "there is some grain of truth to it."

Elizabeth blinked rapidly. "But you and Uncle Phillip have long advocated against the practice. You do not even keep sugar at Weymouth House. It is why you are on such good terms with Mr. Wedgwood."

Aunt Olivia glanced at John and sighed. She placed a gentle hand on Elizabeth's knee. "You uncle inherited a sugar plantation when his father died, dear. It was the most profitable investment he had."

Elizabeth was speechless.

"Because you know Phillip's active holdings very well now," John reminded her, "you are aware they do not include that property."

She closed her eyes to regain her composure, then opened them. "Will you tell me the story?"

It was John who cleared his throat to speak. "Phillip was not yet married to your aunt when he inherited his father's fortune." He leaned back against his desk. "He struggled with the notion that his own family's respectability had rested upon such a venture, but also struggled with what was best to be done."

"Did he sell it?" Elizabeth asked flatly.

"It was not so easy a thing," John said, contemplating something on the far wall over her shoulder. "He could sell the plantation, but he would still be profiting from the sale of human beings and transferring their care to strangers. Their situation was bad enough; he did not wish to make it worse. Were he to keep the plantation to ensure they were treated well, he would be the *owner* of human beings. Neither was acceptable to him." He smiled, his expression nostalgic. "He decided to travel to the West Indies to evaluate the situation for himself."

Elizabeth glanced at her aunt. It was rather shocking to know Uncle Phillip had been to the West Indies and never spoken of it. *Abroad*, he had said. Hardly the same thing.

"He was comfortable, but not yet a wealthy man," Aunt Olivia said quietly. "This was before we courted, but we were already friends of a sort. I asked whether he was certain he wished to travel so far himself and at such risk when he might have a trustworthy local agent report back." Her eyes were glossy, but no tears fell. "He said that in such a case he could trust no one so well as himself."

John smiled. "I clearly recall my father telling me the story. Father was puffed up about it, and of course, I was wild to meet Phillip, who was only just returned. I thought him quite the hero."

"Will not someone tell me what *happened?*" Elizabeth asked with a huff.

Olivia shook her head, her gaze somewhere far away. "Your uncle was horrified when he saw the conditions in which they were living. Against all advice, indeed, all self-interest, he freed every slave, nearly seventy of them, many of them children."

John picked up the thread of the tale. "According to my father, Phillip had the head of each household decide whether they wished to remain or leave. For those who wished to stay, he partitioned off the land he owned and made a gift of it, so they would have a place to live and fields to work. For those who preferred to leave, he arranged their travel. I do not know where all they went."

Olivia added, "Phillip mentioned that many stayed. Though he tried to persuade them it might be dangerous, he would not force them to leave. Some took passage to the East Indies, and one family came back to England with him." She smiled tiredly. "There were two sons, I believe, who became farriers and did very well."

"I would wager," Francis said from side of the room where he was now slouched against the wall, arms crossed over his chest, "that his actions labeled him an eccentric at the very least."

John nodded. "My older brother was like many in the ton. He thought Phillip mad to cut up his fortune in such a way. But my father was extraordinarily proud of him. Phillip had already shown a good deal of promise in his investments, so in the last years of his life, my father funded your uncle, offering him a healthy percentage of any earnings until he could get back on his feet." He shared a look with her aunt that Elizabeth did not understand.

"When he returned to England, he was a different man than I had known." Aunt Olivia's gaze was turned away from them all, briefly lost in her memories. After a moment, she added, "He stopped going to his club because he was often ridiculed there, but never did it shake his conviction that he had done what was right. He was determined to build a new fortune, one he felt was honorable, and simply set about it. Never once did he complain about beginning over again." She paused. "Never once." She smiled at Elizabeth. "And then we danced."

"Why did he never say anything?" Elizabeth asked, lifting her eyes to her aunt's. "He ought to have been celebrated for what he did."

"He did not like to discuss it," Olivia said. She moved forward to perch on the edge of her chair. "He was profoundly troubled by whatever it was he saw when he arrived and always worried he had not done enough."

"Well," Tavistock said wryly, "I shall be only too pleased to go tell *this* story at the club."

John nodded. "It will make the rounds of Parliament as well." He held out his hand to Elizabeth, and after a moment, she took it. "Perhaps you have some friends to visit, my dear?"

"I do." She took a breath. "Mr. Darcy's aunt, Lady Matlock, might be of help. I could write Georgiana."

John appeared displeased but nodded.

Encouraged, Elizabeth pushed ahead. "Did Mr. Darcy send you the note warning you about the rumor, John?" Elizabeth asked directly. "I seem to recall Aunt Olivia telling me he had."

John pursed his lips. "He did."

"May I ask him to visit?" She knew it was a challenge, but she wished to offer him a chance to relent. She was disappointed.

"Not yet, Lizzy," he said, shaking his head. "There are still matters between us that must be put to rest. Please try to understand."

Elizabeth swallowed the response that sprang to her lips. What good would it do? "Very well," she said.

Darcy read through the draft of the marriage articles and sighed. As long as Elizabeth remained Bedford's guest, he could not so much as send a note around. He presumed the same was true for her. If Mrs. Russell was in better health, he might at least have a message about his betrothed from her aunt, but given the circumstances, he was not expecting one.

Richard entered the study without a word and strolled to the decanter. After pouring himself a glass of port, he took a chair and sat, crossing his legs and staring at Darcy.

"Are you finished moping over that contract?" Richard asked.

"No, not quite," Darcy replied sourly. "Have you learned anything about Wickham?"

It had been nearly a week since their arrival in London, and they were no closer to locating the source of the letters, the shot, the thefts, the rumors. Seducing the maid, stealing items while the master was away, speaking venomous words into willing ears—these were all in keeping with what he knew of Wickham's character. Darcy was growing increasingly irritated waiting for the scoundrel to resurface—and there was no doubt he would.

Richard had not been banned from the duke's residence, so Darcy had suggested that he discreetly pose some questions to the staff. His cousin had been more than happy to take up the employment. He had already questioned everyone on Darcy's staff, but they had discovered precious little. Mrs. White had Bingley's direction locked in her desk—she had been asked to keep his whereabouts quiet, as Darcy jealously guarded his privacy. Susan had related that her "friend" had asked more than once about Mr. Darcy's whereabouts, but she had not known them. Darcy believed her—once caught, the girl had freely confessed to stealing, and had shown them several other books that had been removed first—books Mrs. White did not have on her list. They were all valuable and would not immediately be missed. Wickham had grown bolder since.

But Wickham was also clever. Darcy was certain he had sold each item nearly as soon as he had it in hand, perhaps had a buyer even before it was purloined. They would not catch him with stolen goods on his person. Darcy had several agents searching the pawn shops in the hopes of reclaiming at least some of the items.

Darcy would not press charges against Susan, who supported her mother and a younger sister. Mrs. White had, of course, dismissed her, but he had made sure her mother's rent was paid through the next quarter-day to give the girl a chance to find some other employment. Richard had scoffed at that, telling him he was too soft. But Darcy knew how persuasive Wickham could be. The loss of her position without a reference was punishment enough.

"As a matter of fact," Richard replied calmly, "I do have news."

Darcy's attention shot back to his cousin. "What is it?"

Richard's lips curled lazily into a smile. "His Grace will have nothing to charge you with now," he said, satisfaction ringing in his words. "The man has been at Bedford's staff, too."

Elizabeth allowed the footman to hand her into the carriage. She was pleased to be out of the house at last. Her aunt, who was feeling better this morning, had nearly pushed her out, claiming she was underfoot. Elizabeth had sent out her post, including the business of opening the Kensington house for residence a month earlier than planned. Most of the servants had been pleased at the prospect of earning additional wages, and her housekeeper had started the cleaning with the family rooms. She would tell John that she was leaving, but she would do so when he had no opportunity to stop her.

With her removal from St. James's Square discreetly underway, she had sent a note to Amanda and had the pleasure of a nearly immediate response: "Yes, you must come in the morning!"

Elizabeth glanced out the window to the corner and saw a young man holding a newspaper, every so often glancing across the street. Was he waiting for someone? He caught her watching him just as another man walked past; he turned to follow. Was that the man he had intended to meet? Or was he running away? She closed her eyes to try to memorize his looks. Dark hair, probably dark eyes, straight nose—it was difficult to see more from such a distance. Shorter than Mr. Darcy, about Mr. Fitzwilliam's height, dressed respectably but not richly. The carriage began to move, headed in the opposite direction, and she allowed herself to set aside her curiosity to enjoy the pleasant anticipation of meeting a friend.

❧

Amanda engulfed Elizabeth in a fierce embrace. "Elizabeth!" she cried, "It is so good to see you!"

Miss Amanda Cooke was a young woman who stood barely five-feet tall. Her slender waist and fine bone structure often left Elizabeth feeling not unlike a lumbering giantess. But it took no time at all for one to dismiss her friend's diminutive size, for in her fragile frame resided a martial spirit inherited from her family.

"I have missed you, Amanda," Elizabeth replied, holding her friend tightly.

"Is not your Aunt Russell with you today?" her friend asked when they released one another. "I have missed her as well."

"Am I to be thrown over so quickly?" Elizabeth teased, then grew more serious. "Aunt Olivia wished to speak to my cousin and was pleased to have me gone, I think."

There was a definite sparkle in Amanda's brown eyes as she asked, "Is His Grace in trouble? Or are you?"

Elizabeth smiled a little but did not answer.

"My goodness," Amanda said good-naturedly, shaking her head in disbelief. "You have only been in town a few days! What have you done to put your aunt into high dudgeon so quickly?"

"Me?" Elizabeth cried, feigning offense. "Why do you immediately assume *I* am the one in trouble?"

Amanda winked at her. "Have you again stolen His Grace's letters to draw upon?"

Elizabeth shook her head. "I was ten, and I thought they were in a stack to be burnt!" She laughed. "I am sorry I ever told you that story. I am still not convinced John has forgiven me."

"Well, he did have to appear with them in the House of Lords," Amanda pointed out.

"He did," Elizabeth recounted. "And he was told that whoever had drawn on his speech had improved it tenfold."

Amanda laughed and clapped her hands together. "Oh, I am so happy you have come. We shall have such a good time this season, all of us together."

"I did have something serious to discuss with you first," Elizabeth said, coming to the point. "I mentioned it in my letter . . ."

"Oh, the rumors about your uncle?" Amanda waved a small hand in the air. "I brought it up at dinner last night and Penny's grandfather remembered when the news was all over the ton. He was tickled to have the entire company's attention for once. I believe his words were, 'There is no new thing under the sun.'" She gave Elizabeth a wicked smile. "I daresay there is a letter on its way to Sophia even now—and you know her influence among the gossips is vast. It shall take time, my dear, but we will set things to rights."

Elizabeth squeezed her friend's hand. "My uncle was a good man. It is painful to see his name attacked, and you know these stories never disappear entirely."

"I know," Amanda said, all sympathy, "but we will do our best for him."

They sat in companionable silence for a moment before Amanda seemed to shake herself. "Let us speak of happier things, yes? I have someone I wish for you to meet."

"Not for me, surely," Elizabeth said warily.

Amanda laughed gaily. "No, you distrustful thing, for me."

"Truly?" Elizabeth asked, pleased. Amanda had been pursued by several different suitors in the years she had been out, but she had never shown a marked preference for one. "Does this someone have a name?"

"Captain Farrington of the Royal Horse Artillery." She glanced away, and her cheeks pinked.

"I see you favor the man," Elizabeth replied, elated to see her friend so affected. "You have had time enough in society to know your mind." She gave Amanda a grin. "And you have always preferred military men." She narrowed her eyes. "Though I did expect you to be loyal to the Navy."

Amanda grabbed a pillow from the chair next her and slapped Elizabeth's arm with it. Then she held it against her stomach and toyed with the fringe. "I do like him, Elizabeth, very much indeed. But he has not indicated whether he shall offer for me. I must not lose my head."

"Or your heart," Elizabeth warned. She leaned over to nudge Amanda's shoulder with her own. "I suspect that he will reveal his intentions in short order. No man who desired your hand would wish to spend the season watching other men compete for your attentions."

"I should hope not," Amanda said stoutly. "I am not one to loll about, waiting for a man to make up his mind."

Elizabeth smiled. "And he would not be the man for you were he to behave in such a way."

Amanda peered into Elizabeth's face. "You sound as though you have had some experience with a suitor of your own since I spoke with you last," she said with a sort of friendly suspicion. "You know that you must tell me all."

Elizabeth glanced around the room. It was just the two of them. There were no servants here, for they had wanted a long visit to catch up, and Amanda had decidedly banished them all.

"Very well," she said. "But while my father and aunt have consented, it has not been announced. It must remain between us for now."

"And Penny and Sophia," Amanda added gaily.

Of course. What one knows . . . Elizabeth shook her head, but she was pleased. "Yes. My sisters, my parents, Aunt Olivia, John and Francis, you, me, Penny, and Sophia. And of course, Mr. Darcy and his cousin. Oh, and Jane's Mr. Bingley." She grinned. "But no one else!"

Amanda giggled. "You have my word." She gazed at Elizabeth with an expectant expression.

Elizabeth gathered her thoughts. "Do you recall that I mentioned Georgiana's brother had come to stay at an estate near my father's?"

"You never did tell us where that was, precisely," Amanda reminded her.

"My aunt asked me not to—but regardless, do you recall?"

"Of course." Amanda's eyes grew large. "No . . . not Mr. *Darcy!*"

Elizabeth nodded silently.

Amanda's mouth opened, then closed. "Mr. *Fitzwilliam* Darcy, of Pemberley in Derbyshire and heaven knows what else?"

Elizabeth nodded again.

"You sly thing—you never breathed a word but to say he was nearby!" Amanda's expression was almost comical, a cross between disbelief and glee.

"I did not wish to speak out of turn."

Amanda ignored the demurral. "Mr. Fitzwilliam Darcy," she repeated, "the man who has been relentlessly pursued by countless women of the ton for years, even if they are already married? Who has been fawned over by practically every mother with an eligible daughter? The same man who has tried his level best to hide in every ballroom I have ever had the luck to see him in? *That* Mr. Darcy?"

"That Mr. Darcy," Elizabeth confirmed.

Amanda grasped Elizabeth's wrist. "How many times have you drawn your Mr. Darcy?"

Elizabeth blushed. "Do you mean all together or just this week?"

137

Amanda's dark eyes widened and she slapped a hand over her mouth before she was overtaken by gales of laughter.

"Are you ready, Aunt?" Elizabeth asked, offering her arm. Aunt Olivia took it and nodded.

"I have long wished to return to Kensington, my dear," she said. "It was Phillip's last gift to us."

Elizabeth felt her heart contract a bit at the sentiment. "Fortunately, the day is not too cold for December, and it is not so very far."

"I believe I can sit in a carriage to Kensington," her aunt said with a soft smile. "It is a shorter distance than your walk to Netherfield."

A footman gave them a worried, dubious look as he handed each woman up into the carriage. They settled on the seat and Elizabeth bent to adjust her aunt's wrap. Aunt Olivia stilled Elizabeth's hand. "I am not a child, Lizzy." She drew her cloak around herself.

Elizabeth suppressed a smile. She glanced idly out of her window and spied the same man standing at the corner of the park. She had seen him once before—she felt it odd that he was here again, but after all, the square was a busy place. He might have regular business in the area. He was reading a folded newspaper, like before, but when he looked up, Elizabeth was ready to trace his features. She noted the light and the shadow, a small mark near his eye, the tightness of his jaw, as though he was angry. The lines around his eyes that denoted laughter were somehow at variance with the calculating smile that disappeared the moment he turned his head to greet a lady walking past. Elizabeth drew it all in her mind before the Russell carriage pulled away, rattling over the stony street. She settled back in her seat.

"I loved that walk," Elizabeth said in answer to her aunt, dreaming of fields, stiles, and muddy hems. "We could walk anywhere at Longbourn, just the girls and me."

"It is what I wished for you to have," Aunt Olivia said, patting Elizabeth's hand. "Good memories to sustain you."

Elizabeth knew what that meant. She was not foolish enough to believe she would have such peace again. But there were many compensations for the life she had been prepared to lead. There was freedom in being able to assist her sisters, in providing charity for those who required it. Most of all, there was a freedom in being allowed to chart her own course in terms of her finances. Very few women had that freedom. To have found a man she loved who would allow her to continue to do so even after they had wed? It was beyond her dearest expectations. She had been thinking of that man all week, drawing him every day, and she very much hoped to see Mr. Darcy before dinner. *Perhaps I can convince him to stay for the meal.*

"I do wish John had been more reasonable," said Aunt Olivia, seeming to understand Elizabeth's thoughts. "But sometimes men cannot see beyond their pride, I am afraid."

"Mr. Darcy is not like that," Elizabeth said defensively.

Her aunt raised her brows. "Truly?"

"Well, perhaps a little," Elizabeth admitted, thinking of his early struggles not to fall for a woman he believed penniless and without connections. *But he overcame it.* "He would not have kept Georgiana from seeing her betrothed."

"You believe that," Aunt Olivia replied knowingly, "if it gives you comfort."

Elizabeth frowned, and changed the direction of the conversation. "Uncle Phillip was not like that."

Aunt Olivia laughed. "Oh, he most certainly was."

"Uncle *Phillip?*" Elizabeth asked, surprised.

Her aunt smiled. "Do you think your uncle was a perfect man, my dear?"

Elizabeth pressed her lips together before speaking. That was exactly what she thought. "He was, nearly."

Aunt Olivia patted Elizabeth's knee. "He was a very good man, my dear. But he was far from perfect." She chuckled. "I worked on him for many years before you met him."

"He freed all of his father's slaves before you began courting," Elizabeth reminded her. "I think that speaks to my point."

Aunt Olivia nodded slowly. "That was a critical experience in his life." She clasped her hands together and laid them in her lap. "I would not have married the man I knew before he left for the West Indies."

"Whyever not?" Elizabeth inquired.

Her aunt paused, her eyes closed. Then, just as Elizabeth was about to repeat her question, Aunt Olivia began to speak. "Phillip was determined to be a wealthy man. He was tired of being the poor cousin to the family of a duke. He had seen good success but had grown utterly conceited. He was obsessed with making money." Aunt Olivia stared ahead, a wistful expression transforming her features. "Not so that he could marry or do good with it, mind you—he had not yet considered what to *do* with his earnings. He simply wanted to feel that he himself was not so *very* far below his relations." She shook her head. "I always enjoyed our conversations. For all the faults I saw in him, he was never condescending to me. But I could never have married a man so absorbed in all the wrong pursuits."

"But then he went to the West Indies," Elizabeth prompted when her aunt paused again.

Aunt Olivia nodded, her thoughts far away. "But then he went to the West Indies."

❧

The day was unusually sunny and warm for December. Darcy prayed the cheerful weather boded well for his discussion with Bedford. The fact that the man had even agreed to the meeting he interpreted as a good sign. He patted the pocket inside his jacket. He had a letter from Devonshire to share.

Apparently, Bedford had arrived not long before them, as they passed his empty carriage when they entered the square. It was nearly one in the afternoon, and Darcy had spent most of the morning trying to suppress the hope that he might be able to see Elizabeth after his meeting with her cousin. When they entered the house, however, they heard Bedford's angry voice down the hall. They were shown into the study where the duke whirled from his position at the window and promptly accosted them.

"Did you encourage this, Darcy?" he demanded. "This idiocy?"

"What are you talking about, Bedford?" Darcy asked, his impatience with being kept from Elizabeth clear in his tone. "I am here for my appointment."

Bedford dropped into the chair behind his desk and rubbed his forehead. "They are gone."

"Who is gone?" Richard asked.

"Elizabeth has gone to Kensington," Bedford said, still upset. "And she has taken Olivia with her."

Darcy grabbed the back of a chair so tightly his knuckles turned white. "I was willing to be separated from Elizabeth, Bedford," he growled, "only because I did not wish to cause problems between you and I thought she was *safe* here. How could you let this happen?"

Darcy's cousin shot him a warning look.

The duke was not used to being questioned—that was clear enough in the scowl he gave the men. "It is not as though she asked permission, Darcy. She left this morning while I was out. She wrote me a letter." He scoffed. "A *letter*."

"Did they have an escort?" Richard asked, his face stoic and his voice even.

Thank heavens one of us has his wits about him, Darcy thought gratefully.

"Yes," Bedford said, drawing out the word. "It is the only reason I am not chasing after them like a lunatic."

"Then perhaps we should proceed with our meeting, Bedford," Richard suggested. "Afterward, Darcy and I will travel to Kensington, if you will be so good as to give us the direction."

Bedford appeared as though he was about to protest. Darcy leaned over the back of the chair, his voice clipped but even. "I suspect she is far more likely to receive us than you at the moment, Your Grace."

"Besides," Richard said with a grim smile, "we have some interesting news."

Elizabeth walked to the windows in Aunt Olivia's room and threw back the curtains. "The last time I saw this room, it was all peeling wallpaper and rough-hewn floors," she said, pleased with how bright and airy the room felt even in December. "It is beautiful now."

"I will not say that I was correct about the color," her aunt said haughtily.

Elizabeth laughed. "I believe you just did," she teased.

Aunt Olivia was not in the least disconcerted. "Perhaps, and if I did, I would be in the right."

"I shall beg pardon and remind you that I was all of sixteen when we were choosing the coverings," Elizabeth pointed out. "I hope my taste has improved since."

"You were almost seventeen by then," her aunt said tartly, but Elizabeth caught the amusement in the older woman's upturned lips. She moved to help her aunt remove her pelisse. Aunt Olivia sat on the bed.

"The floors are wonderful, too," Elizabeth said, reaching down and pulling up a rug that covered the finished wood.

"The windows are full south," Aunt Olivia pointed out. "I knew it needed a cooler color."

Elizabeth shook her head fondly. "Is this the room you prefer, then?" she asked.

Aunt Olivia sat at the vanity and placed her gloves neatly on the table. "Is the pianoforte still in the sitting room?"

Elizabeth peered around the door into the adjoining room. There, snug against the inner wall, was the Broadwood Square her uncle had purchased for her aunt. There was a music room with a larger, finer instrument downstairs on the first floor, but this one had been intended for Aunt Olivia's personal use.

"It is still here, Aunt," Elizabeth reported as she felt a tug at her heart.

"Then this is the room I choose, dear," Aunt Olivia said, satisfied. "Please call my maid. I should like to rest a bit."

Elizabeth gave her aunt a kiss on the cheek. "Thank you for coming with me."

Aunt Olivia gazed steadily at her, but it was not a stare. It was an embrace. "You are our daughter, Lizzy."

Elizabeth recognized the declaration Olivia had made on the way to Longbourn. She turned from the bell pull and nodded. "I am."

Darcy turned as someone entered the study. It was the maid from the carriage who was led in, accompanied by Mrs. Eustace. Though she was as small and slight as Susan had been, the girl before them was in every other way different. Though clearly anxious, she did not cry. Instead, she stood before the men deferentially but resolutely.

"Well, Mrs. Eustace?" the duke asked.

The housekeeper nodded at Delilah.

"When Mr. Fitzwilliam was speaking to me," the girl began, "I remembered something."

Bedford gave Richard a resentful look. "You have been speaking with my staff?"

Richard shrugged. "You did not forbid it."

"I have not forbidden a number of things," Bedford said, casting annoyed. "Shall you feel free to raid my pantries or examine the contents of my safe because I have not disallowed it?"

He seemed to recall the presence of the servants, then, and stopped what might otherwise have grown into a longer rant. Darcy noted Richard's irritation as well, though it was detected by the slow tapping of his hand against his thigh rather than a grimace.

"Shall we not hear what information has been gleaned?" Darcy asked carefully.

Bedford grunted and waved a hand at Delilah. She swallowed hard.

"I never thought of it before," she said. "Mr. Williams is a friend of Harry's, and lately, he is here quite often." She made a face.

"Harry?" Bedford asked, his forehead furrowing. He glanced at his housekeeper. "Footman?" Mrs. Eustace nodded.

"You do not like Mr. Williams, Delilah?" Darcy asked, earning himself a scowl from Bedford for interrupting.

Delilah shook her head, and answered, but not without a cautious glance at the duke. "He is *too* charming, if you know what I mean, Mr. Darcy. My mum warned me about men like that."

Mrs. Eustace gestured for the maid to continue.

"Well, sir, Mr. Fitzwilliam asked about the post, and I remembered something strange. A few weeks ago, I saw Harry take Mrs. Russell's letters."

Mrs. Eustace prompted the girl. "He put them back later . . ."

"Yes," Delilah said with a nod. "But after Mr. Fitzwilliam asked his questions, then I was thinking . . . Why did he not just take them to Mrs. Russell? Why remove the letters only to bring them back?" She shifted from one foot to another. "It was curious. And then . . ."

Bedford leaned forward, his expression intent. "And then?"

Delilah's eyes dropped to the floor. "Well, I was thinking about Harry and the letters, and then I remembered that his friend, Mr. Williams, was hanging about after Mrs. Russell was taken ill. He asked what the fuss was about, and I . . ." She lifted her head and straightened her shoulders. "I told him Mrs. Russell was ill and we were leaving to fetch Miss Russell home."

The duke's eyes shut briefly, his lips drawn together so tightly that the skin around them turned white.

"I did not think much about it, Your Grace," the girl said in a shaky voice. "I did not know *where* we were to go, and I had forgotten about the letters . . ."

"Thank you, Delilah," Bedford said with a sigh. "You may go."

Delilah curtsied, casting an anxious look at her employer before Mrs. Eustace escorted her out.

The man stood in silence for a time until Richard broke through the quiet.

"Clearly, there is more to this than just a maid stealing things at Darcy House," he said. "Shall we share our resources rather than remain at each other's throats?"

"I only care about Miss Russell and her aunt," Darcy said. "Being at odds only helps Wickham."

"The man's name is Williams," Bedford replied, resigned. "Are you sure he and Wickham are one and the same?"

"The maid at Darcy House called him Wilson, but the description of the man was the same. So yes, I am as sure as I can be without seeing him," Darcy responded. "His methods of seduction and persuasion are a match for the man I knew." He withdrew the letter he had been carrying and tossed it on the desk. "Wickham left his employer in Devonshire last spring when the man died. His son quickly discovered that Wickham had been stealing money for years and turned him out of the house."

Bedford rubbed the back of his neck. "I do not retract my statement about the Darcys bringing this man into our lives. But as Olivia has rather forcefully pointed out, *you* are not the Darcy at fault."

As I told you a week ago, Darcy thought irritably.

The duke stood. "I apologize." He held out his hand. It was hardly enough, but the man was a duke. Darcy knew was lucky to get an apology at all. He took the man's hand. Then Bedford sat to write out the directions. "When you see Lizzy, will you attempt to get her to return?"

Darcy nodded. "I cannot promise success, Bedford, but I will try."

Bedford sanded the note, and as soon as it was dry, handed it over.

As Richard took the paper, Darcy cleared his throat. "I would suggest, Bedford, that you have your staff conduct an inventory. You may find that you, too, have things missing."

Bedford frowned, but Darcy remained impassive.

"I shall," the duke replied.

Richard inclined his head towards the door. They made their farewells and called for their carriage.

Elizabeth left her aunt resting and returned to the ground floor in response to a summons from her butler, Mr. Perry. He was an imposing man—tall, strong, in his forties but with the appearance of a much younger man. Elizabeth had liked the idea of hiring a butler who might also take part in protecting the house. She was an independent woman, but her uncle and aunt had raised her to be prudent as well.

"I am sorry to disturb you so soon after your arrival, Miss Russell," he said with a bow. "But Mr. Yeager has asked to see you down at the greenhouses."

"Is he here?" she asked. "Or waiting for me there?"

"He is waiting," Mr. Perry said. "Shall I call for Taylor and Clark?"

Elizabeth hesitated. She nearly declined the escort out of habit. She had spent months in Hertfordshire and been perfectly fine. It took only a few minutes to ride to the greenhouses, and Mr. Yeager would be expecting her. It would be quicker to go alone. But she soon thought better of it. Aunt Olivia would scold her, and Mr. Darcy would give her that disapproving glare of his, only it truly would be disapproving this time. Even Kensington, as safe as it felt, was not Hertfordshire. Given the events of the past few days, being alone for even a short ride like this was unwise.

Elizabeth returned her attention to Mr. Perry, who was awaiting an answer. She almost laughed at the curled lip. *It is not as though Mr. Perry was asking you a question, you ninny. He was telling you to take them. Ah, well, I shall get used to it again.*

"Yes, thank you, Mr. Perry," she said, and Mr. Perry's lips straightened. "I shall go change and meet them out front. Is Kensington in the stables already?"

"I believe so, Miss Russell."

She nodded. "Please ask that she be saddled for me and brought around."

"Yes, Miss Russell." Mr. Perry stepped away and Elizabeth headed for the stairs.

146

It took some time to make their way through the clogged city streets out to Hyde Park and then just beyond the city limits to Kensington. The rows of houses gave way to small groves of trees with bare branches, some scattered bushes, the occasional large home in the distance, and acres of farmland.

The rumbling of the wheels over the cold ground lulled each man into a kind of private introspection. Darcy had not been sleeping well, instead spending hours ruminating over the letter wielded by his Aunt Catherine, and he had at last come to a conclusion. The writer had meant to get him on the road to Kent. It was possible, he supposed, that Wickham meant to steal him blind in his absence, but his instinct screamed that the blackguard was not after more items to sell.

Darcy did not travel with a team of outriders, nor in a coach pulled by six horses. His journeys included at most two outriders and a coach pulled by four—comfortable but not particularly fast. A trip to Kent from London was relatively brief and made over secure roads. At Easter, he generally traveled with Richard in the carriage and no additional escort at all. For such a summons as his aunt might have been expected to issue when she received the letter, there was every possibility he would have made the trip alone. *Alone and largely unprotected.* Wickham had proven himself adept at getting information. He had managed to get others to steal for him. Darcy's travel plans would not have been difficult to discover.

The more he considered it, the more he had come to the dark conclusion that Wickham was still after the fortune he believed Georgiana could provide—and he was not above either abducting a man—or killing one—to get it.

"What is that dark cloud hovering over your head, Darcy?" Richard asked, his own expression forbidding.

Darcy evaluated his cousin's features. "I surmise you are considering Lady Catherine's letter, as am I."

Richard sighed. "I admit that I am. Have you come to the logical conclusion?"

"But it is *not* logical," Darcy insisted. "Georgiana would remain with the Matlocks were I attacked. She would be more difficult to reach, not less."

"But if it looked like an accident . . ."

It struck him them—the shot that had hit nothing, the branch in the road. "Do you think he meant to cause an accident with Bedford's coach?"

"Perhaps. Bedford is a more dangerous target. If he had startled the horses and tipped the coach," he grimaced, "or run the coach over the branch and sent you all flying . . . he would not have repined, I think." His eyes seemed far away as he thought out loud.

Darcy frowned. "So he waits for an ideal situation, causes an accident, and then waits until—when? Georgiana would still be with your parents."

"Darcy," Richard said gently, "if something of that nature were to occur, you have to know the entire family would remove to London, and then . . ."

"All the men would travel to Kent . . ." Darcy rubbed his forehead. It was an unpleasant thing to consider, even in his imagination. If there had been a clear ambush, the women would be vigorously protected. An accident would not raise the same level of concern. "Leaving only the women in London."

"A decided risk," Richard said thoughtfully, "but were he willing to take it . . ." He paused. "If he were to remove Georgiana in the night, it might be past noon before we would hear of it in Kent. Georgiana is not an early riser and would not be missed until just before breakfast, something he likely knows from her former companion. He could have an entire day on us before we could give chase."

"Georgiana would not go easily," Darcy replied, his stomach sinking at the different ways in which his sister might be forced to comply. "But with that kind of time, he could make it to Gretna."

Neither man spoke their greatest fear—that they would never see Georgiana again, that Wickham would taunt her relations with her well-being for the rest of his life. Or hers.

Darcy could not think long on the bitterness Wickham would take out upon Georgiana; whether he arranged an accident or simply made her remaining life unbearable, his sister would be in misery. And nothing would then stand between the man and the prize of Pemberley. He had made changes to his will after Georgiana's near-miss, but Wickham would not know that. Darcy wondered whether Wickham had approached anyone in the solicitors' office. *No women there.* He closed his eyes. Wickham had him turning in circles, waiting for his next move. It was precisely what the miscreant would want.

The carriage turned up a long drive that jogged to the right around a giant oak tree and then curved before a handsome gray-stone edifice with Palladian columns near the front entrance. The lawn sloped slightly down from the building and was dotted with sheep. A three-sided shelter was built to the west of the house at the bottom of the gentle incline, a small barn some distance farther in the same direction largely hidden by a stand of trees.

"Handsome house," Richard said. "It is easy to see why she might prefer it to St. James."

Darcy nodded solemnly. St. James's Square was a fashionable address and the duke's home was enormous, but the activity all around it was somewhat mixed. Though she had likely been well tended, he had to own a little surprise that the Russells had resided there even when Elizabeth was a child. Pall Mall was not far away, and even during the day there might be less savory characters making their way about. There was prestige there, but not peace.

Here, even so close to London, just over three miles from his own domicile in Mayfair, it was as though he was in the country. Even with all the troubles that had crowded upon him fast and thick in the past week, nearly all of which remained unresolved, he could feel the tension in his back beginning to ease. *Elizabeth*, he thought, his eagerness to see her at last growing stronger with every moment.

Richard was still speaking as Darcy made to rise. "Darcy, are we going at this the wrong way? If it was Wickham firing at the carriage— then he followed the *duke's* carriage, not Lady Catherine's."

Darcy was only half-listening. They had arrived, and he nearly leapt down the steps as they were positioned. He needed to see Elizabeth.

Before they could approach the door, there was a clattering of hooves from one side of the property, and a horse came galloping back towards the stables. Darcy froze. It was an Arabian. With a side saddle. And no rider.

CHAPTER NINE

Elizabeth met her escort at the front of the house. A young man offered her a knee, and she mounted Kensington in a smooth, practiced move. She straightened her skirts and thanked the man. He nodded, tipping his cap to her before shoving it back on his head and turning for the stables.

Clark and Taylor were former Army men, recommended for the position by several of the men she had hired to work the farm. Francis had interviewed them and had them investigated; he was pleased with what he had discovered. So impressed was he that he had teased her about stealing them for Anna. They had been hired to ride escort for Elizabeth and her aunt as they enjoyed the London season, but their changed plans had not flustered either man.

Clark was the smaller of the two, though neither man was large. They were lean and wiry, reputed to be excellent riders and exceptional shots. They did not speak much, instead keeping their focus outward as they rode. Elizabeth felt a little foolish, riding between these two silent men. But Francis had given the men their orders; she would not gainsay them.

She tried to concentrate instead on the pleasure of the location. She was happy to have an opportunity, at last, to view all the work that had been accomplished in their absence.

There was a sparse stand of trees just behind them and a set of boulders across the way. Taylor signaled his partner and rode off to check behind the latter. Elizabeth watched him go—he was a fair distance away when she thought she heard something move behind her. She turned, catching a shadow moving from the trees into a brushy area just beyond. She meant to point it out to Clark, but he was already on the move. He whistled shrilly, two fingers in his mouth, and at the signal, Taylor immediately wheeled around and urged his mount into a gallop back in their direction, the horse's hooves pounding heavily against the ground.

The whistle startled Kensington, and the Arabian's head turned away quicker than Elizabeth could respond. She tried to calm the mare and tighten her hold on the reins, but Kensington skittered to the right and tossed her head. Then there was the *crack* of a shot, and the horse was off.

Elizabeth fought to remain atop Kensington as the frightened mare sped away. The horse did not remain in the center of the trail but was rather precariously keeping just to the side of it. Elizabeth tried to guide her back to safer ground but had not fully succeeded when she saw a thick, low branch directly in their path. There was only a second before she hit it—too low to duck, no time to go around.

She dropped the reins, turning forward as she grabbed at the limb instead; she was certain that falling to the ground after hanging from the bough would do less damage than flying off the mare at this speed. But they were traveling too fast; her hands could not find a purchase. There was a sharp pain as she struck the branch hard—too hard to arrest the momentum that flipped her completely over it. She instinctively tucked her chin to her chest as she dropped, hitting the ground flat on her back.

"Unnnnhh," Elizabeth heard as all the air was forced from her body, and then there was nothing but the struggle to breathe and a growing panic when she could not manage it. After what seemed an eternity but was likely only a few seconds, she heard a guttural kind of moaning, but she was unsure of its source. She could feel her arms and legs but could not summon the energy to move them. Her eyes rolled back as her world shrank to a small point of light. *Breathe,* was all she could think around the burning in her lungs and the pain that surrounded her. *Breathe.*

From far away, she felt a hand on her shoulder and another slipping under her to trace her spine, her ribs. Then there was a second set of hands, gentler, warmer, dragging her up into a semi-sitting position, lifting her arms, carefully pulling her shoulders back while something—legs or knees—pushed her stomach forward.

Her lungs opened and she took in a sliver of air. Then, like someone dying of thirst who has been handed a drink, she sputtered and strained, trying to take in more.

"Easy," she heard a deep voice say. "Easy, Elizabeth."

She gasped and gulped and wheezed and finally, finally, took in a full breath. She opened her eyes halfway, her head fell back, and she focused on a familiar, beloved face hovering worriedly above her.

"Fitzwilliam?" she asked, the air icy in her lungs. She felt oddly disconnected from her voice. Her vision began to swirl and fade, pulling her into the dark.

Darcy stripped Kensington of her sidesaddle and leapt on her bareback. He urged her to a gallop, only to pull up short when he saw a gun being trained on him.

"Fitzwilliam Darcy!" he shouted as he held up his hands, growing frantic when he saw that the man was shielding someone lying in the dirt. "I am betrothed to Miss Russell!"

The man eyed him warily but evidently knew the name. He nodded, putting the gun away, and Darcy slipped off the horse. He took it all in, ignoring the tremor in his hands. Elizabeth was flat on her back on the side of the road, legs slightly apart, arms wide, palms turned up towards the sky, fingers half-curled. Her hat was gone. Some of her hair had pulled free of its pins, fanning out haphazardly around her head. Her face was pale and pained. Not moving. Not breathing. Though . . . thank God, she seemed to be trying. He was at her side before he realized he had moved.

"Clark," the man said roughly, identifying himself as he felt Elizabeth's ribs to check for damage. Darcy wanted to slap the man's hands away but was drawn instead to the strangled sound emanating from Elizabeth's throat as she tried to pull more air into her lungs.

"Her back ain't broke, ribs neither," Clark said with authority. He rocked back on his heels. "There's air getting in, just not much. Normally it starts up again on its own, but . . ."

It put Darcy in mind of someone drowning, and suddenly, he knew what to do. He moved behind her head and shoulders. He crouched, pulling her carefully into a sitting position with her back against his chest. He slid his arms under hers, bending his arms back towards his chest as though he was carrying a load of firewood. At the same time, he pushed his knees into the small of her back and slowly nudged her abdomen forward. She gasped, took a shallow breath, then a larger one. Her eyes opened.

He supported her head with his arm and hand while he shifted to her side. He looked down into her face, grateful to see the recognition in her eyes—but the almost unintelligible "Fitzwilliam?" was less than reassuring. As he watched, her eyelids fluttered closed again. Something cold expanded in his chest and clutched at his heart.

"Elizabeth?" he called, trying with everything he had to keep his voice from breaking, "*Elizabeth.*"

"We have to get her back to the house, sir," Clark told him firmly. "Taylor's after him, but we need to move Miss Russell to safety."

Darcy shook his head tightly, still securing her. Elizabeth's body was limp, her head rolled towards him. She was breathing in shallow but regular puffs of air, but there was no way to know if she was otherwise injured. "We cannot move her yet. Just wait a few moments." *Please, Elizabeth, wake.*

The man made an inarticulate, impatient noise in his throat but nodded.

"Elizabeth," Darcy called. He set his knees fully on the ground and laid her down gently. "Elizabeth, we need to move you, sweetheart. Can you open your eyes?" He stroked her cheek and tried to swallow his fear.

When her eyelids flickered and opened, his own breathing calmed. He tried to offer her an encouraging smile. "Where are you hurt, Elizabeth?" he asked, keeping his voice low and controlled.

She was silent, thinking, and then said, "Sides. Back." Her voice was rough, but it was clearer now.

"What about your head? Neck?"

She considered it. "No."

Clark grunted. "We should get her up and see if she can walk."

"Do you think you can do that, dearest?" Darcy asked Elizabeth. They had little choice but to move her, but if she found it too painful, they would find another way.

"Yes," she said hoarsely, and held her arms out. "Help me."

Darcy glanced at Clark and noted the approval in his eyes. Each man took an arm and assisted Elizabeth to her feet. She stood uncertainly, but she did not complain, and her legs, at least, were uninjured. He caught Kensington's reins and Clark did the same for his mount, but it was clear Elizabeth was in no condition to ride. It would not be safe in any case, not until Taylor made it back. He wrapped an arm around her waist for support as they slowly walked between the two horses and they reached the safety of the house.

It was not until they arrived and the housekeeper began calling out orders that Darcy realized Richard was nowhere to be found.

God, I hope you find him, Richard, he thought darkly. *Find him and bring him here to me.*

"He got away," was the grim report they had from Taylor, whose coat sleeve was torn and bloody. "But I hobbled him."

Darcy crossed his arms over his chest. He was frustrated and angry. Elizabeth was upstairs with the housekeeper and her aunt. After a week apart, again he could not see her. To hear that they were no closer to ending these attacks was infuriating.

Richard entered with Clark, each holding the arm of a squirming youth of about eleven years. He was clad in torn trousers and a threadbare coat. Clark released his hold on the boy. He tossed some clean cloth, a needle, and thread on the desk.

"This was the one in the trees," Clark replied. "Mr. Perry confirmed he was the messenger. Says he was paid a shilling to deliver the message."

He motioned at his partner. "The shot came from behind Taylor—someone was in the rocks."

Richard's expression was grave. "Is she well, Darcy?"

Darcy nodded. "She was able to walk back to the house."

His cousin nodded. "Good." He shook the boy a bit roughly and addressed him. "Very good for you, indeed."

Clark approached Taylor and gestured at the man's coat. He removed a flask from his coat pocket. Taylor rolled his eyes, but did as he was bid, and Clark began to minister to the wound.

"Tell us what you did," Richard growled.

"Nothing." The boy crossed his own arms over his chest though Richard still held his upper arm. His bottom lip stuck out.

"What is your name?" Darcy asked. His voice was not kind, but it was not threatening as Richard's had been.

"Billy." The boy tried to step away from Richard, but he was held tight.

"Billy," Darcy said, "a gentlewoman was hurt today, and Mr. Taylor was shot. You must tell us what happened, or you will be the one held accountable for it."

The boy was sullen and silent.

"You must know," Darcy said thoughtfully, "he meant for *you* to be held accountable rather than him."

The boy glanced sideways and remained quiet.

Richard snorted. "Do you think *you* are the one in charge here?" He released Billy's arm and grabbed his collar. With apparently little effort, Richard held the boy in the air, his small legs kicking hard. He was given a shake and set back on the floor.

"I can do this all day long, Billy," Richard said flatly. He nodded at a thick brass hook on the wall. "I could just hang you up like a picture and leave you there." He paused. "Would anyone miss you, do you think?"

The boy frowned and drove the toe of his boot against the floor. "He told me to take the message and then hide in the trees and scare the

156

lady's horse after she rode past," the boy said through gritted teeth. "I saw no harm."

"Ow!" Taylor complained loudly as Clark poured some alcohol over the wound.

"Ai, keep still, you great clodpole," Clark said, holding a small basin beneath Taylor's arm, trying to catch the alcohol and blood in it.

Taylor frowned at his partner. "Fiend seize it," he swore. "Warn a man, Clark."

Clark rolled his eyes. "Stop jumping around. No sense wrecking a fine rug over a scratch. This ain't bloody Busaco."

Taylor cursed under his breath but held his arm out where Clark could get at it.

Darcy blew out a breath as Clark prepared to stitch Taylor's arm. The boy was eyeing them, too, his eyes wide.

"You saw no harm in startling a gentlewoman's horse?" Darcy asked, his composure growing thin.

The boy clamped his lips shut.

"Billy," Darcy continued, "I need to know who this man is so that he does not hurt anyone else. If you help us, you will not be in trouble."

Richard clearly did not appreciate that statement. He glared at his cousin over the boy's head. Darcy met that glare with one of his own. *It is not the boy I am after, cousin.*

"He gave no name," Billy said with a scowl. "Just gave me a shilling to go to the house and promised another for hiding in the bushes. He ran off without paying that."

Darcy surveyed the urchin, the chill in his voice turning glacial. "You cannot believe I will pay you for what you did today." The boy had the sense to avert his gaze.

"Tall," he blurted. "Not like you," he said, pointing at Darcy. "Like him." He nodded his head backwards, at Richard. "Dark."

"Is that the best you can do?" Taylor asked.

Billy shrugged.

"String him up on the wall," Clark suggested. "See if he gets hungry enough to remember anything."

"He wore fancy boots," the boy added, grudgingly. "His clothes was kinder old, though."

"Worthless," Richard sighed. He relaxed his hold and the boy darted for the door. With one wide swing of his arm, Richard had him again. "Now you hang," he told the boy, who cried out in protest. He spun the belt of Billy's coat around so that the buckle was in the back, then hung it on the brass picture hook. The boy wriggled angrily like a fish on the line.

There was a knock at the door.

The men looked at one another. Darcy called out, "Enter."

To his great surprise, Elizabeth was on the other side. She stepped in and glanced over at the small boy wriggling on the wall. She pursed her lips and turned her attention to the men. She cleared her throat. "Would you gentlemen care for anything?"

Darcy moved to guide her back out into the hall. "Elizabeth," he chided her mildly, "what are you doing downstairs? You should be resting."

She looked at him askance. "As it turns out, standing is less painful than lying down." She patted his arm. "The cool bath helped a great deal."

He must not have appeared convinced, for she shook her head at him. "Would you like some coffee or tea?" she asked. "Or a light meal?" She waited, but when he said nothing, she added, "I have port coming for Mr. Taylor. I am afraid there is nothing stronger in the house." She arched one eyebrow. "Are we feeding the child you have suspended from the wall or are we now revisiting the Spanish Inquisition?"

Despite the anguish of the day so far, he felt a smile tugging at his lips at the pointed remark. Elizabeth must be feeling better if she was teasing. "I think Richard intends to let him remain a while. He has not been precisely . . . forthcoming."

She rolled her eyes. "He is a child. He probably saw nothing beyond the few coins he was given."

"Should we be kinder to the boy who caused your injuries than he was to you, Elizabeth?" Darcy replied, unyielding. "I am afraid I am not so forbearing."

Her expression softened. "Very well," she acquiesced. "I know I would feel the same had you been hurt."

He touched her cheek, then let his hand drop. "Susan was unwilling to give us a description," he admitted. "She was too afraid."

Elizabeth nodded, pensive. "You believe the boy can." Her lips parted slightly. "Oh." She grabbed his wrist.

"Are you well?" he asked immediately, sliding a hand under her elbow for support. A few hours were not nearly long enough to forget Elizabeth lying limp in his arms. Truthfully, he did not think he would ever get past it. The memory made him angry, made him want to hang the boy upside down from his heels, but for Elizabeth's sake, he was attempting to remain civilized.

"I think I may have *seen* him, Fitzwilliam." She turned abruptly towards the stairs and he caught her grimace at the hasty movement.

"Elizabeth," he said, still holding her arm. "Be careful, love." He motioned to a maid who was approaching. "Let the maid fetch what you need."

Elizabeth smiled but said nothing for a moment. "My paper and pencils," she finally said in a voice not much above a whisper, "in my chambers." The maid curtsied and hurried away.

Elizabeth perched awkwardly on the edge of a chaise in the drawing room. Her back was continuing to cause discomfort. She had held a hand mirror up with her back to the full-length glass so she could see the damage; bruises were already forming, the red marks beginning to turn blue. The darkest of them appeared just below her shoulder blades, though Mrs. Gaines assured her the cold bath would speed healing. While her ribs showed no signs of discoloration, they ached nonetheless. As a result, it was painful to move her arms and shoulders the way she normally would when she drew. Even her fingers felt stiff. Still, an image was slowly developing on the paper.

Dark hair in need of a trim. Thin face, laugh lines around his mouth, a smile that did not reach his black eyes. She closed her own eyes for a moment, going over each small section of his face in its turn, lingering over the details. He had a small mark at the end of his right eyebrow. Freckle or birthmark, she did not know, but like everything about him— his clothes, his eyes, his mien—it was dark. She filled it in.

Mr. Darcy sat next to her, observing her work. Mr. Fitzwilliam stood near the window with his back to them, hands on his hips. When she at last lifted her hand, Mr. Darcy gave a satisfied grunt. She let him take the picture. He gazed at it for a minute.

"Richard!" he called. He placed a soft kiss on her forehead. "I think you should address Richard by his Christian name if you are to call me by mine. It can become a bit confusing otherwise." He stood.

Ah, yes. *Fitzwilliam.* She smiled, recalling her aunt's advice. "On the contrary, it is economical. I call one name and am rewarded with two men responding to my summons."

Then Mr. Fitzwilliam was standing before her, a gleam in his eye. "I should be pleased to have you call me Richard, *Elizabeth.*"

"Very well, Richard," she agreed, giving him a small smile. It felt odd to use his Christian name, but she accepted that it *was* more practical. He was nearly her cousin in any case, the same as John and Francis. She would grow accustomed to it.

Richard took the picture from his cousin and glanced at it. He nodded slowly and then looked up at his cousin. The men communicated with no more than a lifted eyebrow from one and a smirk from the other. Elizabeth was very pleased to see proof, yet again, that they were so close. She knew how difficult being responsible for a family name could be; it pleased her that her betrothed had not been alone. Though she was loath to think on it, she had to admit feeling relieved that she would not be alone, either, when the time came.

"Younge?" Richard asked.

Richard nodded. With a grin and a wink, Richard left the room, but not before making a show of ensuring that the door remained open.

"Take the boy off the wall," she called after him.

"I am the only man you should be summoning, Miss Russell," Mr. Darcy—no, *Fitzwilliam* –growled in her ear as he returned to his seat. It tickled. "My cousin will have to find his own wife."

She would not be diverted, even pleasantly. "I presume from your response that the man was indeed George Wickham?" she asked.

He frowned and nodded. "It is. I am not surprised, but I am pleased that we at last have some surety." He took her hand. "It is a fine likeness. Even Richard recognized him, and he has not seen Wickham in many years." His expression was boyishly rueful. "I suppose I should be thankful it is not *my* face you are sketching this time."

"I do not only draw people when they are behaving badly," she responded, thinking of the collection of portraits she had drawn of her intended.

"Forgive me, love. My experience is somewhat limited," he replied, smiling.

Elizabeth gave him a playful shove, and he placed a kiss on her palm—she hummed a little at the tingle.

"You say he was watching Bedford's home?" Fitzwilliam asked.

She nodded. "He was there when I went out visiting a few days ago, and he saw us leave this morning as well." She flipped her hand over to grasp his again. "He might have been there more often without my noticing," she said, resting her head on his shoulder. Her side protested, but she needed the contact. "I feel incredibly foolish that I did not realize he might follow us. It certainly did not take him long to learn Mr. Yeager's name."

Fitzwilliam ran his thumb over the palm of her hand. "It is not information most would think important to conceal, and as we know, Wickham can be very charming."

"I am not usually so rash," she said with a contrite shake of her head. "But I could not remain at St. James. I missed you so dearly."

"And I you, Elizabeth," he replied. "But I would rather have had you safe. Bedford was not wrong about the sorry state of my affairs." He rested his cheek against her hair. "I have warned the earl to guard Georgiana as well. I will not be easy until Wickham is caught."

"As we know," Elizabeth retorted without moving her head, "it is not only *your* family that has been the source of Mr. Wickham's ire. He knows that my uncle and aunt spoke with your father about him before he was sent to Devonshire, and he seems to know I am the one who wrote Georgiana last summer."

"Well," Fitzwilliam said. He went no further.

She sat up. There was still something that was not clear to her. "I do not understand what his purpose was here today," she admitted. "He shot at Mr. Taylor, but he could not have known Kensington would bolt as she did." She smiled weakly. "We shall have to train her to withstand Mr. Clark's whistle."

"I do not wish to frighten you," Fitzwilliam said, his expression somber, his thumb tracing circles on her skin, "but I believe he meant to take you. Perhaps hold you for ransom, perhaps force you into a marriage to gain your fortune. I cannot say for certain, but his object was you."

She felt cold. "Did he not realize I would be attended?"

Fitzwilliam sat up straight and cupped her cheek with one large hand. His eyes examined her for a moment before he replied, "He probably meant to kill them." He cleared his throat—it had the sound of a low rumble, and she was inexplicably comforted by it. "The boy actually did you all a favor, calling your attention as he did before Taylor reached the rocks. Richard believes, and I agree, that he likely meant to kill Taylor at close range and then deal with Clark. Better odds to take them one at a time. As Mr. Yeager had not sent for you, he would not have been alarmed when you did not arrive."

Elizabeth closed her eyes. And if Mr. Wickham had succeeded? What then?

"As it was," he continued, "he attempted to shoot Taylor in the back." He touched his forehead to hers, clearly uncomfortable with the disclosure. "Fortunately, he was never a very good shot and a man on a moving horse is a difficult target. However," he added, "Taylor is certain he wounded Wickham. If that is indeed the case, he cannot have gotten far."

Elizabeth sat quietly as she took it all in. "I am pleased," she said, "that you are willing to speak of these matters with me." She ignored the twinge in her ribs as she reached to take his other hand. "It is not easy for me to hear them, but it is better to know."

Fitzwilliam twisted his lips into a sort of half-smile, half-grimace. "It is not easy for me to say them to you, but Georgiana informed me after Ramsgate that remaining silent left her vulnerable. You reminded me of it at Netherfield when you demanded to read your aunt's letter for yourself."

I have missed him so much. Elizabeth closed her eyes, taking in the pleasure of his endearments, the excitement of his nearness, his scent. It was an intoxicating mixture of sandalwood, musk, and . . . she wrinkled her nose.

"Fitzwilliam?" she asked, pulling back and planting an unrepentant kiss on the end of his nose.

"Yes, love?" He half-smiled at her.

"My aunt would like to see you. She asked, in fact, last week, before you were . . ." she gestured uselessly.

He nodded. "I see. Is she well enough to receive me today?"

"Yes," Elizabeth told him. "Although you may wish to refresh yourself first."

He gave her a wary look. "And why is that?"

She stared at him before chuckling. "Well," she began, a tease on her lips. *Be good, Lizzy*, she warned herself. "Aunt Olivia is rather fastidious." She patted his cheek. "And you smell like my horse."

Olivia watched the children enter in response to her invitation. They were so very handsome together, her Lizzy grown so womanly and beautiful, her intended so tall and strong. The way he held the door for Lizzy and placed a very light hand on her lower back as she stepped through made Olivia want to weep, and she hated weeping—even when they were happy tears. Therefore, no sooner had Elizabeth stepped into her aunt's room with young Fitzwilliam Darcy in tow than she was asked to leave it.

"Aunt?" Lizzy asked, confused.

"I do not need you here for this conversation, Lizzy," Aunt Olivia said tartly, shooing her away. "I wish to speak to your betrothed alone."

Elizabeth made a face and raised her hands in mock supplication, an undercurrent of humor in her tone. "Fine, Aunt Olivia. Clearly, I am not wanted. May I play the pianoforte while I wait?"

Aunt Olivia considered the request. "Yes, so long as you shut the door and play very loudly."

Elizabeth rolled her eyes, only to be brought up short.

"Is that how I have taught you to behave, Miss Russell?" her aunt scolded. "I do not recall eye-rolling as an appropriate response to an adult conversation. Shall I send you up to the nursery?"

Lizzy's eyes lit up. "The nursery is not open, Aunt," she said, tipping her head to one side in a teasing gesture.

"You should see to that," Olivia shot back with a pointed look at Lizzy's betrothed. The poor boy's ears were already red, and his cheeks were not far behind. She took pity on him, recalling how long it had taken Phillip to grow accustomed to her sportive banter. "Please, my dear," she said softly, "I would like a few moments with your young man."

"Very well," Lizzy said, and Olivia reached out to squeeze her hand. Lizzy turned to face Mr. Darcy. "Any requests?"

He smiled shyly at her. "Anything by Handel would be wonderful, Elizabeth."

Oh, Olivia thought, wistful, *he is so formal. More like his mother in that than his father.*

Lizzy sent him a quizzical look and reluctantly took her leave, closing the door between the rooms.

Olivia gestured to a chair. "I must apologize for receiving you in my chambers," she said. "I have not been well and helping Lizzy earlier has done me in."

"She is being incredibly stubborn and refuses to rest," he said quietly. "I cannot imagine playing the pianoforte is comfortable for her, yet she insists she is well." He took the chair she indicated and lowered himself into it. "If you have any advice on that score, I should dearly love to hear it."

Had Olivia not known his father, she might have missed the dry wit in the statement. As it was, she simply looked him over. "Stubborn?" she asked, pretending surprise. "*My* Lizzy? I cannot imagine what you mean."

His eyes twinkled at that. *My goodness,* Olivia thought. *Good looks and a sense of humor. Lizzy has done well.* She could see his father in his face, and whatever else he had been, George Darcy *had* been a handsome man. *I recall Fitzwilliam when he was in leading strings. I did not think him so promising then. But when he returned from his first year at Eton, so intelligent and well-mannered . . .*

The light notes announcing the beginning of Handel's *Chaconne Variations in G major* wafted into the room, muffled by the shut door but still clear. She smiled, closing her eyes to listen for a minute. It was so like her Lizzy to select music based on her feelings. This variation was light, even luminous—it revealed a sort of happiness Olivia thought Handel had lost as he aged. After the day they had experienced, the choice was almost astonishingly optimistic.

When she opened her eyes, the youngest Mr. Darcy was gazing past her, toward the music, his eyes burning with a low heat, his lips drawn slightly up on one side. She watched him until he became aware of her observation, when he blushed and cast his eyes down to the floor.

"Do not be embarrassed, Fitzwilliam," she said, entirely serious. "It does me a great deal of good to know you love her so well."

He cleared his throat, clearly uncomfortable, but to his credit, he looked directly at her. "I do, Mrs. Russell."

"Excellent," she replied. "I have some things to say and two rather significant requests to make."

He gave her a single nod. "Whatever I can do will be done. I promise you."

Olivia paused to collect her thoughts. "In light of what happened today, I believe we both know that removing from John's home was perhaps not the best course of action. However, Lizzy has been making decisions for the both of us for more than two years. She is unaccustomed to being thwarted in such a way."

Fitzwilliam nodded. "I would not have allowed it should I have known."

His eyes showed everything to her, and Olivia was struck by the fear she saw there. To be ruled by it would be his undoing.

"You will argue, you know," Olivia told him. "And despite what your marriage vows will say about the wife obeying the husband, you have not chosen that kind of a wife. Do not issue dictates. Loving persuasion is your best course of action."

"And if she will not be persuaded?" Fitzwilliam asked, a tinge of frustration in his speech. "What if she is putting herself at risk as she did today?"

"Mr. Darcy," she said, shaking her head. She laced her fingers together and pursed her lips. "Fitzwilliam. Elizabeth has not received any letters from Georgiana since the summer. Were you aware?"

"Georgiana mentioned she had not heard from Miss Russell, but I was unaware Miss Bennet and Miss Russell were one and the same until fairly recently," he said, bemused. "Why . . . "

Olivia held up a hand and he stopped. "I know the girls wrote at least a few letters. Both Georgiana's letters to Elizabeth and Elizabeth's to her were to pass through me. Neither John nor I wanted Elizabeth's whereabouts known. Oddly, Mrs. Bennet's insistence on Lizzy using the Bennet surname helped with that."

"I still do not . . ."

Olivia issued an impatient grunt. "Do not be obtuse, Fitzwilliam. If those letters have gone missing—and I am not so far gone as to believe them only mislaid—then someone on staff in the duke's household is up to no good. How can we say she would be safer there than she is here?"

His countenance darkened. "I will allow that you are correct about the duke's staff. Still, Elizabeth was not attacked when she remained at Bedford's home, Mrs. Russell."

Olivia watched him carefully. "So you have discovered who it was, then?" she asked. "Might I ask why I was not informed?"

Mr. Darcy scratched the back of his head, her certainty seeming to catch him unaware. "You were already gone. A footman named Harry Sykes was taking your mail and then returning it. We sent for him, but he had already left the house."

Clearly not all the post was returned. Olivia sighed. "So, despite your assurance that Lizzy was safe in the duke's home, she might not have been. And she did not remain in the house at all times, did she?" There was a touch of asperity in her tone.

He shifted in his chair. "Mrs. Russell, I . . . "

"Let us stop arguing and get to my point, Fitzwilliam," she said firmly. "You will never be able to keep Lizzy entirely safe. She is an heiress now and will be a very wealthy woman in her own right." She did not add *soon*. "Her position will attract a certain level of attention. While the details of her inheritance are not common knowledge, her connections would suggest it is significant." *Even she does not know how significant.* "You cannot anticipate every possible situation. Phillip knew that. I know it. Lizzy knows it."

Olivia almost pitied the man, but she hoped, at the least, to save him a good many arguments with her headstrong niece. At best, she hoped to alleviate the guilt she knew he felt. "You do what is reasonable to keep yourselves safe, and then you go on with your lives." She smiled. "You cannot wrap her in cotton and store her safely in the attics."

He did offer a wan smile at that. "No matter how sorely I am tempted," he joked.

"Oh, Lord." Olivia tossed up her hands. "Can you imagine the hollering?"

He made an odd sound in his throat she could not quite call laughter. "I can."

"Very well," Olivia said. "Now, to my requests. First, I wish you to be married soon." She gave him a beseeching look. "Very soon. John has a special license."

Fitzwilliam nodded. "He said as much. He would not hand it over to me as he worried Elizabeth would not invite him to the wedding without it."

Olivia scoffed. "Lizzy is nothing if not forgiving of those she loves. As soon as he apologizes, he will be back in her good graces. We shall simply have to tell him when to arrive." She eyed him. "When would that be?"

"I would prefer to have my family here," he explained, taken aback by her insistence, "but we must be sure it is safe for them to travel. If the need is *pressing*, and Elizabeth agrees, we can marry as soon as possible."

"By the end of the week, perhaps?" she asked, suddenly feeling every inch a doddering old woman.

He gave her a solemn look. "I shall speak with Elizabeth."

The light, airy notes from the pianoforte filled the silence between them—the contrasting scores played by each hand representing two people conversing happily, exchanging ideas, making plans. It was the perfect choice for an engaged couple.

Olivia swallowed. *He is very accommodating. I would have liked something grander, but given the circumstances . . .* "Thank you," she said.

"Of course," he replied, his own hands clasped, thumbs pressing together. "You mentioned a second request?"

She paused for a moment, listening to Lizzy finish the song, then to the silence as her girl chose another. When that song was Handel's *Yes, I'm in love,* she risked a glance at the young man who sat next to her bed. He was smiling with both sides of his mouth now.

"She is telling us that we are taking too long," Olivia said with a little laugh. "Very well, let us be brief." She laid a hand on the young Mr. Darcy's arm. "My second request is related to the first. Lizzy does not want to hear that I am dying, Fitzwilliam. But I am."

He met her earnest entreaty with a somber "I understand."

She gave him a sad smile. "You see it, do you not? You who have experienced so much loss."

His expression was mournful, but he nodded.

"I want to attend Lizzy's wedding. And I want her to be married to the man she loves when she grieves me. She will need you to support her through the loss the way you supported me."

His forehead creased. "I only wrote you a letter," he replied, bemused. "Mr. Russell was a fine man, and he was good to me. It was, truly, the least I could do, having missed his funeral."

"You told me stories about him in that letter. Things he did for you."

He nodded again. "But I do not have stories about you."

She patted his knee. "I know. Let *her* tell them. *Encourage* her to tell them. She will begin to remember me as I was." Olivia paused here, then said emphatically, "Otherwise she will try to make an angel of me and that will never do." She released a small laugh. "It will help her, and in the process, you will learn a great deal about your wife."

He placed his hand over hers, warm and comforting, and the ache for Phillip was nearly unbearable. But she said none of that.

"I give you my word," he said, his voice deep and low.

Olivia smiled at him. "Then we are done," she told him. Exhausted and grateful, she sank back into her pillows just as the final chords stilled and drifted away.

CHAPTER TEN

There were only the two of them at dinner. Had it not been for the disaster of the day preceding the meal, Darcy would have been elated. Instead, they were both simply weary.

Elizabeth's aunt remained in her chambers, and Richard had left hours ago to seek out Mrs. Younge, after Darcy had given him her last known direction. Richard had commented on the strength of his memory while pointedly informing Darcy that he was not wanted on this errand.

He thought it was not so astonishing that he recalled where the woman had said she lived. Mrs. Younge had, after all, tried to take his sister from him. Darcy was not pleased to be left behind and was only mollified when Richard explained that he wished to take Mrs. Younge by surprise.

"She would recognize you in an instant, Darce," he argued. "She has never met me. Let us not give her a reason to flee."

Mrs. Younge. She had appeared so steady, so responsible. Her references were impeccable—he had checked them personally and discussed them with his cousin. He suspected that Wickham had worked on her only after she had taken the position, a rather impressive feat considering the risk to her livelihood. The cad's timing would have been perfect, of course—after Mrs. Younge was hired, but before she had formed any sort of bond with Georgiana.

He had been so relieved to have disrupted Wickham's plans in Ramsgate that he had not given the man's plan itself adequate consideration before today. He was not only seducing young women, those who had little experience with men such as him. Instead, Wickham had manipulated a maid into stealing from Darcy House, convinced a footman in the home of a duke to pilfer correspondence and persuaded a widow—who had a great deal to lose by throwing in her lot with his— to follow his designs. Darcy had put Wickham's failure to fool Georgiana down to the reprobate's fading charms, but Wickham was better at his schemes, not worse. He had not given his sister enough credit.

"A penny for your thoughts, Mr. Darcy," Elizabeth said playfully as the soup arrived. Darcy breathed in the aroma. Chestnuts, onion, thyme, butter, fresh bread . . . he realized he was ravenous. "I am thinking about eating, Elizabeth." *I am. Now.*

Her expression was dubious. "Are you." It was not a question.

A footman lifted the lid off a small tureen, steam curling up into the air, before he served them both. Darcy swallowed a spoonful of the soup, and nearly moaned.

"Have you Mrs. Thistlewaite concealed in the kitchens?" he asked, only half in jest. "This is marvelous." Suddenly, being left behind by Richard seemed a stroke of luck.

Elizabeth shook her head. "No, but the cook used her instructions. She was delighted when I asked for several receipts before we returned to Longbourn. Her chocolate cream, unfortunately, is never shared. She said she needed to keep something to herself so I would be sure to return." She sipped her soup. "A wonderful woman, Mrs. Thistlewaite."

She fell silent after that, dipping her spoon delicately into her soup and lifting it to her mouth. Darcy noted that her movements were cautiously measured. He could feel himself about to ask her whether she felt well enough to be downstairs, but he closed his lips tight. *Do not tell her how she feels, Darcy*, he reminded himself. *She is aware.* Instead, he concentrated on his meal. *Perhaps she came down for Mrs. Thistlewaite's soup,* he thought, his spirits lifting. *I believe it might restore even a consumptive to full health.* He took the final spoonful and savored the taste on his tongue.

Eventually he reached for the fish, serving Elizabeth first, then himself. He took several bites, and then, his hunger not so sharp, he stopped with his fork suspended in mid-air. Elizabeth was eating. She was not conversing, though she normally took the lead. She was not looking at him. Her eyes were entirely on her food. She was intentionally ignoring him.

"Will it always be like this?" he asked, both irritated and amused.

"I do not know what you mean," Elizabeth replied smoothly. "I am simply eating my meal."

"You are waiting me out, Elizabeth," he told her bluntly.

She did not smile, but he was sure she was hiding one. "Am I?"

He responded with a good-natured grunt. "You are."

"Then perhaps you should simply tell me what was occupying your mind, Fitzwilliam." She put down her fork and sat primly, hands in her lap. "I know you were not thinking only of the food. You are not your cousin."

He put another piece of fish in his mouth and chewed it thoroughly. She waited patiently, and he was caught between wishing to tease her more and wanting her to eat. "Very well," he said at last. "I am concerned that Wickham has more talent for manipulation than when he was young. When he failed with Georgiana, I did not consider him as being a continuing threat. It was a serious miscalculation, and you have paid the price for my error."

"You had no way of knowing that he was more than a fortune hunter," Elizabeth assured him. "He can charm people to steal or lie for him. His position as a private secretary seems to have given him the skill to produce a reasonably good forgery." Her forehead creased. "However, none of that speaks to violence."

Darcy shook his head. "I should have known. He came to see me after Father died. He threatened me when I told him there was nothing in the will for him. He had never been violent, as far as I knew, and I dismissed him. Thought I was done with him. Then he showed up in Ramsgate."

She sat still, quiet, before adding, "If it was money he desired, it is strange he did not simply forge your father's name to a bank draft years ago. Or yours."

Darcy set his own fork down and touched the corner of a napkin to his mouth. "He may have tried, but he seemed content to steal from his employer until last summer. To tell the truth, I do not write many drafts. I keep strict accounts and send a quarterly list to my solicitor, who sees the creditors paid." He placed the napkin back in his lap. "When I *do* write a draft, I always add a numerical code to my signature. My solicitor and I quite enjoy choosing new ones." He took another mouthful of the flounder. After he swallowed, he said, "My father dealt with an unscrupulous merchant once, so I suggested the idea to him."

Elizabeth nodded at the roast chicken. "How old were you then?"

"Oh, seventeen, I suppose, and rather enamored of numbers."

She smiled. "I should very much like to see that," she said, as he lifted a piece to her plate and added some of the pickled asparagus. "Thank you." She picked up her fork.

"Perhaps," he said dismissively, and saw her narrow her eyes. His own lips began to twitch up, but he bit the inside of his cheek to stop them. "Very well," he said airily. "I shall show you once we are married. For it is a *Darcy* secret, love."

"Fitzwilliam Darcy," she reproached him. "How many *Darcy secret*s have you yet to reveal to me?"

Oh, good God, woman, Darcy groaned to himself. He checked the room before touching her hand and saying softly, "A great many, as it happens. But those are best left for *after* our vows." He served himself and tucked into the meat.

Elizabeth's head turned one way and then the other, her cheeks now suffused with a very becoming shade of pink. Her expression was both piqued and puzzled.

She does not understand, but she will never admit it. He attempted to keep the smug look from his face but failed.

Elizabeth picked up her knife and fork. "That is quite enough from you, Mr. Darcy," she said curtly.

He chuckled. After such a day, it felt very good to laugh.

Despite Mrs. Russell's warning, Darcy was not convinced that having the women remain in Kensington was safe. However, Olivia

Russell was ill and Elizabeth, though she had refused to rest, was clearly denying her own discomfort. A carriage ride over the cobblestones would be a painful journey. Thus, rather than raising the question of St. James or even holding the conversation he knew they must have, he had instead *lovingly persuaded* her to retire. The housekeeper had trailed behind her mistress with some sort of parsley poultice and a vinegar rub. Elizabeth had jested about being a part of dinner rather than dressing for it, but she had removed upstairs at last.

Taylor and Clark had slept the rest of the afternoon in anticipation of standing guard overnight. It was their job to protect the Russell women, they had told Darcy flatly, and they would not be leaving the premises unless they were escorting Miss or Mrs. Russell. They had delivered their message in such a way, Darcy realized, to put him on notice that the ladies would not be *unprotected* at any time.

Darcy took no offense. He knew it was not strictly proper for him to remain in Elizabeth's home, even with her aunt in residence, but after the events of the day and his conversation with Mrs. Russell, he simply could not bring himself to leave. Elizabeth had not inquired about his plans; as the housekeeper was occupied, she had left orders for Mr. Perry to arrange for a room. Mrs. Russell might raise an eyebrow at him in the morning, but he found he could withstand any scolding quite cheerfully.

Truth be told, Darcy would have thrown a blanket on the billiards table and slept there if necessary. Thankfully, Mr. Perry had merely nodded at his mistress. Then he had turned to Darcy, given him the disapproving frown every butler worth his pay had in his arsenal, and remarked that there were ten bedrooms in the house. He would see to having a *suitable* chamber prepared for Miss Russell's guest. Darcy only hoped the room Mr. Perry selected would not be on the roof.

Upon concluding his conversation with Mrs. Russell, Darcy had written several letters. One was to Bedford and another to Matlock House in London. He had already written to his uncle about Lady Catherine's appearance in Hertfordshire and his concern for his sister. In this latest missive, he had both announced his engagement and explained his impending nuptials, though he warned that the precise date was yet to be approved by his bride. He had also mentioned their current situation, if somewhat obliquely, so his uncle would know that the situation had not settled; the earl would need to alert his men in town as well.

In Matlock's quick response, Darcy had been informed of their intention to be in town for the festive season, but given the safety concerns, he had not given an exact day. He knew his uncle well; the earl would refuse to change his plans, but he would alert his outriders and hire more protection. There was a part of Darcy that hoped they were already in town. He was certain Georgiana would plague him forever were she not present at his wedding to her dear friend.

As it had for the past week, the problem of Wickham simmered in the back of his mind. The man was wounded now; he could not have gone far. Were Wickham wise, he would lay low until he was well and then make his escape.

Mrs. Younge's establishment was an obvious choice. Her house was in a nondescript neighborhood of the city. As he had been sacked from his position in Devonshire, Wickham would be looking to remain discreet and conserve his resources. Until Mrs. Younge began to complain about him making love to every female servant in town to forward his own ends, the woman would feel the full measure of the scoundrel's approbation—a handsome, clever man raised as a gentleman. A man who promised her a share his windfall if she would only offer him some trifling assistance. He knew from his own experience that Wickham would make it sound as though the money were laying on the ground just waiting to be collected.

A footman approached with a note on a silver salver and Darcy took it up immediately. It was a message from Richard. Mrs. Younge had been identified on her way home from posting a letter. She was still in the same residence, and Richard wrote that the woman clearly knew *something* but was not willing to speak. They would leave men behind to watch her establishment. He tossed the message aside.

Would Wickham cut his losses and run? Or would he make another attempt to wreak havoc? He leaned back in his chair. If the man intended to finish this, he would likely return to Mrs. Younge. If he meant to leave the country, as he would have to do now, he would make a trip to his bank. Wickham, wanting to appear the gentleman, had always preferred to bank at Thomas Coutts & Company. Hopefully that had not changed.

He could write Mr. Coutts to alert them should Wickham clear out his accounts. Better yet, Bedford could make the request.

Darcy took another sip of his port, turning the events of the last week over and over in his mind as the candles burned down. When he was finally informed that his room was ready, he stood. *One way or another, Wickham, you shall have to surface.* He scowled, controlling his features only when he saw the footman blink and glance away nervously. *And when you do, you will be sorry you ever came back into my life.*

❦

Elizabeth rose to find that the general aches of her misadventure the day before had improved somewhat. She was still sore, particularly where she had spied the worst of the bruising the day before, but the pain in her sides had ebbed away, only bothering her now when she reached suddenly to one side or the other. She believed she had her new housekeeper to thank. The woman had clucked at her the night before, saying that she had helped raise eight nephews, and her new mistress's injuries were not unlike those she had tended many times before. Elizabeth smiled at being compared with a group of wild young boys. How could she pretend to be affronted when the comparison was so apt?

Goodness, she thought suddenly, *I no longer need Aunt Olivia to scold me. Her voice is in my head.* She felt a wave of guilt and changed the direction of her ruminations.

Elizabeth's mind had been whirling as she pondered their predicament throughout the night. She had struggled to find a comfortable position for sleeping, but in such a state of unease, it was unlikely she would have been able to rest in any case. In the light of early morning, she had come to some conclusions.

Even wounded, she was sure that a man who had shot a gun at the Duke of Bedford's coach would not give up his prize easily. *It indicates frustration, recklessness. And I am certain it was him. Nobody else so bold or so foolish as a man who has been thwarted twice so near his goal.*

Every reflection brought her back to the same place. George Wickham had been abruptly and unexpectedly removed from his privileged position in the Darcy family. He had gone into his final

176

meeting with his patron expecting, perhaps, to have his inheritance explained to him. Instead, he had been offered a profession and a swift farewell, nothing at all left to him in the will. *It must have been a terrible shock.* Years later, when Mr. Wickham thought he had a chance to elope with Georgiana and gain control of her substantial dowry, he had again been denied. Both times, it had been a Russell in the middle of things. Surely the animosity he felt for the Russells was at least as sharp as that he held for the Darcys themselves.

He would not turn down Georgiana's fortune should it fall his way, she thought somberly. *But I must now be his first object. To harm me would satisfy both his needs. Money, of course. John would pay a great deal to recover me. But also revenge. If he hurts Georgiana, he would see himself as hurting only Fitzwilliam. If he hurt me, he hurts Fitzwilliam* and *Aunt Olivia—and me, of course. His revenge would be complete.*

She wondered that a man in his position would take such a risk—he could not believe he would remain free for long after insulting a duke in such a personal way. He might plan to escape the duke's reach, though it would require he leave the country altogether. She considered that notion. It *would* make sense to take his stolen fortune and try his luck elsewhere. Had he managed to abduct her, would she have been forced to accompany him? Would he have left her somewhere in England or would she have suffered an accident at sea?

Elizabeth's mouth grew dry, and she clenched her fists defiantly. *No. He would never have succeeded.* Despite her accident the day before, her guards had kept her safe. Mr. Wickham had never gotten near her. She shut her eyes, remembering instead Fitzwilliam's anxious face hovering over hers, the comfort of his arm around her waist as he helped her walk back to the house, his solicitude at dinner when she knew he was anxious to be elsewhere, dealing with the man himself. She had not asked him to stay, concerned he might say no. Fitzwilliam was easy in her company, but she knew his reticent nature. He was ever mindful of propriety. It had been unfair of her, perhaps, but she felt safer, calmer, with him nearby. So she had given orders that a room be made up for him, and to her relief, he had issued no protest.

When Elizabeth had composed herself, she took the stairs down to the kitchen. Sitting alone at the servant's table was a scruffy urchin who smelled like the stables and was currently trying to stuff two poached eggs in his mouth at the same time. She took a plate and put a few slices of toast on it, then sat across from her young guest and slid the food over to him.

His eyes were wary. "Cook said I could," he said, his mouth still full. He pushed the rest of the eggs in and chewed with some difficulty, his cheeks puffing out.

"I am the one who asked Cook to feed you. I am not here to take your breakfast away," Elizabeth said. "Your name is Billy, correct?"

He eyed her as he worked on the eggs, finally swallowing them. "Maybe." His hand snaked out to grab a piece of the toast. Elizabeth glanced around until she found a bit of butter on a butter plate near the larder. She retrieved it and set it down next to the boy, whose eyes grew wide with wonder.

"*Maybe* you are Billy?" she asked lightly. "Are you not sure?"

He shrugged. "Dunno my real name. Billy's good as any."

Elizabeth nodded, unsurprised. There were thousands of boys like this in London.

"Why did you tell Cook to feed me?" Billy asked.

"You appeared hungry," was Elizabeth's blithe response. The boy frowned. "Do you like horses?" Elizabeth asked.

He eyed her suspiciously. "'Course."

"Well, I might have work for you here, if you promise not to get up to any mischief."

He considered it. "I canna promise that, miss."

She smiled—he was being honest, at least. "No? Not even for the chance to work your way up to a groom? It would take time, of course, and a lot of work. The head groom would have to be very pleased with you, but the pay is steady, and it is more than a shilling." She hesitated before adding, "A groom can take care of the horses—even ride them out for exercise."

He reached for another slice of toast and dumped the butter on it. He chewed slower now, a thoughtful expression on his face. "Would I get to eat like this?"

Elizabeth responded gravely. "That is up to Cook, but I believe everyone here is well fed. The staff stays very busy with their duties. I need everyone to be strong enough to do their part."

He grabbed the second slice of bread. "I guess I could do it," Billy concluded.

"Good." Elizabeth stood. "Finish your meal. You shall need it."

Billy swallowed and reached for the glass of milk to his left. "Thank you, missus."

"You are welcome, Billy," she replied.

When Elizabeth arrived in the breakfast room, Richard was already there, discussing something with Fitzwilliam. She squelched her disappointment at finding him occupied.

"Good morning, Richard," she greeted him. "Fitzwilliam," she said, feeling a little shy.

They were pouring over a document, but Richard put it away when she approached. "More letters, gentlemen?" she asked, irritated that she was not being included in their conversation. She could tell from the frown on Fitzwilliam's face that it was not good news.

"Just one that was waiting at Darcy House this morning," Richard said quickly. *Too quickly. It is quite early for the post.*

She sighed and rubbed a hand over her eyes. "I am too tired to argue with you both. Please tell me what it says."

Richard glanced at his cousin, who nodded. Richard handed her the letter and moved off to the sideboard, where a cup of coffee was poured for him.

Elizabeth took the page and began to read. It was a short, terse letter. Were she not a lady, she would have given voice to the curses that rose to her lips.

There is a man who loiters on the corner near Aunt and Uncle's townhouse, Fitzwilliam, who looks a great deal like Mr. Wickham. My aunt and uncle are sure it is my imagination, but I know I have seen him. He was waiting when we arrived, and I believe he is waiting still. Please come, brother. I know Uncle will listen to you.

It was signed in a shaky hand: *Georgiana Darcy*.

After a quick breakfast, both men took their leave. Elizabeth stood outside to say her farewells. Richard gave her a quick bow and nearly leapt up into his saddle. Fitzwilliam took her hands.

"Be careful, Elizabeth," he said. "We shall see to Georgiana and then you and I need to have a conversation about the wedding."

"Shall I see you tonight for dinner, then?" she asked.

He nodded. "That is my intention." He gave her a searching look. "It was good of you to give that boy a job."

"He must earn it if he wishes to keep it," she replied. "But I am hopeful. I think he will work hard if given the chance."

"There he is now, straight to work," Fitzwilliam told her softly, indicating the back of the house. "It appears you may be right."

Elizabeth did not turn to look, but she did nod and squeeze his hands before changing the subject. "Your cousin is invited to dinner as well, provided he can behave himself."

"Then I should probably not accept your kind offer," Richard called. "Come, Darcy."

She let go of his hands and immediately felt lonely. "Will you be back in time to ride with me?"

"You plan to ride today?" His disapproval rang in the increased volume of his speech.

"I do," she responded, her voice rising to match his own. "Otherwise I shall grow quite afraid of it."

"No, Elizabeth," he said, shaking his head vigorously. "I forbid it."

"You *forbid* it?" she asked, incredulous.

"Of course. You took a serious fall yesterday and we still do not know where Wickham is hiding," he said, patronizing her as though speaking to a child. "Wait but a few days and I shall go with you."

"I will make no such promise, Fitzwilliam Darcy," she snapped. "I have Mr. Taylor and Mr. Clark, and you shall not stop me."

"Your guards would no doubt appreciate it if you did not make their job so difficult."

Elizabeth placed her hands on her hips. "You are not my husband, Mr. Darcy."

"*Yet*, Elizabeth," he told her tersely. "I am telling you not to ride today."

She scowled fiercely. "I am not your younger sister, either. See to Georgiana, Fitzwilliam."

He gave her an exasperated look. "We will speak of this later," he told her firmly.

She pursed her lips and found his eyes were drawn to them. "We shall. *After* I ride."

"Darce!" yelled Richard from near the road. "Are you coming?"

Elizabeth stormed back inside before Darcy had even turned to mount his horse. He watched her all the way inside, breaking away only when Mr. Perry closed the door. Finally, he swung up into his saddle and rode away.

Elizabeth spent the morning indoors, taking care of all the details one must when a house is newly opened. When she had seen to everything she could and had inquired as to the satisfactory progress of dinner, she dressed in a clean riding habit and a warm fur muff. She passed Mr. Perry on the way. Her eyes sought the clock. The butler gave her a single silent nod as he held the door open and she strolled out to the stables.

When she arrived at the stable-yard, one groom was brushing down the carriage horses and the other was instructing Billy on something. Billy tipped his hat to her and the grooms called out their well-wishes. The head groom, whose name was Isaac, doffed his hat and offered a quick, stiff bow.

He gestured to the stable. "You are here to see Kensington?"

"I am," she replied.

He replaced his hat and led her in. Kensington stamped one hoof on the ground when she heard her mistress's voice. Elizabeth reached over the gate to rub the mare's neck and received a snort in reply. Elizabeth unfurled a fist to reveal two small pieces of sugar, and Kensington took them from her hand immediately.

Isaac shifted from one foot to another, his posture uneasy, his words halting. "Now that I have you here, miss, I was meaning to ask whether we might be expectin' more horses to arrive." He motioned to the empty stalls and raised his eyebrows. "I fear I am not earning my pay."

She gave him a small smile. "I believe we will, Isaac, but how many I cannot say. I will send word as soon as I know."

"Very good, miss. Shall I lead Kensington out and saddle her up for you?"

Elizabeth patted the horse a few more times, pensive, and then nodded. She watched as Isaac led Kensington away, then closed the gate on the stall before turning to follow them.

And found herself face-to-face with the man in her drawing.

"Mr. Wickham," she said quietly. The man was leaning on the post of a stall between her and the door through which she had entered, his weight all on his left leg. "Did you sleep here?"

He smiled at her, a lascivious expression that only made her angry.

"No," he said, and took a halting step towards her. "Your greenhouses are much warmer."

"Ah," she said, nodding and stepping back. *I ought to have thought of that.* "It *is* cold today, is it not?" She held up her muff. "I understand why the greenhouses were more comfortable last evening."

Mr. Wickham gave her a curious look and took another step. "You wish to speak of the weather?"

"I have many things I wish to discuss with you," she replied, matching his step forward with another back. *There are six sets of stalls behind me to the rear door.* "Beginning with why you sent my aunt that letter and then shot at my cousin's carriage."

He chortled, a hollow sound that sent cold chills up and down her spine. "I wanted that sickly old bat terrified. I seem to have succeeded, judging by her looks yesterday." He smiled again, a nauseous, pained grimace.

A hot fury flared in her chest and she stopped moving.

"Besides, judging from your very descriptive and hopelessly naïve letters to your beloved aunt, Darcy is in love with you, as much as he is capable of it. Stupid prig. I have you all dancing to my tune, now—and it is all funded by the sale of Darcy heirlooms." Wickham leaned forward and hissed, "Will he save Georgiana or the woman he says he loves?" He sneered. "Does he love you more than his sister?" He waved his hand around the empty stable. "It appears not." He reached into his waistband, under his coat. "Shall we go, Miss Russell?"

Elizabeth pulled the muff up her arm to reveal a small pistol in her hand aimed at his chest. "I think not," she replied.

He put his hands up, palms out, but kept talking. "Do you even know how that toy works?" he scoffed, taking another limping step forward.

"Come any closer and you shall have your answer," Elizabeth assured him. She took two large steps back.

"I presume that means that you do not," he replied, as he continued to move towards her.

Five stalls.

"You question *my* skill?" she goaded him as she darted back. *Quick, now.* "I cannot possibly be a worse shot than you."

Four stalls.

Wickham lunged.

No sooner had Elizabeth cleared the fourth stall then Fitzwilliam and Richard exploded out in front of her as though they had been shot from a cannon, one from the right stall, the other from the left. Before she could do anything more than remove her finger from the trigger of her pistol and lower her arm, Wickham was on the ground, and Richard had his weapon. As soon as Richard rocked back and his heels and stood, Fitzwilliam hauled Wickham up from the floor by his lapels and forced him backwards into one of the stalls, slamming his enemy's back against the wall, his forearm pressing into the man's throat. Wickham continued to thrash, trying to hit Fitzwilliam and escape. Richard gave Wickham's injured leg a hard kick, eliciting a pained cry.

Elizabeth was shocked by the swiftness with which the men had moved. *I was supposed to back up much faster,* she thought, concealing her trembling hands in her muff. *I would not make a good soldier.* She squared her shoulders. She would not be afraid. She would not.

"Come, now, Mr. Wickham," Elizabeth chided, "did you truly believe you could fool the three people who know Georgiana Darcy best?"

❧

Richard maintained a steady stream of taunting words that faded in and out of Darcy's hearing. "Terrible attempt to forge a letter from a girl" gave way to "street rats are loyal to coin, not employers." There might have been something about Billy telling Wickham the men were leaving and placing him to overhear the argument between Elizabeth and himself. He did note that Richard was pulling Wickham's arms behind him and tying them together tightly.

His vision narrowed to Wickham's thin, flushed face. There was no contrition there, not even for being caught at last. No, there was only a contorted sort of frustration and fury as he struggled like a bug on a pin, face red, arms bound, derision on his lips and burning vulgarities falling from his mouth. The instant Richard finished his task, Darcy shifted his hold, grabbing Wickham by the waist of his trousers, placing his other hand directly on Wickham's throat, and shoving the man roughly up the splintered, wooden wall until his boots barely touched the dirt floor. He heard choking noises replace the curses. *Better.*

"Not that we would avoid a terrific quarrel were he ever to speak to me in such a way," Elizabeth was saying with a brittle kind of humor. *That* Darcy heard clearly, along with the very small tremor in her voice. She had been so composed he had *almost* believed she was not afraid. She might have fooled his cousin and even Wickham, but she could not fool him. *I will kill Richard for this insane plan.* Elizabeth had agreed to it only because his cousin had spoken to her alone.

It had taken a few minutes before he had calmed enough to realize that the missive was *not* from Georgiana. It had been a credible forgery, but the plea had been rather tearful. Obviously, neither Mrs. Younge nor Wickham had understood his sister. *Tearful* was not the way she would have written, even at such a moment. Besides, he had already alerted his uncle. Any threat Georgiana felt would have been taken seriously. When Elizabeth had returned the letter, he had perused it again, attempting to discern its purpose. Perhaps Wickham intended to take the money and run while they chased a false trail to retrieve Georgiana? Darcy had only been pulled from his thoughts when Richard called Billy in from the kitchen. Elizabeth had already agreed to his cousin's plan. He had agreed to use the boy to flush Wickham out, hoping Elizabeth would not need to participate, but the man was slippery as an eel—her presence had been required to make him reveal himself.

As much as Darcy hated to admit it, the plan had worked. Wickham had not told them everything, but he had said enough. The admission of his thefts from Darcy House were enough to see the man hang, though he was more likely to be transported. But he had boasted about the letter that had sent Mrs. Russell to her bed as well as taking the shot at the duke's carriage. Bedford would have something to say about that. Not that the duke would be doing much talking.

Darcy wanted nothing more than to crush the villain's windpipe, wanted it badly, could imagine all the life draining from the reprobate before him. He felt a dark sort of joy as he pressed his forearm forward.

Then he felt one small, familiar hand on his arm and the darkness dissipated. Not the desire—the desire to end Wickham's life remained. But he brought those less noble feelings under a tenuous sort of regulation. He slackened the pressure on the man's throat and allowed him to collapse to the ground, wheezing and choking.

"Please leave, Elizabeth," he growled.

"Fitzwilliam?" she asked, and he *felt* her apprehension. He did not move his eyes from Wickham to her, however, lest he lose his anger. He did not wish to lose his anger.

185

"I will not kill him, Elizabeth," he promised, though the words were difficult to say. "But I shall not leave him unmarked. I would rather you not be here for that."

Her hand remained.

"Perhaps you could write your cousins and let them know where they can pick up the pieces," Richard added.

Elizabeth did not reply, but she did turn to leave, slipping past them all. Darcy saw her glance back once, nervously, before disappearing into the winter sunshine.

Once Elizabeth was away, the head groomsman filled the doorway, blocking most of the light. "Shall I send Taylor and Clark in, sir?" he asked, boisterous and menacing all at once. "They be rather keen to join in."

Darcy did not reply. He was too busy enjoying the way Wickham's face had paled. "This is just the beginning, Wickham," he said. "For once we are finished with you, we shall turn you over to the duke." He smiled. "He is seriously displeased."

In the end, it was Richard who answered Isaac. "Send them on in," he said, exultant. He rubbed his hands together. "The more the merrier."

※

"It was terribly foolish, Lizzy," Aunt Olivia rebuked her. "I can see why you did not inform me earlier. Why not just have the boys take him up immediately?"

"You will be pleased to know that Fitzwilliam objected strenuously," Elizabeth replied, abashed. "However, Richard believed Mr. Wickham would be only too happy to brag to me if he believed he had succeeded." She fussed with her aunt's bedclothes, straightening them and tucking them around the older woman's legs. "I was very well protected."

"I am sure the men are perfectly capable of getting him to confess," her aunt replied, pulling the blanket out again.

Elizabeth frowned as she poured out the tea. "And I am sure we now know he was confessing the truth of his actions rather than yielding to torture." She handed her aunt a cup. "You know how John would have handled this."

Olivia pursed her lips but nodded.

"I am sorry for your anxiety, Aunt Olivia, but truly, I was always safe." She took up her own cup with a steady hand. She had recovered quickly, and she knew why. "Fitzwilliam would never allow me to be hurt." She bit her bottom lip and gave her aunt a pleading look. "You cannot tell me you would have done differently."

Aunt Olivia harrumphed. "*I* am an excellent shot."

Elizabeth smiled. "Did you tell the Archbishop that in your interview?"

Aunt Olivia just gazed sadly at her. "No, dear. It did not take many words to convince him that there were extenuating circumstances surrounding your wedding."

Elizabeth ignored Aunt Olivia's response. Pretended it did not exist, that there was no reason for a special license other than for John to show off.

She withdrew from the conversation to think about Fitzwilliam. She had been able to feel the trembling rage in his arm when she touched it. She trusted that he would keep his promise not to kill Mr. Wickham, but she had wanted that promise more for Fitzwilliam's sake than Mr. Wickham's. She felt no compassion for the man who had threatened her aunt and made her ill; such implacability was a foreign feeling, but she could not regret it.

As a peer, John had the right to apply for a special license—but he wielded influence that went far beyond that. He might use his power to discreetly dispose of Mr. Wickham, and the law would never touch him. Elizabeth did not believe John would kill the man any more than Fitzwilliam would. It was not his way. But placing him in a position that would make the man miserable, would make him suffer—that he would only be too willing to do. An idea occurred to her, and for the first time since breakfast, she smiled.

When the men returned to the house several hours later, they repaired upstairs to refresh themselves. Elizabeth gave orders for their care, and listened, impatiently, to their low voices and high spirits.

I do not understand men, she thought, then sighed to herself. Dinner was in an hour. She would go upstairs to change and insist on an accounting when she met them at the table.

When the men did come down, she was surprised to see that Francis was with them. She motioned to a maid, and with a quick nod at her cousin, the girl scurried away to set another place at the table.

"Francis," she said, confused, "what are *you* doing here?"

He laughed and slapped Richard on the shoulder. "I came in response to your message, Lizzy. I could not allow these scapegraces to have all the fun."

Fun? "Where is Mr. Wickham now?" she asked. She did not inquire *how* he was.

"My men have him out in the stables, Lizzy," Francis said, taking her hand and kissing it. "Darcy asked me back to dine, and I have indeed worked up a bit of an appetite. You do not mind, I hope?"

"Of course I do, Francis," she replied pertly. "You always eat more than your share."

He grinned at her. "You had better get the food on your plate expeditiously tonight, cousin—I am not the only hungry gentleman who dines with you tonight." He offered her his arm, and she took it, unhappy that he had anticipated Mr. Darcy. She huffed at his self-satisfied grin.

"I made sure to request another of Mrs. Thistlewaite's dishes tonight, Mr. Darcy," she said as they all sat, using his formal name in deference to their company. "I know you and Mr. Fitzwilliam both enjoyed the roasted partridge you had at Netherfield."

Richard's eyes lit up. "A meal fit for royalty," he told Francis.

The meal continued without conversation other than the sounds of gratification that occasionally erupted from one man or another. Elizabeth ate the food on her plate without tasting it. She tried to wait until one of the men introduced the subject, but they were more interested in filling their stomachs than satisfying her curiosity. Finally, she put her utensils down and called them to attention.

"I should like to know what happened after I left, Mr. Darcy," she said plainly. He gazed at her, reluctant, and she said, exasperated, "I do not need the . . . details. I simply wish to discuss the plans for Mr. Wickham's removal."

"Before we get to that," Francis interrupted, swallowing a final bite of partridge and reaching for another piece of bread, "I should like a further accounting of how the man was caught." He tossed the bread on his plate and raised his eyebrows at Elizabeth. "I know about your part in this. But how did you know he would be in the stables?"

"Wickham somehow believed that his confederates could not be used against him," her betrothed said, his expression impassive. "But Elizabeth made a friend of the boy this morning and he agreed to put a word in Wickham's ear." He grinned. "For a price, of course." He toyed with his fork. "We were fairly sure Wickham was listening to our argument about Elizabeth riding without me today." He shook his head. "We had hoped to catch him out then, but he did not reveal himself."

"He is best cowering somewhere on his belly," Richard interjected.

"So," her intended continued, "we were forced to continue with the second plan, which was to draw him into the stables. Not long before Elizabeth came outside again, the grooms made themselves busy elsewhere and Billy waved Wickham inside." He stabbed at his food with his fork. "I wish we had thought to check the greenhouses last night."

Richard shook his head. "Staying in the greenhouse was due more to his leg wound than any cunning on his part. He thought to use Elizabeth's horse when he took her—without the horse, he was stranded. He got away from Taylor, but it took everything out of him."

"Not quite," Francis murmured, "but it has now." Richard grinned.

"I believe we mentioned the letter purporting to be from Georgiana," Fitzwilliam said. "Richard and I left the house earlier, appearing to be heading for Matlock House, and then doubled back."

"You left Elizabeth standing alone outside?" Francis asked sharply.

"No," he said with a shake of his dark head. "I waited until she was inside."

Francis grunted and reached for more partridge.

Richard picked up the story. "Once we knew Wickham was near, we snuck into the stables from the other end but had to duck into our stalls more quickly than we had hoped." He addressed Elizabeth. "Wickham popped up to have a look right before you entered." He reached for his wine. "The . . ." he bit off what he was about to say. "The *man* was only too happy to boast about his crimes once he thought he had her alone."

"It is just like him to play one hand too many," Fitzwilliam said grimly. "He was wounded far worse than Taylor. At the least he ought to have dropped from sight until he healed." He addressed Elizabeth directly. "But he had drawn too much attention to linger in London and was too close to his goal." His eyes burned into hers. "He admitted he meant to take you for ransom." Francis uttered a surprised protest that they had broached this topic before his cousin, but Elizabeth rewarded her betrothed with a smile. *He respects me enough to be honest.*

"I promised I would tell you these things," he told Elizabeth. "You must promise to tell me if they are too much to bear."

Elizabeth shook her head. "You mentioned this possibility earlier, and I had already concluded that he meant to take me. It is good to know that at least my judgment has not failed me." She gave him a half-hearted smile.

He nodded. "Tavistock will take Wickham to Bedford tonight. I cannot imagine His Grace will be lenient."

"Thank you for telling me," Elizabeth said, suspecting that she had not been told all but willing, now, to let it drop. She addressed Francis. "I have a suggestion to make."

Darcy and Richard saw Tavistock off, the carriage rumbling away in the dark with six outriders. Wickham had been tossed onto the carriage floor as limp as a dish rag, bound hand and foot. Four men, including Tavistock, climbed into the carriage and sat on the benches. Darcy caught a glimpse of Tavistock placing his boot on Wickham's head just before the door closed.

Once the coach was gone and it grew quiet, Richard grasped Darcy's shoulder. "Well done today, Darce," he said.

Darcy said nothing, just turned and plowed his fist straight into Richard's gut. His cousin bent over double with a "whoosh," and sank to his knees in the dirt.

"Do not *ever* use Elizabeth in one of your schemes again, cousin," he said menacingly.

Richard coughed and put one palm on the ground. "You hit like a woman."

Darcy wheeled around to return to the house. Behind him, he heard Richard forcing himself to his feet, and an admiring voice say, "A *large* woman."

Darcy searched the drawing room, the parlor, and the dining room before he saw Mr. Perry in the hall. The butler acknowledged him and said, "I believe Miss Russell is in the library, sir."

"Thank you," he said, already walking to the room.

There was a fire in the hearth and the candles in the sconces were all lit, but Elizabeth was sitting in the coldest, darkest part of the room near the back window. She was leaning against one large wing of a leather armchair, likely to keep the worst of the pressure off her back. Her legs were drawn up beneath her.

"Elizabeth," he said with a sigh. She appeared so small, so miserable. *One punch was not enough,* he thought, and began to contemplate other ways to get Richard alone.

She sat up at the sound of his voice, dabbing at her cheeks with the corner of a handkerchief. He took a dozen long strides to reach her, then gently took the cloth to wipe her tears himself.

"I am so sorry, Elizabeth," he told her, his chest tight with remorse. "God, I am so sorry."

But it was not her confrontation with Wickham that was causing her grief.

"Fitzwilliam," she said between half-disguised sobs. "I am not ready to say goodbye."

CHAPTER ELEVEN

December 9, 1811

Darcy watched Elizabeth bounce up and down as the Bennet carriage approached the house. He smiled down at her, his heart full. Given the need to deal with Wickham, they had not wed by the end of the week, but now it was Monday, and her family was arriving for the ceremony on Tuesday. She would be his, truly his, tomorrow.

Elizabeth had spent all her tears and was no longer denying her impending loss. Darcy believed, however, that she was in no way reconciled to it. Once they were wed, he would be allowed to properly comfort her when the time arrived. For now, they would celebrate.

As Darcy stood observing, a seemingly inexhaustible number of Bennets tripped happily down the steps from their small carriage. Mr. Bennet alighted first and turned to hand down his wife, who regarded the house uncertainly. Next was Miss Bennet, smiling, as usual, then Miss Mary. Both young women came to Elizabeth immediately and folded her into an embrace. He stepped back to allow their greeting and Elizabeth smiled brightly at him.

Darcy recalled Elizabeth's comment about not being able to fit eight people in their coach for the Netherfield ball, so he was sure they were at the end when he saw Miss Kitty, then Miss Lydia, emerge into the daylight. His eyes darted back to the coach when there was more movement. Astonishingly, Cleopatra Bingley was exiting, wearing a wide-brimmed straw bonnet trimmed with a brown ribbon and adorned with at least ten green and yellow feathers gathered together in a bunch on one side. He blinked. How did *that* monstrosity fit in a coach strained at six? *And where is Bingley?*

His uncle and aunt had arrived in London on Saturday with Georgiana. He was anxious to see his sister, but rather suspected she was more anxious to see his betrothed. Georgiana's letter to Elizabeth, arriving Saturday evening, expressed her approbation of the match in no less than four pages of tightly scripted exclamations. He smiled, recalling how it had made Elizabeth beam.

His ruminations were interrupted when one last figure made its way deliberately out of the Bennet equipage. *Please do not let that be Miss Bingley,* he pleaded silently. It was not. Appearing on the steps, a little pale and slightly better-fed than he recalled, was his cousin, Anne de Bourgh. Mr. Bennet handed her down and went to join his wife.

Darcy was shocked. *What the blazes?* "Anne?" he called, heading towards her. "What are *you* doing here?"

She gave him an owlish look. "I am here to stop your wedding, of course."

That brought him up short. He shook his head to clear the shock. "What . . ."

Behind him, Elizabeth began to giggle, and Anne's pale face was graced with a thin smile. "In truth, cousin," she said coyly, "I am here to make absolutely certain the wedding goes ahead as planned." She made a show of looking behind her and lowering her voice. "But do not tell my mother. She has sent me here to object."

"But you are here with the Bennets," he replied, confused.

Anne now began to laugh. "I have ridden from Hertfordshire for your wedding squashed next to a woman who keeps an aviary in her traveling bag, and you are stunned by *my* appearance?" She strolled over to his side, every move delicate, and hooked her arm through his. "Someone had to go retrieve my mother and send her back to Kent— you *know* she would have remained at Netherfield ranting and raving for weeks before Mr. Bingley would even *begin* to think about asking her to leave. She did depart, but only with the promise that I would make trouble for you." She clasped his arm. "Have I succeeded?"

He laughed warmly. "You are a treasure, Annie," he told her, rubbing the back of his neck. "Thank you for coming."

"Thank your betrothed, cousin," she responded gaily, releasing him to take Elizabeth by both hands. Anne leaned in to bestow a kiss on each of Elizabeth's cheeks. "When I asked her sister Jane to write and inquire whether I would be welcome, Elizabeth insisted on my presence." She gazed at Elizabeth for a second. "I am very happy to make your acquaintance at last, Elizabeth. I have heard so much about you from your sisters."

"I am so pleased you could be with us, Anne," Elizabeth replied cheerfully. She whirled to face Darcy. "Are you *very* surprised, Fitzwilliam?"

"Stunned," he admitted weakly, and both women laughed.

"Come inside, everyone," Elizabeth called. "Come warm yourselves by the fire."

Before they followed Elizabeth indoors, Anne turned to Darcy, her eyes dancing with mirth. "Should you like to tell my mother about Elizabeth's family and what I imagine is her fortune, cousin, or may I?"

Darcy chuckled, still recovering from the surprise of her presence. "You more than anyone deserve to tell her, Annie, if you wish."

"Oh, *thank you*, Fitzwilliam," Anne said, and her face glowed with gratification. "I do. I truly do."

※

Darcy followed Elizabeth's father inside and stood in a corner with his back to the wall. "Frightened, my boy?" the older man said with a smirk.

"We are vastly outnumbered, sir," Darcy replied, straight-faced. "It is a tactical position."

"Well said, son," Bennet replied lightly. He watched the activity in the room before inquiring, "Have you anything to add to the information in Lizzy's letter?"

"Is it wise to have the conversation here?" Darcy asked, uncomfortable. His eyes, as always, found Elizabeth, who was speaking with Bingley's aunt. It warmed his heart to see her ease with other people, even those who might be considered, well, odd. She was always kind, had even been kind enough to overlook his insult at the assembly. *Thank God for that.* Now if he could only convince her to burn those drawings . . .

"Almost no place better," Bennet retorted. "We are in a room full of women who are anticipating a wedding. We shall be completely ignored."

Darcy had to agree—they had been left entirely to their own devices. "Very well. A few more pieces of the puzzle did come to light. The duke's footman, Harry Sykes?"

"Yes?"

"Evidently, the man took Wickham's example to heart. He was able to forge Wickham's signature and abscond from Coutt's with nearly all of Wickham's savings. I believe the discovery of this was what made Wickham so desparate in the end."

Bennet sounded amused. "Hoist with his own petard."

Darcy shrugged. "Indeed." He did not speak again until Bennet prompted him.

"So quiet still? Must I ask if there was anything else?"

Darcy shifted his feet. "Only that Mrs. Younge wrote the final letter and was arrested in consequence. It was a passable forgery, truth be told, but it was certainly not as well done as the one supposedly from my father. Because he was wounded, Wickham had no way to return to check the work before the letter was sent. My cousin believes Mrs. Younge had just returned from posting it when he arrived to speak with her."

"Not the brightest of criminal minds, in the end."

"Had he merely remained a thief, he would have done better," Darcy had to admit. "Instead, he allowed his anger to rule him. Angry men are seldom wise."

They stood quietly, then. Darcy was watching Elizabeth conversing with Mrs. Bingley and Miss Lydia when Richard and Bingley appeared with Mr. Perry.

"Ah," Bennet said drily. "Reinforcements."

The home's most formal drawing room was a bit old-fashioned. It was not precisely to Elizabeth's taste, but she thought the room pretty enough. Aunt Olivia had not bothered to do much here other than have a painter touch up the chinoiserie. The walls were adorned with delicate trees in soft blues and creams, silhouettes of birds resting on the branches. Mrs. Bingley was busily arranging a collection of her stuffed birds on a work table near one of the large windows in the front drawing room. Elizabeth walked over to see what she was doing.

"Elizabeth," the elderly lady preened, "will the wedding be held here?" She lowered her voice. "What an exquisite room."

Elizabeth touched a bird with a green head, red body, and black and white tail. "Mrs. Bingley, is this a masked trogon? From South America?"

The older woman's face shone with delight. "You know it?"

Elizabeth nodded, recalling a book in her father's library. "I have seen pictures. It is a beautiful bird."

"Oh, it is," Mrs. Bingley cooed. "Some ladies keep them as pets, but I ask for them when they pass and have them stuffed. They are ever so exotic." She touched each on its head as she spoke its name: "Rufus-collared kingfisher, oriental dwarf kingfisher, they are from the Orient, and would appear quite to advantage in this room." She nodded at the wall. "Those birds look like pheasant-tailed jacana. They are from India."

Lydia edged her way to the table to listen as Mrs. Bingley continued.

"This is the regent bowerbird, from Australia, where the convicts go. As is the gouldian finch. And this," she said with a fond smile, "this is the regal sunbird." She was nearly reverent. "He is from Africa!"

Elizabeth smiled. Mrs. Bingley knew a little something about her birds. That was an interesting revelation.

"Have you been any of these places?" Elizabeth asked.

"No," Mrs. Bingley said with a sigh. "My late husband always promised we would travel the world, but business, you see . . . and I am no longer young enough for such adventures. But I can just imagine seeing these birds flying in their own homes. It must be extraordinary."

Lydia asked a few questions about the birds as Elizabeth gazed around the room. Fitzwilliam was standing with her father and they were speaking together, Mr. Bennet's eyes dancing with mirth and her intended's shoulders lifting in a shrug.

"Perhaps I could hide one in Miss Bingley's reticule, Lizzy," Lydia whispered in her ear. "Would that not be a fine joke?"

"It is not polite to torment her, Lydia," Elizabeth warned her sister, though she personally felt it a grand idea. "Besides, she is rather clever— she might do something to you in return."

Lydia considered that for a moment. "I do not think she is as clever as she believes, Lizzy. She thought Mr. Darcy was in love with her! I am glad she has gone visiting."

"Miss Bingley perhaps hoped for an offer," Elizabeth corrected Lydia. "It is not the same as believing him in love."

"What is the point of marrying if not for love?" Lydia asked. "I shall not marry without it. Not when you and Jane are marrying men who clearly adore you." She twisted her hands together before adding, "I deserve such a man, do I not?" She frowned. "I should not like it if my husband teased me before my children, Lizzy. Papa thinks Mama does not notice, but she does."

Elizabeth glanced quickly at her father and patted her sister's hand. "All of us have faults, Lydia. Do not worry. You have plenty of time to decide upon the kind of man you prefer as a husband. There is no rush."

Mr. Perry opened the door. "Mr. Fitzwilliam and Mr. Bingley," he intoned.

Oh, I wondered where Mr. Bingley had taken himself to, she thought. *He must have gone to collect Richard.*

"Mr. Bingley!" Mrs. Bennet called, entirely ignoring Richard. "You have come at last!"

Jane blushed, but Mr. Bingley moved to join her directly, and soon the three were chatting amiably, with only occasional bursts of nervous glee from her mother. Kitty joined them, but Mary wandered over to Elizabeth and Lydia, who had left Mrs. Bingley to the arrangement of her display.

Mr. Bennet excused himself from the men and made his way to Elizabeth. "Is Aunt Olivia upstairs?" he asked, as Mary began a conversation with Mrs. Bingley.

Elizabeth nodded. "She is trying to rest so that she can remain for both the ceremony and breakfast tomorrow."

"Do you think she would be willing to see me?" he asked, his eyelids drooping and the corners of his mouth tugging down.

She smiled, though it hurt. "Just ask her maid if she is awake. I think she would be quite pleased for a visit."

He stepped away but stopped and turned.

"I nearly forgot," he said. "You wrote me, but you never mentioned what had been done with Mr. Wickham."

Elizabeth shifted her feet. "He has been . . . *impressed*, I believe is the term. John paid the Navy to take him, as he is so inexperienced. He tells me Mr. Wickham is currently sailing to join the West Africa Squadron."

"Hmm," her father replied with a sly smile. "Forced to swab decks and suppress the slave trade. An elegant solution and yet I doubt it was the duke's."

When she answered, there was satisfaction in her tone. "I thought that as he was so very concerned about Uncle Phillip's dealings with the institution that he might like to be involved in its prohibition himself."

Her father said only, "Indeed," but there was humor in the word. He made his way out of the room.

Fitzwilliam approached her shortly after, Richard in tow. She took her intended's arm and leaned against him but addressed herself to his cousin. "Richard, have you spoken with Georgiana?"

He smiled. "I have. She was a bit upset she was not to see you today."

"Oh," Elizabeth said, disappointed. "Why ever not?"

"Because, my dear Miss Russell," he replied, offering an exaggerated bow, "my mother has declared that you already have a great deal of company and should not be imposed upon."

"Oh, Georgiana is never an imposition," Elizabeth scoffed. "She should have been here to meet my sisters."

"Which I told my mother, along with delivering your invitation to dinner," he explained. "They have accepted and will be here a little later."

"Oh, wonderful!" Elizabeth exclaimed. "I cannot wait to see her!"

"What shall we do while we wait?" Richard asked, waggling his eyebrows.

Damn Richard, Darcy thought as he clapped his gloved hands together to force some warmth back into his fingers. *His ideas are terrible, yet somehow he is always able to get them implemented.*

Mr. Bennet might have quashed the notion, but he was still upstairs with Mrs. Russell. Mrs. Bennet had been too engrossed with Bingley's aunt to do aught but wave them off. Richard always had been good at using those fleeting moments of adult inattention as a child, and his skill had only improved. He had been a master in the past sen'night. Which is why they now all found themselves out of doors in the very cold December weather, the day before Darcy's wedding, teaching the women how to shoot.

Darcy had assisted his betrothed, who was now encouraging each of her sisters. Elizabeth had received instruction before, but she was an indifferent student, which did not bother Darcy in the least. She could hit a target up close—as they would always travel together, and he planned to hire a small army to protect her, it was more than adequate.

Richard was demonstrating a stance for Lydia when Jane turned to Elizabeth. "Have you heard, Lizzy, that Charlotte Lucas is to wed?"

"No," Elizabeth replied, and Darcy wondered how such a thing could have come about in less than a fortnight before begrudgingly noting that not only his engagement, but his wedding would occur in little more than the same amount of time. "I had no idea. Who is her intended?"

Jane pressed her lips together when Lydia snorted, and Richard had to pause. "She is to marry our cousin, Mr. Collins."

There was an astonished silence from those of their party who had not been aware.

"Mr. Collins?" Elizabeth repeated, her expression indicating her disbelief. "Clever Charlotte Lucas is to wed Mr. Collins?"

"Not so *very* clever," Kitty said softly, sending Lydia into silent but shoulder-shaking laughs.

"I suppose I did not know Charlotte so well as you, Jane," Elizabeth said slowly. "She did tell me once that she would be happy to know as little as possible of the defects of her marriage partner." She turned to Darcy, "Truly, I thought she was in jest."

"The man lit up a curtain in front of her, Elizabeth," Darcy said, shaking his head. "I am afraid she *has* seen the defects in her partner and has chosen to ignore them." *What a life she has chosen.*

"Charlotte *is* clever, Lizzy," Jane admonished her. "Mr. Collins is awkward, and he may not be the cleverest of men, but he is neither wholly without wit, nor is he vicious." She took a seat on a wide stump. "Perhaps at seven-and-twenty Charlotte feels it would be imprudent to turn away an eligible offer." She brushed off her hands. "I must say, I believe Charlotte will make an excellent mistress for Longbourn."

Elizabeth had not considered that, but had to agree. "Perhaps Papa should teach *Charlotte* how to run the estate. She would certainly have a better chance at preserving his work, and she would be able to manage Mr. Collins." She pursed her lips. "I wish her luck. It is not an inconsiderable task she has accepted."

Darcy silently agreed.

Lydia turned back to Richard and eventually managed to shoot, hitting the edge of a paper target. Jane took her turn, but she did not like the loud report nor the recoil and returned to Bingley. Kitty would not even make the attempt—she shook her head and backed away.

"Well, Miss Mary?" Richard asked jovially. "Would you like to learn?"

Mary had watched them all without comment; now she tugged thoughtfully on one lock of her hair and nodded. She stepped up to Richard and listened to him carefully. Then she stood in the stance he showed her, grasped the weapon with both hands, steadied it—and shot a bullet through the center of the paper circle fifteen feet away.

Darcy did not react outwardly, but Elizabeth's eyes opened wide. "Do that again, Mary," she insisted. "Can you do that again?"

Mary cocked her head to the side. "I do not know," she admitted.

Richard was delighted. He trotted out to the target to move it a little farther away. "It is too far, Richard," Darcy called.

Miss Mary pursed her lips. "I am willing to try, Mr. Darcy."

Richard returned, showing Mary how to reload the pistol. When it was ready, she again took up the correct stance, held the weapon with both hands, and pulled the trigger.

A small hole appeared in the paper a half-inch above the first. They all turned to look at Mary, who ignored them and handed the pistol back to a smiling Richard.

"That confirms it," Elizabeth declared proudly. "Mary rides with me."

Elizabeth dressed early for dinner, as she expected the party from Matlock to arrive before they would normally come down. She was wild to see Georgiana. It had been two years—more—since they had been in one another's company, and their letters had been waylaid since the summer. She had been extraordinarily busy but thought that Georgie had likely been rather dull in the country with no girls close in age with whom to speak. Still, she would be here soon and all of that would be forgotten.

Fitzwilliam was waiting for her at the bottom of the stairs. "You look beautiful, Elizabeth," he said with that tiny smile she loved. "I do not believe I have seen that gown before."

She was wearing a deep rose gown with a scalloped hem, a single strand of pearls around her neck and the matching ear-drops, simple but elegant. "That is because I did not take it to Longbourn," she informed him. "I sent most of my best gowns ahead so as not to stand out."

He shook his head. "It is not the gown that makes you stand out, Elizabeth."

"Oh," she said with a laugh and a blush, "you may continue to flatter me all you wish, Mr. Darcy. I quite enjoy your compliments."

"I try," he said wryly, in imitation of her cousin from Kent, "to give them as unstudied an air as possible."

She met his eyes. "I am looking forward to being married to you, Mr. Darcy."

His smile was uncharacteristically broad. "I am anticipating that moment as well, Miss Russell." He laid his free hand over hers where it rested on his arm. "Shall we?"

Just as they arrived in the front hall, a blur of white threw itself at Elizabeth. Darcy was forced to grab her before she tumbled to the floor.

"Georgie!" Elizabeth laughed, tossing her arms around her friend. "I believe you have missed me!"

"Good gracious, Georgiana Darcy," a middle-aged woman fussed from the doorway. "You are not a child to greet people in such a way."

"Yes, Aunt," Georgiana said, her tone contrite, but her face all that was merry. She hugged Elizabeth tightly. "My apologies, Elizabeth, brother." She released Elizabeth long enough to embrace Darcy.

"Of the two of us, Georgiana," he said, amused, "I believe I could withstand that sort of welcome more easily than Elizabeth."

"But it has been so *long*, brother!" she protested, before turning back to Elizabeth. "Oh, Lizzy!" Georgiana crowed. "You are truly to be my sister! It is too delightful to be expressed in words—and I know, for I have tried!" She clasped her hands together. "I am to stay the night with all your sisters," she announced, her joy readily apparent.

"You know, Georgie," Elizabeth replied, her expression one Darcy identified as *saucy*—"we have not been able to practice our teasing in an age. When we are all together at Pemberley, we shall have to sharpen our wit on your brother. I mean to vex him a great deal."

Georgiana laughed, and Darcy forced himself to frown. "I beg your pardon, Miss Russell, but you *already* vex me a great deal." He turned to Georgiana. "*Et tu*, Georgiana? You have been here less than two minutes, and already you are taking up arms against me, your favorite brother?"

"My *least* favorite brother," Georgiana teased, and pretended to consider the idea. "Oh, wait, my *only* brother."

Darcy cast his eyes heavenward. "I believe you two have no need for additional practice. Now, I believe our aunt and uncle have requested an introduction." He motioned to the Matlocks.

Georgiana's hand flew to her mouth and she stepped back. "Oh, Lizzy, forgive me. Uncle, Aunt." She turned to her relations, both well-dressed and attractive. Lord Matlock was built solidly, like his second son, and Lady Matlock was—Elizabeth searched for the word—*stately*. "Please allow me to introduce Miss Elizabeth Russell of Weymouth House in Yorkshire. Miss Russell has been my very dear friend since I was all of six years old. Elizabeth, these are Lord and Lady Matlock, Richard's parents and my uncle and aunt."

"Delighted, Miss Russell," the earl said, as Elizabeth curtsied. "We have waited a long time to meet you in person."

"Thank you, Lord Matlock," Elizabeth replied.

"Oh, you must call me uncle, and my beautiful wife"—here Lady Matlock gave her husband an appreciative glance—"aunt, as Georgiana does." His gaze was warm. "We shall be family in less than a day, my dear."

"I thank you, uncle," Elizabeth replied, and gave him a brilliant smile. She turned to Lady Matlock. "Aunt. I am Elizabeth, or Lizzy."

"You are a dear girl," the countess said approvingly, her eyes alight with interest. "I cannot tell you how pleased we are that Fitzwilliam is settling down at last." She took Elizabeth's arm and began to walk her towards the drawing room. "Now we just have to work on Richard. Is he within?"

❧

Elizabeth opened her eyes to the promise of sunlight and a cold chamber. She heard servants in the hall—perhaps she could ring for someone to build the fire as she would sleep no more this morning. She rose to pull the bell and wrapped a dressing gown around her as she sat down at her vanity.

"Today," she told the glass, "today you wed."

Elizabeth had never thought much about marrying; even today, it was not the decorations or the finery or the wedding breakfast that set her heart racing, but thoughts of her intended. Being alone, truly alone, with Fitzwilliam Darcy. "To learn all the Darcy secrets," she teased her reflection, then, more shyly, "I am all anticipation."

It was only a half-hour later, with the sun filtering weakly through the windows, that her sisters began to appear. Jane and Georgiana were first, followed by a sleepy Mary, who rubbed her eyes as she entered. They all had tea together in her room before they decided to send the maid away and prepare Elizabeth's hair themselves.

"I am trusting you both," Elizabeth warned, "not to create a pyramid or a feathered nightmare." She paused. "With all respect to Mrs. Bingley, of course."

Jane and Georgiana took great delight in deciding upon a style and weaving Elizabeth's thick waves into a complicated chignon with soft curls framing her face. They would not be going out of doors so there was no need for a bonnet, and Georgiana suggested a bandeau instead. Elizabeth was forced to remain seated, Georgiana's hand holding the style in place while she pinned Elizabeth's hair. Elizabeth explained where to search, and Jane soon selected a white bandeau decorated with tiny, light blue glass beads.

"Oh," breathed Georgiana. "It is lovely against your dark hair, Lizzy."

Elizabeth had chosen a white satin gown she favored but had never worn. *I shall wear stronger colors when I am married*, she thought, and then smiled to herself. *Married. To Fitzwilliam.* The gown itself was embellished with blue and green embroidery at the hem and waist in crescent patterns that reminded Elizabeth of ocean waves. When her hair was at last complete, she was nearly afraid to move for fear of loosening the pins holding the style in place, but Mary laughed at her fears.

"There are so many pins in your hair, Lizzy, I believe you could go out into a gale and it would not dare move," she said pertly.

Kitty and Lydia knocked and entered the room without waiting for a response.

"Oh, Lizzy," Kitty exclaimed, "you are so beautiful!"

Lydia touched one sheer sleeve gently. "May I have this dress to wear when *I* marry, Lizzy?"

Elizabeth shook her head fondly. *Mary is right. I do not think my hair dares move.* "Lydia, by the time you marry, you shall want a newer, more fashionable gown. I promise to shop for it with you."

Lydia was satisfied with the offer. She walked slowly around her sister, appraising her from every angle. "Mr. Darcy is going to be well pleased, Lizzy."

Kitty nodded her agreement.

Elizabeth smiled nervously. She knew he would not care what she was wearing, but she did hope he noticed. She wondered whether he had arrived; her toilette had taken an excessively long time this morning.

"There," Jane announced, examining their handiwork. "You are finished."

There was another knock on the open door. "Not quite yet," came a voice of the woman Elizabeth loved best of all. "May her mother and I speak with Elizabeth, girls?"

"Aunt Olivia!" she cried, twisting in her chair. She held one hand out to her aunt and one to her mother. "Mama," she said, smiling, "I am happy you have come."

Elizabeth's mother reached out to cup her daughter's cheek, her countenance calm but happy. Elizabeth held it there a moment, then rose to lead them both a settee in the small drawing room off her bedroom. Elizabeth smoothed her skirt behind her before sitting on a chair facing them.

"My dear girl," her mother said, touching a handkerchief to her eye, "you are beautiful."

"Thank you, Mama," Elizabeth replied, and then smiled. "It took a great deal of work on the part of Jane and Georgie to make me so."

"False modesty is unbecoming," Aunt Olivia said sternly, but her eyes twinkled as she said it.

Elizabeth winked at her aunt, who shook her head.

"Impertinent girl," Aunt Olivia replied, her lips pressed into a wistful smile. "I have told your mother that this house is yours, Lizzy, and she was surprised to hear it. I told her that neither she nor the girls will ever have to worry about having a place to live."

Elizabeth shook her head. "Mama, I believed Papa has told you as much."

Mrs. Bennet nodded. "He did, it is true, but he so often makes a jest of things that I could never be entirely easy. The girls have dowries enough to support them," she said, "but I worry all the same."

"Mama," Elizabeth said, "I promise you shall always have a home. The dower house is on Bennet land, and if you are willing to work within the budget Papa sets, we shall see it put to rights for you."

Mrs. Bennet leaned forward to pat her daughter's hand, calmer than Elizabeth had seen her in her entire stay at Longbourn. "I *would* prefer to remain in Hertfordshire, and the dower house is on the Meryton side of the estate. It is very kind of you, my dear." She stood. "You are a stunning bride, my Lizzy." She stroked Elizabeth's cheek with the back of one hand. She sighed, rather dramatically, Elizabeth thought. "I thought I had lost you. But your aunt has explained it all to me. I only wish I had listened sooner." She dabbed at her eyes with her handkerchief again. "I was so determined to protect my heart that I wounded yours. I am so sorry."

"Mama," Elizabeth replied with a great sense of relief, "it is all in the past. Let us go forward now."

"That is precisely what your aunt has said," Mrs. Bennet replied. "I shall, Lizzy." She smiled wanly. "I shall try." She kissed Elizabeth's forehead. "I will go downstairs now and tell everyone you are ready."

Elizabeth watched her leave before turning to her aunt. "Aunt Olivia!" she exclaimed with a shocked laugh. "What did you *say* to her?"

Aunt Olivia still sat on the settee, hands folded properly in her lap. "I heard from one of the maids that she had begun to complain."

"I do not believe Papa has told her much of anything beyond the initial dowries," Elizabeth admitted. "Arriving here must have been a surprise."

"I told her enough to put her mind at ease. She complains, you know, because she is afraid."

"She might have been spared that," Elizabeth said.

"She might have been," Aunt Olivia agreed quietly. "The dowries for you and your sisters never depended upon you coming to live with us, but we did ask your father to send one of you girls to Weymouth House. Thomas felt you were the right girl. I believe he knew your mother would be angry with him and decided to allow her to think we had insisted."

It sounded like something Papa would do. "It was unkind," Elizabeth said quietly, thinking of a life at Longbourn with her mother, "but it was the right decision. I love Mama, but . . ."

"In any case," Aunt Olivia continued, "Thomas did not explain, nor was your mother willing to listen if he had. They are both at fault. As are your uncle and I for not understanding what had happened and tending to it sooner." She smiled. "We are all of us imperfect, dear. But we all love you."

Elizabeth sat down on the settee. "It is hardly your fault, but I thank you, Aunt."

"Well, that is that," Aunt Olivia replied, rather self-satisfied. "Now, I have something for you. I had to fend off your groom to give you this," she said gleefully. "He had his own ideas."

"Oh dear," Elizabeth said with a chuckle. "You must have been formidable indeed."

"Not at all," Aunt Olivia demurred. "For he is not to be thwarted in such a direct way. I appealed, rather, for the right to give you a gift from your Uncle Phillip. To that, he had no answer." She slid a rectangular box from her sleeve. "Phillip selected this for you before your coming-out. He meant for you to wear it at your ball. He would be thrilled to see you wear it today."

Elizabeth's eyes began to sting. "I wish he could, Aunt Olivia."

The older woman handed her the box. "I believe he will, dearest."

She took the box from her aunt in trembling hands and carefully opened the lid. Inside was a necklace of small but perfect oval sapphires trimmed in gold and set off by a single teardrop sapphire in the center.

She said nothing at first, content to run her finger along the stones. "Uncle Phillip chose this for me?" she asked.

"He did," Aunt Olivia replied gently. "Here, turn away so I may . . . ." She took the necklace and fastened it around Elizabeth's neck.

Elizabeth placed her hand over it where it lay on her chest. "I am so very grateful to you and Uncle Phillip," she whispered. "Everything I have is due to you."

"Do not be ridiculous," Aunt Olivia said, but her tone was affectionate rather than brusque. "Everything you have is due to *you*. We might have offered you the world and still have seen you fail had you not worked diligently to become worthy of the gift."

"You are not supposed to argue with me," Elizabeth retorted, unable to hide a grin. "It is my wedding day."

"Then do not say silly things, and I shall not have to correct you," Aunt Olivia retorted.

The women looked at each other silently for a moment, and then both laughed.

There was a knock at the door.

"Come," Elizabeth called, and John stepped through. Elizabeth stood. She ran her hands along her skirt, trying to pull out wrinkles that were not there.

John blinked twice, his eyes suspiciously glossy, before he cleared his throat and said, "I see Phillip has given you his gift after all." He took Elizabeth's hand and kissed it. "You are beautiful, my dear." He bowed deeply to them both and held out a hand to Aunt Olivia.

"Livy," he said quietly, "may I have the honor of escorting you ladies downstairs?" He inclined his head towards the hallway. "I believe I heard something about a wedding, and the groom is currently pacing the drawing room like an angry bull."

"We should go," Elizabeth replied immediately.

"Nonsense," Aunt Olivia said as she lifted her hands for assistance in rising. Once on her feet, it took her a moment to catch her breath. "It will do him no harm to wait. The boy has grown far too used to having his way in all things."

"Then I wonder he wishes to marry our Lizzy," John teased.

"Elizabeth?" Georgiana called. Her head appeared around the door. "Oh, I did not mean to interrupt," she explained, her cheeks flushing pink. "I will just wait for you out here."

"Not at all," Elizabeth said, waving her inside. "Please come in. Do you know my cousin?"

Georgiana nodded. "We were introduced this morning." She curtsied. "Pardon me, Your Grace, but my brother asked me to give these to Lizzy." She thrust out her hands. In them was a small bouquet of roses.

White roses.

Darcy did not *mean* to pace the floor waiting for Elizabeth, but he was impatient to begin the ceremony. He had not had nearly enough time with her of late and was anxious to claim her company for himself. He would wed, the attendees would be fed, and then they would all go home. *Elsewhere.* He and Elizabeth would remain here in Kensington—he had grown very fond of the house and grounds already. He was especially grateful that Anne had come—he would not feel any guilt sending Georgiana and Anne with the Matlocks to enjoy a prolonged visit while he and Elizabeth began their lives together.

Richard tried to press a glass of wine into his hand, but he resisted. He did not need port to calm himself, he needed his bride. Bingley asked whether brandy would be more to his taste.

"Or a strike to the head," Richard muttered. "May I never wed at all if this is what it does to a stoic man like you."

"I only need Elizabeth to arrive," Darcy said, his manner abrupt. "Leave off."

There was a stifled squeal near the windows. Darcy saw Mr. Gardiner handing Miss Mary a guitar. He had never seen one in person and wondered where the man had procured it.

"Hmm," Richard said. "A Spanish guitar. Are there masters who teach that?"

Darcy shrugged. He had no idea.

Richard's gaze searched the drawing room now filled with relations. "Bingley," he hissed, "where is your sister? She is not trying to storm the rooms upstairs, is she?"

Bingley grinned and shook his head. "Caroline returned to Auntie Cleopatra's home in town last night, rather unexpectedly."

"Hoping for an invitation?" Richard asked.

"Lizzy was generous enough to invite them both," Bingley replied, "but I thought Caroline's presence a risky proposition at best with a duke, a marquess, *and* an earl in attendance."

"Not to mention their wives," Richard added, tugging at his cravat.

Bingley nodded. "My aunt was happy to have Caroline stay a little longer. That being the case, I did not bother to relay the invitation to my sister."

"You *lied*, Bingley?" Richard asked, grinning. "I should never have thought it of you."

"Only of omission, my friend," Bingley replied cheerfully. "It is still a sin, but for such a cause I thought I might be forgiven."

Darcy lifted his face to the ceiling and blew out a gust of air. "You are a good friend, Bingley."

"I am a *wise* friend," Bingley replied, shaking his head, "and Elizabeth will be my sister at the end of January. I do not wish for her," he grinned at Darcy, "or her husband, to be cross with me."

There was a stirring outside in the hallway, and Darcy straightened up so abruptly that Richard flinched. Bedford entered with Mrs. Russell on his arm; he delivered her to the duchess before returning to the back of the room, where Mr. Bennet waited. Bingley hurried to a seat, and Richard put the wine away and resumed his place at Darcy's side.

At last, Mr. Bennet stepped outside and reappeared with Elizabeth.

Darcy's breath caught at the sight of her in the doorway, her hair elegantly coiffed, coppery highlights shining in the cold sunlight that streamed through the windows. The rosy bow of her lips, her creamy skin, the glint of the gold in her eyes—he could barely force himself to remain still.

In one hand, Elizabeth held his bouquet, and his heart ached with tenderness. He caught her eye; her entire face radiated joy. He glanced down at the flowers and back up at her. "Aphrodite," he mouthed, and her cheeks pinked.

Mr. Bennet walked Elizabeth into the room and brought them to a halt next to Bedford. The duke held out his hand in a gracious sign of condescension, and Elizabeth's father shook it. He then formally handed Elizabeth over to Bedford. Elizabeth kissed her father's cheek and then Bedford led Elizabeth to Darcy.

It was difficult to concentrate while the vicar spoke, but Darcy managed it during the brief service. He said his vows and gazed deeply into her eyes as she said hers. He slid the wedding band onto her finger reverently and had to remind himself to breathe when she smiled up at him.

Richard prodded him in the back when it was time to sign the register, but he barely felt it. Elizabeth had taken his arm, her light touch sending a shiver down his spine.

"Thank you for my flowers, Fitzwilliam," she whispered to him as they bent over to sign their names.

"Thank you for marrying me, Elizabeth," he whispered back.

Elizabeth was still removing hair pins when Fitzwilliam entered the room with a lit candle in his hand. She swallowed hard when she saw him in his dressing gown but giggled when he stood facing her empty bed for a moment, clearly wondering where she might have gone. At the sound, he turned to see her still sitting at the vanity. When his eyes met her own, his expression softened.

"Where is your maid?" he asked, setting the candle down and coming to help.

"I sent her away," Elizabeth said. "I wished to wait for you by myself." She nodded at the growing pile of pins. "I have been a bit precipitous, I am afraid. I knew our sisters spent an hour taming my hair, but I did not realize it would be so difficult to undo."

Her scalp tingled as his fingers combed through her hair, carefully searching for pins and removing them. "You have a talent for this," she told him.

"I had a much younger sister," he reminded her.

"She was, and is, a very fortunate girl," Elizabeth replied, leaning back, reveling in his touch. After a moment, she recommenced her work. "We must be nearly finished," she said with a laugh.

There was a faint clink as Fitzwilliam dropped three more pins into her pile. "Nearly," he agreed.

Finally, she found the last pin and placed it on the table. She stood to face him, her hair flowing down her back as she shook it out. It was long and thick, and she was pleased that he seemed to appreciate it. He reached out to run his hand through it from her crown to the ends, stepping so close that she was able to lay her cheek upon his heart, the palms of her hands resting on his chest.

He leaned down and touched her lips with his own, pulling back only when she released a soft sigh. He took a step back, her hands in his, and stared at her—just stared, his eyes dark, intense, recalling the picture with which she had confronted him. Of their dance at Netherfield. She knew it was love, had known it for some time. But . . . ardent. *Ardent.* Her husband reached for her dressing gown.

"*Ohhhh,*" she exhaled, as understanding dawned.

CHAPTER TWELVE

January 1, 1812

Elizabeth was delighted when her aunt insisted on joining them for dinner. She and Fitzwilliam had a great many matters to discuss as they began their lives as a married couple, and it pleased her that Aunt Olivia was well enough to participate in at least some of the conversation.

"Now," Fitzwilliam said, as the remnants of their meal were cleared away, "we agreed to discuss where you would prefer to live in town, Elizabeth. I know Darcy House is on the small side for a family, but we could use the adjacent home as well."

Fitzwilliam stood to offer his arm to her aunt and they all made their way to the drawing room. He spied a drawing on the wall and addressed Georgiana. "I see you and Father have reemerged at last."

"It travels with me," Georgiana replied. "I am never without it."

"Yes," Mrs. Russell said, giving the girls an affectionate smile. "That was one of Elizabeth's earliest efforts, was it not, Lizzy?"

He husband started; he leaned in to examine the drawing. "Why did you not say something?" he asked as he led them all back to the settee.

"I wanted to see if you would discover it on your own," Elizabeth gently taunted him. "Alas, you never did."

After they were settled closely together and near the fire, Elizabeth asked the question she had been considering. "How will you acquire the other townhome, Fitzwilliam?" She was certain from the sly expression on her husband's face that he was about to reveal another surprise, like the annual income of Pemberley being augmented with investments of his own and two smaller estates that were currently let out. "Surely the residents are not interested in decamping."

Her husband had shared a smile with his sister. "We hold the lease on that home as well, Elizabeth. My father intended to open the wall between them and create a single dwelling as a gift for my mother."

There was no need to ask why the work had never been done.

"Are there currently tenants in residence?"

Fitzwilliam nodded and stood to pour himself some wine. "There are. In truth, the cost of the original lease is paltry in comparison to the rents I collect now. It is almost enough to pay for the lease on both properties."

Elizabeth wished to be fair, so she did consider it. The location was fashionable, but in the end, that was all it had to recommend it. Should they embark upon a campaign of improvements to expand its size, they would spend money. If they let out Darcy House, they would make money.

It made more sense to remain where they were, close to the greenhouses and on their own property. "If you do not have a particular attachment to the townhouse, it would be wise to rent out your current residence as well and collect the profit. This home is freehold; thanks to Uncle Phillip, we own the home and the land outright."

"Unless," Aunt Olivia added, "you worry about the location. We still have the property in Russell Square, Lizzy."

"I love it *here*," Georgiana announced suddenly, then glanced worriedly at her brother. "Of course, I have not lived at Darcy House since father passed, but town is so . . . "

"Not like the country?" Fitzwilliam asked, when it seemed clear Georgiana would not finish her thought. "As your drawing already hangs on the wall, I believe we know where you would prefer to reside, Georgie."

Georgiana smiled brightly, and Elizabeth shared a look with Aunt Olivia.

"This house was left to me by my uncle," Elizabeth said, touching her husband's arm. "If you do not object, I should prefer to remain here."

"It would be an ideal location to breed those fancy horses you and Elizabeth love so much," Aunt Olivia declared. "You are bound to earn an inflated price for them here in town."

Fitzwilliam smiled. "I owe the next to Richard," he admitted.

Elizabeth shook her head. "Richard still has a decent horse to ride. Jane will get hers first. It can be a wedding present."

"Fair enough," he conceded. "It appears unanimous, then." He poured everyone a small glass of wine before raising his own. The women joined him. "To Russell House."

At his declaration, Aunt Olivia's expression transformed to a mixture of astonishment and tender regard. When Fitzwilliam took her aunt's hand and kissed it, Aunt Olivia actually blushed. When she recovered her composure, she turned to Elizabeth and said, "Spending these weeks with you, seeing you with your young man, Lizzy—it has made me very happy."

Elizabeth embraced her aunt, not releasing her until the older woman swatted her shoulder. "Very well, Lizzy. I know you love me."

Everyone laughed at that, although when Elizabeth sat up, she hurriedly dabbed at her eyes with her handkerchief. She was careful to always have one with her these days.

"One more bit of advice from an old woman," Aunt Olivia said, glancing first at Elizabeth and then at Fitzwilliam. "You two will need to select a staff to help you manage your holdings."

"That has not been necessary in the past, Aunt Olivia," Elizabeth replied. "We each have stewards for our properties and a solicitor here in town." She looked at her husband, whose brow was furrowed.

Aunt Olivia shook her head, amused. "It has never been necessary because you have not been married." She gave her niece a knowing look. "Should you wish to ever see one another, Lizzy, you will both of you hire a personal secretary and solicitors for your various projects. It will take some time for you to sort it out." She sipped a little wine. "It took years before Phillip yielded to the necessity, but we were far happier afterwards." She placed her wineglass on the table and folded her napkin.

"You two have a combined fortune that should ensure the family thrives for many generations—*if* you handle it properly now. Wealth is not only a privilege . . ." She eyed Elizabeth expectantly.

"It is a responsibility," Elizabeth finished. She noticed that Fitzwilliam was nodding in agreement.

"Well," Georgiana said suddenly, an impish grin on her face, "since we are all so very wealthy, perhaps you will accompany me to Bond Street tomorrow, Lizzy?"

"Whatever for, Georgie?" Elizabeth replied, pretending to groan. "Have you not had enough shopping with Anne?" She looked askance at her newest sister. "I suppose it would be too much to hope that you wish to visit Hatchard's?"

"I am sure we can find something," her friend replied, with a toss of her head. Her golden ringlets bobbed merrily. "If wealth is a responsibility, we ought to support the merchants and the modistes. It is the economically responsible thing to do." She maintained a serious expression throughout her little speech only to dissolve into giggles when her brother raised his eyebrows at her.

Olivia Russell sat at her writing table sprinkling sand on a letter to her niece as the candle flickered next to her. She had felt unusually well after Lizzy's wedding. Well enough to remove to St. James's for a week to allow the new couple their privacy and well enough to return when that sojourn was over.

It had been a shock to hear Fitzwilliam announce that he and Lizzy would use the Russell name for this house, but it should not have been. Phillip had thought highly of the boy, and she thought even more highly of the man. Still, the gratitude she felt that Phillip would not be forgotten was surprisingly powerful.

Her gaze moved to the wall. She thought about Georgiana and how the girl carried her small framed portrait of her and her father to wherever she was living. She understood the urge. The portrait Lizzy had drawn of her and Phillip had traveled with her when she had first returned to London, and now hung above her escritoire. It gave her peace to have him watching over her. She could feel Phillip here in a way she did not in town. Although he had never lived here, Phillip had chosen this room for the two of them particularly—the care he had taken with the repairs and restoration was as much for her comfort as for Lizzy's, though they had both intended from the beginning that the home would be willed to the daughter of their hearts.

Yes, she had felt somewhat stronger these past several weeks. She had even joined Lizzy and Fitzwilliam at dinner several times, basking in the bliss of the newly married couple. Georgiana had returned from her visit with Miss de Bourgh only yesterday, and after their business had been resolved, the girls had taken great delight in one another's company. They seemed mostly to relish teasing Fitzwilliam.

Olivia enjoyed the banter, but she was fatigued, retiring long before the others. It struck her now, as she readied herself for bed, that she ought not to put off finishing her letter any longer. That was now accomplished. She folded and sealed it, writing Lizzy's name on the outside in the spidery script old age and illness had forced upon her. How she detested that outward sign of weakness.

"I am ready, Phillip," she said aloud. "Lizzy is settled, and so am I."

"Aunt Olivia seemed well tonight, do not you think?" Elizabeth asked as Fitzwilliam slipped into their bed. "Oh!" she squealed. "Your feet are cold."

"Yours are warm," he said, his sonorous voice making her tingle all over. He turned onto his side and tucked a strand of her hair behind her ear. "Surely my loving wife will not allow me to freeze."

"How am I to warm your enormous feet when they are twice the size of my own?" Elizabeth teased. "Stretch them out towards the bedwarmer."

"*You* are my bedwarmer," he replied, enfolding her in his embrace and pulling her to his chest.

"Your hands are like ice," she protested, her teeth beginning to chatter.

"Just another minute or so and we shall both be warm," he assured her.

"I *was* warm," she chided him as she shivered.

He ran his hands briskly up and down her back. "I know what would heat you up," he whispered in her ear.

"What is that, Mr. Darcy?" she asked, feeling rather bashful.

The wicked smile he only used when they were in the privacy of their rooms was playing on his lips. "Darcy secret number four."

"Oh," Elizabeth breathed, ducking her head. Why she wished to hide her blush, she could not say—certainly it was too dark for Fitzwilliam to see it. "I should like that."

From the time she had decided that she would marry Fitzwilliam Darcy, Elizabeth had imagined what it would be like to share his bed. She had an elementary notion of what would happen, but Aunt Olivia had told her not to be afraid to ask questions of her husband, that discovering their pleasure together was itself a kind of intimacy. The idea that it could be pleasurable had been echoed by her mother, and so Elizabeth had been keen to begin this part of their life together. Elizabeth had done as Aunt Olivia suggested—and what she had learned was that she craved these moments with Fitzwilliam nearly as much as he did with her. The world demanded so much of them, but this—this was theirs alone.

Sharing herself in this way was still new—every time he introduced something else, she was awkward and uncertain all over again. But then he would ask . . .

"Do you trust me, Elizabeth?" He kissed the spot behind her ear that was especially sensitive, and her tremor this time was not caused by the chill in the air.

"Yes, Fitzwilliam," she replied, made almost breathless with the longing induced by his touch. "Yes, I do."

January 12, 1812

Elizabeth woke suddenly. It was still dark, but the sky outside her aunt's window was fading to an ashy hue. Dawn was coming. She stood to stretch her back and rub the ache from her neck. It was her second night in the chair, and she knew she would have to sleep some hours in her bed this morning.

Aunt Olivia's appearance at dinner a week and a half ago had been her last. Her decline had been slow but steady, like a watch whose mainspring was winding down. Though it did not make the coming separation any easier to bear, having Fitzwilliam and Georgiana with her did help.

Georgiana assisted in the sickroom during the day while Elizabeth slept. Fitzwilliam kept everything else running smoothly, speaking with Mr. Yeager in her stead, seeing to whatever business he could as she remained above stairs with Aunt Olivia. He had even come to sit with them the night before. When it was clear he meant to accompany her last evening as well, Elizabeth had refused and sent him to bed.

Her husband was also trying to prepare Darcy House in the hope he could find a tenant before the season. It required daily trips to Mayfair, seeing to the storage of some family heirlooms that should remain with the house, the removal of others to Kensington, reading and updating the inventories, and conducting meetings with his solicitor. He then returned to Russell House to support her in her vigil. Elizabeth knew Fitzwilliam was rushing the preparations. *He wishes to complete them before Aunt Olivia passes and we have so many other matters to arrange.* The poor man was exhausted. It was now Sunday, and she was determined he would rest. Aunt Olivia's advice about hiring more help for their financial endeavors now appeared prescient. *I should never have doubted her.*

Elizabeth was grateful for the weeks they had shared after the wedding. Aunt Olivia had been sure she would not live to see Christmas, but she had been healthy enough to join them for the pudding and to tell a few stories about her own childhood holidays; it was a gift Elizabeth would always cherish.

She held her aunt's fragile hand and placed a kiss on the back of it. "I love you, Aunt Olivia," she whispered.

"Lizzy?" Her aunt's voice was weak but clear.

Elizabeth lifted her head. "Aunt Olivia?" She stood without relinquishing her aunt's hand. "Would you like some water? Or shall I send for some tea?"

"No, dear," her aunt said. It was difficult to see her expression in the gray room. "I would like some music."

"Music?" Elizabeth asked, her weary mind unable to grasp the request. "Now?"

A rasping laugh rose from the darkness. "Beethoven, please, Lizzy? You know my favorite."

She did indeed. As she rose to fulfill her aunt's request, the first streaks of red light stretched across the sky outside. She sat on the bench, positioned herself, and ignored the pain in her heart as she began the first movement of *Quasi una fantasia*.

The keys were cold, but her fingers found their way. She played the notes, finding the music separate from her, somehow—only a minute into the piece, she faltered. There was a gloominess, a melancholy overtaking her and destroying her concentration.

Elizabeth began again and progressed a little farther before she hit a wrong note. The jarring sound of a sharp played out of place made her pause; she could not recall where she had left off.

The third attempt ended when she found herself motionless at the first notes of the second movement, staring at the keys rather than playing them. Her hands hovered over the keyboard, but she could not remember where they should go. She noted with a strangely calm detachment that they were shaking.

There was a rustle of fine muslin and suddenly Georgiana was sitting next to her on the bench.

"I am sorry to wake you, Georgie," Elizabeth said, her breath coming hard and fast. "Aunt Olivia wanted . . ." Tears clouded her vision, but she fought them back.

"I was awake," Georgiana assured her in a whisper. "Would you like me to help you? It is *Quasi una fantasia*, is it not?"

Elizabeth nodded dumbly. "Please," she begged, her hands falling, useless, to her lap. "Please."

Georgiana kissed Elizabeth's cheek and began to play from the second movement. The notes were cheerful and light, like small seeds transforming into beautiful flowers. Then the reprieve was over, and they descended into the storm of the third movement. As Georgiana played, Elizabeth dragged herself back to her aunt's bedchamber.

There was enough light now to see that Aunt Olivia's eyes were closed. Her chest did not rise and fall; there was no color in her cheeks, though there was yet a small smile on her lips. Elizabeth sat heavily on the end of the bed, numb with sorrow, and placed one hand on the blanket that covered her aunt's leg. She did not cry or scream or wail. Somewhere in the distance, the sonata ended. Elizabeth heard soft slippers on the floor approaching the room before someone was flitting away in a hasty retreat. A little time passed before she heard a heavier footstep in the hall. It grew louder as it moved into the sitting room.

Then Fitzwilliam appeared before her, stroking her cheek, taking her cold hands in his.

"Elizabeth?" he asked, crouching down before her, peering up into her face. "Dearest? I am so very sorry, love."

Elizabeth leaned her head against his shoulder, her heart broken. She felt the air shift beneath her as he swept her up into his arms and carried her out of the room where Aunt Olivia laid so still. She clung to him as he sat in a chair near the pianoforte and placed her gently on his lap, wrapping his arms around her and holding her close. She wound her arms around his neck, dropped her head on his shoulder—and wept.

January 17, 1812

Darcy held Elizabeth's hand as John left the room.

There were three solicitors from three different firms. Elizabeth had only known one of them. They would all arrive early Saturday to read and explain the will properly, after the Darcys had time to absorb the information in her aunt's letter. It had been Livy's request, the duke said, and he felt honor-bound to see things done as she had instructed.

Elizabeth stared at the unopened letter in her lap. "I am almost afraid to read it."

Darcy was no less concerned. He had never considered that one might possess too much wealth, but the requirements of Elizabeth's investments and his own going concerns, they were both worn thin. Wealth had to be managed; it was both a boon and a burden. He recalled Mrs. Russell's advice about creating a staff and realized it had not been an idle suggestion.

"Perhaps we ought to adjourn to our sitting room," he suggested. "It will be quieter in that part of the house." She agreed, and they removed upstairs silently, lost in their own thoughts.

Darcy had known that Elizabeth was to be an heiress, of course. She had told him as much, though he had not known how soon that would occur. He knew she owned Russell House, or would, upon her birthday in May. He had fully expected that she would inherit Weymouth House in addition to the funds to operate it. Mrs. Russell had mentioned another home in Russell Square. Beyond that, if he considered it at all, he supposed that Mr. Russell had left a healthy jointure for his wife that she had drawn on in the years she had been a widow. Elizabeth had a jointure from him in their marriage contract; he had coerced her into taking it for the sake of tradition. She had laughed at him but finally agreed. Any additional monies that came to her from her aunt's funds would simply be secured for Elizabeth's use.

The weeks since they had left Hertfordshire had been very full; he had honestly not had much time to think beyond the figures she had outlined for him in her father's study. The need for three solicitors, however, spoke to something more.

The funeral had drawn a large crowd despite the cold weather and the difficulty of travel. He had worried incessantly over Elizabeth, who played the perfect society hostess in St. James's Square each day before crying herself to sleep in his arms each night. He was grateful that she was improving now that all the mourners, including her father, had gone home. Bedford had been trying to warn them about the will, now that he thought about it, but they had none of them been in a state to attend him. What had he said? *I have been managing the less active accounts.* What did that mean?

In the midst of all of this, they had word that her Uncle Gardiner's ships had come into port; Darcy was not surprised to find that they had brought his wife her pineapples, but not the plants. Elizabeth had not betrayed any disappointment. She had simply given the job of growing new ones over to Mr. Yeager. They had discussed the proper procedures for using the tops to cultivate new plants as well as using the slicks and suckers to gradually increase the yield—the gentleman farmer in Darcy found the details of great interest. The land steward had given them a tour of the greenhouse that had been converted into a small pinery. Despite his initial hesitation, Mr. Yeager now seemed eager to begin.

They had eaten one of the pineapples, and it had been delicious; the diversion had been most welcome.

With two ships, Gardiner had been able to double his orders and negotiate an extremely competitive rate for his purchases; he had then sold them to three large concerns at a substantial profit rather than piecemeal to individual merchants. While the smaller merchants paid more, they could not buy in volume, leading to wasted time and, Gardiner insisted, wasted goods. The ships would sail again in the spring; there were already orders in place. A few more lucrative trips like this one and Gardiner would be able to add a third ship to his fleet.

Elizabeth's share was triple the amount of her initial investment. The Darcys had decided to reinvest it all with Uncle Gardiner's company. They had just finished discussing the contracts when the duke had arrived.

They entered the sitting room attached to their bedchambers and made themselves comfortable. Darcy placed a hand over his wife's to still her fidgeting, touching his forehead to hers. "It will be all right, Elizabeth. I love you and I am here."

Elizabeth closed her eyes for a moment. "I do not know what I would do without you, Fitzwilliam," she said, her voice nearly inaudible.

Bedford had suggested that while doing business during mourning was generally frowned upon, there would be matters to which Elizabeth would be required to tend and promised the solicitors would be discreet. Darcy knew Elizabeth was struggling. She understood that her aunt and uncle would wish her to see to her duty but remained anxious to honor her aunt by observing a proper mourning period. He had tried to convince her that the Russells would agree with her cousin, but she still fretted.

"Shall I read Aunt Olivia's letter aloud, Fitzwilliam?" she asked, breaking the silence.

"If you would be willing," Darcy replied. "I should not like to invade your privacy, love, but I fear I am at a loss."

Elizabeth chuckled then, and his spirits lifted. "I should not have been at such a loss, knowing my aunt and uncle as I do." She winced. "As I did." She closed her eyes.

Darcy lifted her hand to his lips. "It will take time, Elizabeth. Be patient with yourself."

Elizabeth lifted the folded piece of paper, running her fingers over her name on the

outside, then turning it over and touching the wax. "They saved Longbourn from ruin, you know," she said quietly.

"Your father told me," Darcy replied. He knew she was wavering, waiting until she could find her courage. He had no doubt she would, but he would wait as long as she needed.

It took several minutes before she squared her shoulders and broke the seal. She unfolded the pages slowly.

"My dearest girl," she read, and caught a painful breath. He motioned for her to stand and maneuvered her to his lap. She sat, leaning back against him with a contented sigh, and he kissed her ear before she returned to the letter.

"Do you recall the day you arrived at Weymouth House with endless questions and I told you never to stop asking them?" Elizabeth sniffled. "You were so curious about the world, something girls are told is not their province. Well, it is their province, Lizzy, and you are proof of that."

"You are, you know," Darcy told her, his voice husky.

Elizabeth wiped a tear from the corner of her eye. "I was forced to add this missive to the will," she read, "for I intend to explain a few things and make a demand or two now that you can no longer argue with me."

Darcy laughed softly, and Elizabeth swatted his arm playfully. "First," she read, "you are not to go into deep mourning. It is a waste of time and fabric." Elizabeth shook her head. "Yet I know my obstinate girl too well to suspect I shall prevail entirely."

"She knew you well indeed," Darcy teased, but Elizabeth only gazed at the paper. He kissed her again, this time near her temple.

Elizabeth continued. "Here is your charge. I shall allow you to mourn me as appropriate for an aunt. Three months. One month would be preferable, but no more than three. No black dresses, Lizzy—not one. They make you appear as a crow, and you are not Mrs. Bingley, dearest. A black ribbon on your bonnet is more than sufficient. When that nonsense is over, I want you to dance with John and your husband at your first ball and I want you to enjoy it."

Elizabeth let the hand holding the letter drop into her lap. "Three months and no mourning clothes!" she muttered, running one hand down her black bombazine skirt. "The woman was mad." She rested the back of her head on Darcy's chest.

"She may have been," Darcy agreed. "You are hardly a crow." He laughed softly. "Perhaps a magpie."

Elizabeth huffed, but gave no sign she wished to read the rest.

"May I?" he asked, gesturing at the letter.

She sighed and nodded. "Please."

Darcy read over Elizabeth's shoulder. "*I am certain you are now uttering something entirely unladylike.*" This time he laughed openly while Elizabeth tossed her hands up, letter and all, exasperated. He waited for her to recover before picking up where he had left off.

"I beg you to spare your demonstration of pique, my dear," he read, trying not to smile, "for I shall not see it. I am gone at last to be with Phillip and I need none to mourn for me. But for loving you I would not have tarried so long; however, there were things I needed to finish here. Remember, it is you who now has business to tend. To that end, I wish to outline what you will learn in the will."

Yes, Darcy thought, *there will be a great deal of business to conduct, and it cannot wait for the end of a lengthy mourning period. Mrs. Russell knew it. Bedford knows it. I hope Elizabeth will see that it is not a slight to her aunt to carry on.* Elizabeth handed him the letter.

"Shall I finish it, then?" he asked.

"Yes, thank you." She shifted so she could lay the side of her head on his shoulder.

He found the place where he had stopped. "Lizzy," he read, "when you were thirteen, your uncle realized that you possessed both the acumen and the discipline to carry on what he had built, provided you were carefully taught. You have been prepared very well for what you are about to assume. Do not doubt that you can do this, especially with Fitzwilliam's assistance. Remember, Phillip chose you—and he was not wrong."

Darcy let those words of encouragement hang in the air before continuing.

"There are accounts that John has had in keeping about which you are unaware. First, there is my widow's portion. I was the youngest child and married rather late. Between my father and my brothers, my dowry had grown to ten thousand pounds, quite a sum in those days. Your uncle Phillip invested it in the funds. It was conservative for him, but the dear man refused to take any chances with it, even adding to it as he became more successful. As the principal grew, he took some of the interest to invest. Thirty-nine years is a long time for money to sit growing, but I have never needed it. This is how we amassed the sum I now give to you."

"Fitzwilliam," Elizabeth said, peering at the paper and sounding a little dazed. "does that say *eighty-eight thousand* pounds?"

Darcy blinked, but forced it out of his head for the moment. The sum made the jointure he had insisted upon in the marriage contract appear rather paltry. "It will allow us to provide for our children, dearest," he said, commanding himself to at least appear calm before returning to the missive. He was not as tranquil as he pretended but thought one of them should at least *attempt* to remain grounded. He helped Elizabeth stand before standing himself and walking towards the wall.

"Where are you going?" Elizabeth asked. Her voice was reedy and uncertain, and he returned to her side at once.

"Only to ring for a servant, Elizabeth," he said, squeezing her hand and waiting for her to look up at him. When she did, he gave her a crooked smile. "I brought some brandy back from Darcy House. I think before we continue," he remarked, gesturing to the letter in his hand, "I will need something stronger than tea."

Elizabeth pursed her lips and gave him a smile that was both sweet and cheeky. "Two glasses, please."

They read through the business carefully, but the letter went on, offering the treasure of reminiscence. Because of the stories her aunt wrote out, Darcy knew that Elizabeth had fallen off her horse twice her first week riding on her own but had refused to give up. He learned that she was rather good at fishing but hated taking her catch off the hook. That she sometimes had laid flat on her back in the middle of a floor to better study the art on the ceilings at Weymouth House. That she had scandalized George Darcy by teaching Georgiana to do the same one spring afternoon at Pemberley. That she had drawn nearly every creature indigenous to West Riding, and that those drawings were safely packed away in the attics. That when she loved someone, she drew them over and over again.

Elizabeth was not the only artist in the family. Mrs. Russell had painted a picture of her own—one of a country girl with a loving heart and an insatiable desire to learn about the world around her. The letter, Darcy realized, had been as much for him as it was for his wife.

"Lizzy," he read as the letter concluded, laying his cheek against her curls, "you have been the light of our lives from the moment you descended the carriage with your papa and forced yourself to walk rather than dash up the stairs to meet us. You have been every bit our long-awaited daughter, and we will forever be grateful to your parents for sending you to us. You gave two old people new life, my delightful girl, and now it is time for you to live yours."

Elizabeth read the final words. "Our love will be with you always. Aunt Olivia."

Darcy folded the letter and held it out to his wife. She took it and for a few minutes they sat together without speaking.

"I know it is early," Elizabeth said softly, "but may we go to bed, Fitzwilliam?"

"Of course, my dear," he replied. He stood with her still in his arms and carried her the short distance to their chambers. "Which Darcy secret shall we explore tonight?"

She snorted against his neck, and he laughed at the tickling sensation on his skin. "Oh, the third one, Fitzwilliam," she said, clinging just a little tighter. "I am excessively fond of the third."

CHAPTER THIRTEEN

March 18, 1812

Elizabeth felt her husband's comforting hand resting lightly on the small of her back as they welcomed guest after guest. All the prominent families of England seemed to be in attendance, particularly those with connections to the Duke—the Byngs, the Gordons, the rest of the Russells, even the von Keppels and the Lennoxes in addition to all the ladies from Almack's and their extended families. Then there were the Darcy relatives like the Fitzwilliams—even the elusive Viscount Milton and his not-very-charming wife had made an appearance. From dukes to baronets, the air was thick with titles. *Small fish,* Elizabeth thought, *big pond.*

The Bennets were also here. Her father had promised not to leave her mother's side—though thankfully her mother appeared overawed and was unusually quiet. The Bingleys were here too, including a very proper Miss Bingley. Even the Hursts had been invited, though Fitzwilliam had been adamantly opposed to that.

"Hurst is a good enough fellow," he had said, "but he is married to a shrew."

"She did send an apology," Elizabeth reminded him gently.

"Not a very good one," he countered.

She had encircled her husband's waist with her arms. Truthfully, she had had no desire to invite the Hursts, but Mr. Bingley had asked them. The manner of his request had been fair—he was in an unenviable position. He felt he must ask on behalf of his sister but understood completely if they felt they could not extend their hospitality. Elizabeth suspected Jane would not have been injured if she had refused, but Aunt Olivia would have told her to allow it.

"They are all a part of Jane's family now, Fitzwilliam," she had answered. "Besides, I shall never have so many friends and family in one place again. I hardly think she shall try to make any trouble. Perhaps if she makes some connections at this ball, she will feel less bitter and behave better."

Her husband had not been impressed with the likelihood of that.

The disagreement had carried on for days, but her husband had finally compromised, explaining to Mr. Bingley that they would issue an invitation, but certain conditions would need to be met. The most important one—Mrs. Hurst was not to approach either him or his wife. She could content herself with all the other notable members of the ton and take her chances there.

Elizabeth was weary from greeting all her guests. She wondered idly whether it would be acceptable to leave her own ball after supper. Thank goodness her friends were here and approaching their turn—Amanda and her dashing Captain Farrington were followed in line by Miss Penelope Finch and Lady Sophia Cecil. She had grasped the hands of each woman and warmly expressed her gratitude for their presence.

"You have left this rather late, Lizzy," Lady Sophia chided, a sparkle in her hazel eyes. "Showing up to your own coming-out ball with a husband. *Really.*"

"Truly, Sophie," Elizabeth said, shaking her head in mock censure, "look at the man. Why would any woman wait once *he* asked?"

Fitzwilliam made a face that had her friends stifling laughter. "As I recall, Mrs. Darcy," he nearly drawled, "you *did* make me wait. Most unfair if you intended to accept me all along."

Penelope waggled her eyebrows and placed a hand on Elizabeth's wrist, "Oh," she said, "we shall have this story from you, my dear." She indicated the long line behind them. "We will let you finish here, but we *shall* have the story."

Elizabeth felt a sudden surge of affection for the man at her side. She had not known it was possible to love him more than she had when they married, but her feelings for her husband continued to grow deeper and stronger every day. She knew Fitzwilliam hated being the center of attention nearly as much as he despised a crush, but he was enduring both patiently for her. For him to then joke with her good friends—to even make himself the source of the jest—it was perhaps the best present he could have given her tonight.

Sophia leaned in. "Is Miss Bingley here, Lizzy? We are greatly anticipating the *pleasure* of her acquaintance."

Elizabeth gave Sophia a warning glance. "Sophia . . ."

It was too late. The line of guests was pressing forward, and Lady Sophia disappeared into the crowd.

Elizabeth glanced over at Fitzwilliam, who was suddenly in a very good mood. She smiled up a him.

He had given way on so much to make her evening special. The Duchess of Bedford and the Marchioness of Tavistock had formally requested the right to purchase a new ballgown for Elizabeth's long-awaited entrance to London society, and Fitzwilliam had graciously agreed, though she believed it had not been easy for him. He had of course given the first dance over to John. In the end, he had contented himself with the supper set and by giving her a thin gold bracelet with a single oval sapphire to match the necklace she had worn at their wedding and was wearing again tonight. She touched the bracelet before tipping her head towards him.

"I believe John has invited the whole of London," she whispered in his ear.

Fitzwilliam's lips turned slightly upward. "He wishes to show you off, love."

She narrowed her eyes. "As do you, I think."

He shook his head. "I do not know what you mean."

Elizabeth examined his face. "Your left eye is narrowing, but not the right. You are congratulating yourself, Fitzwilliam."

"You have been speaking to Richard again," he said, his expression smug despite the annoyance in his tone.

"Am I correct, husband?" she asked, staring playfully up into his face.

"Why would I not?" was his serious reply. "I have married the most beautiful woman in the room, not to mention the most intelligent. I *ought* to be congratulated on securing her." He took her hand and bestowed a light kiss as the last of the guests filed into the ballroom.

Elizabeth felt her cheeks heating up. Three and a half months married, and the man was still making her blush.

Darcy stood to the side and watched as the Duke of Bedford led Elizabeth to the top position; in deference to her cousin's preference, she had called a minuet. It was no longer the fashion to dance the minuet at a private ball as it took too long to display each couple, but Elizabeth had explained that it served several purposes. First, it made Bedford more comfortable to dance something familiar to him. Second, it told the large assembly that Elizabeth's family was more important to her than society dictates or expectations. Third, it was a statelier dance, allowing the gathered guests to get a good look at her. Elizabeth told him she hoped they would be satisfied and move on to enjoying themselves instead of gawking at her.

He knew she would never achieve her third purpose. She appeared more enchanting than ever tonight. Her hair had been swept up, shorter curls framing her face, one long curl laying suggestively over her shoulder. The color of her gown, Georgiana had informed him, was celestial blue. It was trimmed in white and gold embroidery; the sleeves were puffed and slightly off-shoulder, revealing more skin than he thought necessary. Not that he minded, but he could not help but feel those shoulders were his—they should be restricted to their moments alone. His eyes followed her graceful steps and the smile she bestowed on her partner. *Celestial, indeed.*

At last it was over, and Bedford was escorting Elizabeth back to him. The duke held out his hand and Darcy, surprised, took it. He should have known Bedford would have planned to show his approbation, but he had been so wrapped up in Elizabeth he had not given much thought to the other details of the night. Darcy was grateful for the gesture. Few doors would be closed to them now; the problem would be keeping their own door closed.

"Fitzwilliam," Elizabeth whispered next to him, her face aglow. "I cannot wait to dance the first with you at our next ball."

He smiled down at her upturned face. "And all the balls ever after. I feel the same, love." His thumb traced the back of her hand. "Which dance have you called for me?"

Her eyes twinkled. "Oh, I think you will like it very much, Mr. Darcy," she said. "For it is a country dance."

When she whispered in his ear that the song would be "Teasing Made Easy," the reserved Mr. Darcy threw his head back and laughed, shocking the entirety of the ton at one go.

"I see, Mrs. Darcy," came a voice both strained and amused, "that you have now taught your husband how to flout convention."

"Miss Bingley," Elizabeth greeted the woman, warmth in her greeting. "I do hope you are enjoying yourself."

"I am indeed, Mrs. Darcy," Miss Bingley replied. She raised her elegant eyebrows. "The minuet was an interesting choice for an opening dance."

"A request of His Grace," Elizabeth said, placing her hand on her husband's arm.

Miss Bingley's expression softened. "I see." There was a flash of something in her eyes that Elizabeth thought she had seen at Miss Bingley's ball the previous November. Self-deprecating humor. "Your soirée seems a pleasant little gathering, Mrs. Darcy," the woman continued. Elizabeth's artistic eye picked up a small twitch of her lips. *A smile. That is absolutely a smile.* "I thank you for the invitation."

They made their brief farewells as Lord Matlock arrived to collect Elizabeth for the next dance. Caroline Bingley swept away, eventually joining a small knot of attendees where the only untitled gentleman was also quite wealthy.

When the dance was over and she was returned to her husband, he was shaking his head. "Caroline Bingley always lands on her feet," Fitzwilliam said in her ear.

"Oh, just wait," Elizabeth said, nodding towards Miss Bingley. Lady Sophia, Penelope, and Amanda had surrounded Mr. Bingley's unmarried sister and gaily maneuvered her off to the corner for a chat. "She may eventually gain what she desires, but she will have to work for it."

The last thing she saw before the music started was Miss Bingley's eyes opened wide in something akin to panic.

May 1, 1812

"Is he out in the stable?" Richard Fitzwilliam asked his cousin the moment he entered Netherfield's library.

Darcy turned from the largely empty shelves and rolled his eyes. "Yes, Richard, it is good to see you as well. How are your parents? How are the viscount and his lovely wife?"

"Do not get me started," Richard snorted. "You know how we are. In your absence, we all had to pay court to Aunt Catherine this Easter. You may owe me more than an Arabian." He slouched against the shelf closest to the door. "Besides, when you call Maggie lovely, I know you are being sarcastic, and it does not suit you."

"It is not my fault Anne enjoys torturing her mother," Darcy replied calmly. "In fact, I am satisfied she seems to be taking some pleasure from my marriage."

"It was a spectacle," Richard said, crossing his arms over his chest. "Anne had already told her mother everything—that Elizabeth was not a penniless chit who was after Pemberley, that you were not a man being led by his . . ." Here he rolled his eyes. "You know."

"I am pleased to have missed it," Darcy said. He was. He would not have been able to maintain his composure, he was sure of it.

"In any case, she would not believe it. She was ready to fly to Kensington on her broom, intent on denouncing the pair of you for sullying the family honor. Even when Father confirmed that Bedford himself gave the bride away, she would not cease."

"Perhaps you should just tell me how it all ended, Richard," Darcy said flatly, feeling his temper beginning to kindle despite his best efforts. He had wanted to burn the letter Lady Catherine had sent upon the occasion of his marriage—with her impeccable timing it had arrived, full of invective, just after the reading of Olivia Russell's will. He had not wanted to allow Elizabeth to read it, but she had coaxed it from him. He hardly recognized himself in the man who was helpless to refuse his wife. He should not even have bothered to protest.

Elizabeth had found the letter delightful, much to his chagrin. She had pointed out the best of the insults and laughed away his affront. "Your Aunt Catherine is an old woman with nothing to do but order the world to her liking," she had said as she handed the letter back. "When the world does not do as she bids, there is bound to be disappointment." His responding missive had been icily proper, and in it he had severed their relationship until she deigned to apologize. Unsurprisingly, no such apology had been forthcoming.

It had been the happiest Easter he had spent in many years. Elizabeth had asked the Gardiners to come and stay for a few days. He had found them sensible, pleasant, fashionable people. Their four children had delighted in all the room outdoors to roam and play; Georgiana had quite fallen in love with them. In the evenings, Elizabeth sketched the children, all the women played and sang, and the men took turns reading. His holiday had, for once, been a scene of domestic felicity.

Richard pushed himself upright and raised his eyebrows. "How do you *think* it ended?"

"Will Anne come to stay with your mother for the season?" Darcy hoped his cousin's health would continue to improve were she away from Rosings for a time.

"Anne may love to torment her mother, but she does love her." Richard shrugged. "We may get her to town for a month or so, but I doubt she will stay longer."

Darcy nodded. It was something.

"Now, I must ask why you are gathering us all together here at Netherfield, of all places. It is not like you to be secretive." Richard considered his words. "Never mind. It is exactly like you. It seems unusual for your bride, however." His eyes narrowed. "You cannot be expecting already."

Darcy rolled his eyes. "We would not ask you all to travel to Bingley's home to make such an announcement, Richard. Do not be daft."

"Then what is it?"

"Good God, man," he burst out, "cease your whining. You will learn it all soon enough." Darcy was anxious enough about the ensuing family meeting without having to deal with his cousin's petulance. He considered how he might feel were Richard keeping something of importance from him and softened. A bit. "Richard, it is too complicated to go through it now. Please, I promise you will know all very soon."

There was a knock, and Elizabeth's head appeared around the edge of the door. "Fitzwilliam," she called, and smiled when both her husband and Richard turned in response to the name. She stepped into the room, her eyes twinkling. "I love doing that."

Darcy smiled, his eyes linked with his wife's.

Richard made a disgruntled sound in his throat. "It has been *months*," he complained. "Can you not behave yourselves in company?"

"Is there company here, dearest?" Darcy asked his wife.

She made a show of looking around the room. "I cannot *see* any," she replied. She laughed at Richard's exasperation.

Richard bowed to Elizabeth and left, grumbling about something. Elizabeth held out her hand, and Darcy came to take it.

"It is time," she said.

When Darcy finished speaking, there was silence in the dining room. Mr. and Mrs. Bingley, Richard, and three Bennet sisters all stared at him in various stages of shock. He looked to Elizabeth.

"We know this is something of a surprise," she said as she stood and took her place next to him. "It was to us when we learned of it."

"Lizzy, how long have you known? Have you known since last summer?" Jane asked as she regained her composure.

Elizabeth shook her head. "John has been caring for many of the accounts. Aunt wrote me a letter for after . . . before the will was read." Darcy took her hand.

"You have known since *January*?" Richard inquired, his face reddening. "We were all there for your ball in March! One hundred thousand pounds and you did not think to mention it?"

A little more, in fact. Darcy cleared his throat. "As I think you can all imagine," he said with some impatience, "there was a great deal of legal work to be completed before we could tell all of you. This was a bequest for the Bennet daughters, but we were left in charge of a number of concerns."

Elizabeth, said simply, "We wanted to be certain we understood the details before we approached you all."

"Well, I for one am happy to learn more about investing," Mary said bluntly. "I should be thrilled to have your help, Lizzy."

"Me too!" Lydia said, bouncing in her seat. "Shall we each have the whole twenty-five thousand at once?"

"No," Darcy and Elizabeth replied together. The others laughed.

"It is a great deal of money," Kitty said, in her unassuming way. "You are married now, Lizzy. I should hate to take what our aunt left for you."

Darcy cleared his throat again.

"Are you all right, Darcy?" Bingley inquired, his expression amused. "You seem to have caught a cold."

Elizabeth answered for him. "Aunt left me well off, Kitty. This money is what she would have given Papa for you all had he accepted. He did not feel right about it when he had already taken so much. He has promised you shall have it now, as it is a gift from me."

Darcy recalled that conversation with pleasure—Mr. Bennet had been entirely vanquished by Elizabeth, tossing his hands up in the air in a manner reminiscent of her own. The older man had muttered something about officious old women and officious young women, but he had given his permission. Elizabeth had been triumphant in her victory, and she had been even more passionate than usual that night . . .

Richard's suspicious tone broke into his thoughts. "Why am *I* here, Darcy?"

"You are here, Richard," he replied, "because you are being made an honorary Bennet sister."

Elizabeth jabbed him in the side with her elbow.

Darcy grinned, turning his face to hers. "Ow," he said as the other girls, even Jane, giggled. He turned back to his cousin. "Very well, then. Richard, you are here because Mrs. Russell also wished us to include you."

"She was very grateful to you for helping to protect us, Richard," Elizabeth said softly. "Please do not be offended. She did not leave a specific bequest for you but left it to me."

"I will not take money from either of you." He stood abruptly. "I think you ought to know better than that, Darce."

"I told Elizabeth as much, Richard," Darcy responded, "which is why that is not what we are offering."

"Richard Fitzwilliam," Mary snapped, "sit down. You are spoiling what is becoming a lovely afternoon."

Darcy blinked. Richard scowled at Mary but sat down.

"We plan to expand our horse breeding operation to Kensington," Darcy said. "We have already begun building a larger, more modern stable at Russell House and there are plans to add another wing to the house. We would like you to spend more time in town and partner with us."

Richard's frown deepened. "Horses?"

"Horses," Darcy confirmed.

Richard rubbed at his eye with his index finger. "Well," he said slowly, "that might work. Perhaps thoroughbreds as well as Arabians?"

This time it was Mary who rolled her eyes, and Darcy nearly laughed at how embarrassed his cousin appeared as he mumbled his thanks.

Darcy felt his wife squeeze his hand, and he gazed at her. She looked back up at him with the eyes that had captured him from the beginning, and he knew they were brimming with love. For him.

"There is one more thing," he announced. "It will require work from us all, probably for the rest of our lives—but Elizabeth and I cannot imagine moving forward without you all and Georgiana." He paused.

"Oh, what is it?" Lydia asked, her hands clasped in expectation of something wonderful.

EPILOGUE

May 3, 1822

Thomas Bennet shifted quickly to his left as a thundering herd of small children pounded past him through the French doors and into the garden. In years past, he might have been taken aback at such an intrusion into the library, but it was not uncommon at Pemberley.

Over the past decade, he had regained some of the joy of that time when his own girls had climbed into his lap to beg for stories. Most of the children were still young—Phillip Darcy was the eldest of the brood by a year, far too old at nine years of age to do anything so undignified as to sit on his grandfather's lap. He never strayed too far when a story was promised, but he did his level best to appear as though he had heard them all before. Little Charles Bingley, the next oldest at eight, tried to emulate his older cousin in every way.

There were ten grandchildren now, and Georgiana Darcy Astley's two girls, upon whom he doted every bit as much as his own blood, made an even dozen. Because all the families gathered together in this way at least twice a year at their various homes to do business as well as celebrate holidays and christenings and breechings, Thomas Bennet had the very great pleasure of watching them all grow. *Fanny would have loved this*, he thought with a sigh. *She would have been calling for her salts every day, but she would have loved it.*

Upon returning from Lizzy's wedding, he had seen to the renovations of the dower house and Fanny had happily busied herself with the redecorating. It had kept her humming and happy for over a year—she had spent every last farthing of her budget but had not gone over. Even Thomas had to admit that Fanny had made the place shine—but she had never lived there. Instead, Mrs. Grover did.

He was alone at Longbourn now. Fanny had passed three years ago, bemoaning even in her final illness that she had only managed to get four of her five girls married.

To Thomas's surprise, it had not been his adventurous Mary who was the last to wed. Although he had waited until she was of age, Richard Fitzwilliam had convinced Mary to marry him, making her the third of his girls to leave Longbourn. Kitty had followed suit a few years later.

Boisterous Lydia had been the last of the Bennet girls to leave home. Mr. Matthew Ennis, a quiet, serious young man with a pretty estate in Buckinghamshire had asked to court her a year ago, but Lydia was quite happy being fêted as Mrs. Darcy's only unmarried sister. Thomas laughed at the memory—Lydia had suggested that Mr. Ennis ask again when she was older. That she was already twenty-four had not made the slightest difference to her; Fanny would have had something to say about that.

Mr. Ennis had returned six months later to resume his suit. Elizabeth had finally run out of patience with her sister, and insisted she give Mr. Ennis an answer one way or the other. Lydia had chosen to say yes. This was Ennis's first family gathering, and the poor man appeared a little overwhelmed.

Thomas sympathized. When Lizzy and Darcy had come to him after his Aunt Olivia's death to tell him that they had been left a staggering sum bound up in an irrevocable trust to be used for charitable causes, he had felt more than a little lost himself. How could Phillip Russell have made that much money, even in forty years, after having been so thoroughly bankrupted by his own guilt and generosity?

"John's father," Lizzy had said. He had given her Uncle Phillip the capital, ostensibly to allow Phillip to share in the profits, but ultimately, he had refused to accept a single penny. So the duke's share, a rather significant sum, had been put away for charitable giving. Thomas did not like to think of it but considered it likely that this was the source the Russells had used to keep Longbourn afloat in those lean early years when he had taken over the estate and all the debt that came with it.

"I had no idea the principal was so high. Uncle Phillip simply called it 'the fund,'" she had said with a tiny smile.

The fund, indeed. Phillip Russell's fund had amassed over three quarters of a million pounds. Depending upon their annual returns, there had been between thirty to fifty thousand pounds in interest available to be given away each year. The Darcys had insisted from the first that it was too much money and the country's need too great to rely only upon the pair of them to make all the decisions. Thus, philanthropy—anonymous philanthropy—had become the family business. That a good deal of additional business was conducted at these retreats by the men and the women alike, well, that was neither here nor there.

The Darcys were known in society as fabulously wealthy and very well-connected; their guest lists were highly exclusive, primarily limited to close friends and relations. There was a running joke in the family that an invitation to a soiree or dinner at Russell House was nearly as sought after as a voucher to Almack's, and the food was a great deal better. The latter was more than a jest. Upon her retirement from service, Mrs. Thistlewaite had been persuaded to teach the Darcy cooks to prepare many of her dishes. Apparently the Darcys had added a small competency to her retirement in thanks—and in return, Thomas recalled, Mrs. Thistlewaite had given them her receipt for Elizabeth's favorite dessert—the chocolate cream.

At the family meetings over the years, Thomas had listened to a variety of discussions about canning factories and threshing machines and ensuring those who depended on the various estates represented in the room had no reason to become desperate. Kitty's husband, the vicar of a large congregation who held one of Bedford's livings, was an advocate for the poor and argued for charities that served society's most defenseless, especially women and children. No one protested the need, but they all had a great deal to say about which charities were most effective and which should receive their donations. Elizabeth was still on about passenger railways, which she insisted would transform the country and change the future of their horse breeding enterprises. Only Darcy supported her endeavors in this area. In any case, Thomas was sure he would not live to see it.

Thomas enjoyed these gatherings enormously. He relished the debates on legislation pending in Parliament nearly as much as the many games of chess to which he was certain to be challenged. Through the former Captain Fitzwilliam, he knew more than about horseflesh than he might wish. Now in their seventh year of marriage, Mary still seemed happy with him. She had even become an accomplished rider, something of a minor miracle and a testament to the influence of her husband. Their two boys were as enthusiastic and daring as their parents, and Mary, he had noticed, was increasing again. He imagined they were hoping for a daughter this time.

As for the deliberations over how to allocate Phillip and Olivia Russell's legacy, that was for the younger generation to carry on. He had made one suggestion in the first year—that everyone who wished to learn ought to be taught to read. He emphasized that he meant boys and girls, men and women. That idea had been embraced, and both schools and tutors dedicated to the purpose had been funded as an annual gift. After that, he felt he had said enough.

Thomas took a chair he did not often use, one with a tall back and wide wings situated facing the window that overlooked a garden. There they all were, even little Thomas Edward Bingley, the youngest grandchild at two years of age who was still in leading strings. Despite his restraints, the boy was determined to join in the ruckus and was giving his nursemaid a good deal of trouble trying to toddle after his sisters. The scene warmed his heart.

He heard more footsteps entering the room but, caught up as he was in the activity outside, he did not stand to greet the newcomers. Whoever it was, they would only be walking through on their way out of doors.

"Alone at last," he heard Darcy growl from the far corner of the room, and suddenly Thomas realized he ought to have alerted the man to his presence.

There was a light laugh—Lizzy was with him, of course. "Not for long, I am afraid. Are you not worried about the hordes descending upon us?"

Something was being tossed onto a table—a book perhaps—and then there was the unmistakable sound of a kiss. Thomas grinned to himself, caught between embarrassment and laughter. *Not just a peck on the lips, either.*

"Fitzwilliam," Lizzy scolded her husband, though her voice was anything but disapproving. "You must wait for tonight. We have guests. The children . . ."

"If we ever want more children," Darcy replied, "we should not wait too long."

Lizzy laughed again, harder this time. "I believe that ship has sailed, my dear."

Thomas perked up.

There was a long silence, and then Fitzwilliam replied, his voice deep with emotion, asked, "So—it is certain?"

"I felt the quickening this morning," Lizzy said. Thomas imagined her looking up into her husband's face and smiling. "Are you pleased?" she asked.

There were more sounds indicating just how pleased Darcy was—sounds that Thomas wished he could not hear. Then they spoke of something he did not understand.

"Darcy secret number three, tonight?" Darcy inquired, the words muffled. Thomas was certain he did not wish to know why.

"That is how we made Olivia," Lizzy responded teasingly. "Perhaps Russell secret number one?"

"That was William," Darcy quipped. "Must we choose?"

Thomas silently willed them to leave.

Eventually, the two collected whatever it was they had put aside and went out into the garden. Thomas watched as they called the oldest children together for a drawing lesson. There was a great deal of running around and shouting while a few of the older boys disappeared with Darcy; when they reappeared, Darcy was holding something in both hands.

Darcy sat as the older children picked up their drawing materials, and Thomas Bennet felt as though he had been transported back in time twenty years. His Lizzy was giving drawing instruction exactly as her aunt had all those years ago in the garden at Weymouth House.

There was more, though, and Thomas Bennet was sure he had never seen the like. The serious master of Pemberley, elusive and influential member of the ton, wealthy beyond imagining for anyone lower than a duke, was currently abandoning all pretense of propriety. He was sitting cross-legged on the ground like one of the boys, barefoot, the hems of his pants wet, his shirt sleeves rolled up, trying to keep hold of a slimy frog who was unimpressed by the honor of having his likeness taken. The frog finally escaped, leaping wildly from Darcy's hands as he grasped at it, sending most of the girls scampering away and the boys off on a chase. With a great deal of shouting and good-natured commands, the frog was recaptured, and the lesson resumed.

Thomas opened the window to let in the spring sun and air. He peered out far enough to spy what his Lizzy was drawing. It was not a portrait of the slippery, big-eyed amphibian. Instead, it appeared to be a rather deft depiction of the disheveled man holding it.

There was another disturbance behind him, and he wondered how he had managed to choose the busiest spot in Pemberley for his morning reading. This time, however, he was not hidden, and Lydia was soon at his side, dragging Ennis with her.

"What are you looking at, Papa?" she asked, craning her neck to see. "Oh." She turned to her new husband and giggled. "It is just Lizzy. She is always drawing Mr. Darcy."

HEADSTRONG (COMING 2019)

Months after teaming up with Major Richard Fitzwilliam to thwart a terrorist attack in Europe, twenty-three-year-old Marine Staff Sergeant Elizabeth Bennet is back in the States as a civilian. Her training in cyber-security makes finding consulting work easy, and she's learning to find her place in her family again after so much time away. But there is lingering fallout both from the attack and from her life before it that she's not yet prepared to face.

Co-owner of Darcy Acquisitions, CEO of FORGE, and guardian to his younger sister Georgiana, Will Darcy is stretched to his limits. His sister has purposely chosen a college across the country to get away from her overprotective brother. When his cousin, Major Richard Fitzwilliam, sets up an interview at FORGE for his friend Elizabeth Bennet, Will insults her instead of hiring her. Now Richard's angry at him, too. Can Will make amends, and if he does, can he stay away from the tough, witty, troubled Marine with the finest eyes he's ever seen?

ACKNOWLEDGEMENTS

Many people were instrumental in the writing of this novel. I thank all my reviewers, readers, and supporters, those who pointed out errors or inconsistencies and who mused about potential storylines. Thanks to you, the story is better and stronger than it would have been without your assistance.

Special thanks to my intrepid beta Sarah Maksim, whose incredible brainstorming skills, keen eye for humor, and quick turn-around had a great influence on the development of this story. Thanks also go out to my tireless editor, Sarah Pesce at Lopt&Cropt.

Finally, thanks must always go out to my family, who put up with my many hours spent typing away on my computer when I might have been cooking, cleaning, or doing the million other things it takes to run a house. Thank you for your love, support, and the invaluable gift of time.

ABOUT THE AUTHOR

MELANIE RACHEL is a university professor who first read Jane Austen at summer camp as a girl. She was born and raised in Southern California, but has lived in Pennsylvania, New Jersey, Washington, and Arizona, where she now resides with her family and their freakishly athletic Jack Russell terrier.

Facebook: facebook.com/melanie.rachel.583

Website: melanierachel.weebly.com

Made in the USA
Monee, IL
29 August 2019